Also by Shaun Sinclair

The Crescent Crew Series

Street Rap

King Reece

Published by Kensington Publishing Corp.

Blood Ties

SHAUN SINCLAIR

KENSINGTON PUBLISHING CORP.
www.kensingtonbooks.com

DAFINA BOOKS are published by

Kensington Publishing Corp.
119 West 40th Street
New York, NY 10018

All Kensington Titles, Imprints, and Distributed Lines are available at special quantity discounts for bulk purchases for sales promotions, premiums, fund-raising, and educational or institutional use. Special book excerpts or customized printings can also be created to fit specific needs. For details, write or phone the office of the Kensington special sales manager: Kensington Publishing Corp., 119 West 40th Street, New York, NY 10018, attn: Special Sales Department, Phone: 1-800-221-2647.

Dafina and the Dafina logo Reg. U.S. Pat. & TM Off.

ISBN-13: 978-1-4967-2107-5
ISBN-10: 1-4967-2107-1
First Kensington Trade Edition: February 2019
First Kensington Mass Market Edition: August 2020

ISBN-13: 978-1-4967-2106-8 (ebook)
ISBN-10: 1-4967-2106-3 (ebook)

10 9 8 7 6 5 4 3 2 1

Printed in the United States of America

Prologue

The man on the other side of the door did not know he was about to die.

Unfortunately for him, he had crossed the wrong man. A man who took lives for his bread and butter. Sadly, this was not business. This was personal. If it were business, the man would have been dead already, for the assailant knew more ways to kill a man than there were stars in the sky. However, he wanted this victim to pay homage to his greatness as he gasped for his final breath.

After all, wasn't that the primary thrill?

The assailant pressed his ear to the door. He could hear The Fugees' new song "Killing Me Softly" playing on a stereo.

Could he have company? Impossible! The assassin had staked his victim out all morning.

The assassin attached his ear to the door once more, his mask impeding his hearing a bit. After quiet observation, he was satisfied that his victim was alone.

He raised his silenced pistol to the door and squeezed. POP! The handle disintegrated under the powerful .45 round.

The assassin kicked the door open and surveyed the room simultaneously. Immediately, he spotted his victim. His victim seemed to be anticipating his arrival as he pointed a weapon of his own and squeezed off a stray shot before sprinting towards another room.

The assassin didn't even flinch from the assault. In one smooth motion, he retrieved a dagger from his pouch, and flung it into his victim's neck, dropping him on contact. The man yelped in pain, but his screams fell on deaf ears.

The assassin calmly walked over to his victim, who had fallen clumsily onto one side with the knife lodged into his neck. Blood oozed around the blade and down his neck onto the thick black carpet. He bent to one knee to look at his victim eye-to-eye. For a while, he said nothing, just peered deeply into his mark's eye as if trying to extract his soul with his penetrating gaze.

The victim stared back just as deeply. If he could move, he would have been putting up one hell of a fight, but the dagger lodged in his neck paralyzed him. His only defense was an unflinching stare. So, two predators engaged in an intense mind game. One, a predator by nature. The other, a predator by trade. Eventually, the supreme warrior ended the battle.

"I told you not to fuck with me," the assassin reminded his victim. His victim recognized his voice at the exact moment he recalled his transgression.

He began to panic. "P-please, man," he begged as sincerely as a street soldier could, which wasn't much. "I had to defend what's mine. Ya understand dat, right?"

His assailant cocked his head to the side thoughtfully, then nodded his agreement. "But you forget one thing," he replied.

"What's dat?"

"*There is no protection from me. I am my only defense!*"

"*B-but wait man. If I had known it was you, we could've worked something out. I-I- maybe would've h-handled it different,*" he pleaded.

The assassin smiled. There it was. Submission. They always bowed down in their final moments. Always. No matter the size, stature, reputation, or wealth . . . they all bowed down in the end.

The assassin raised his silenced pistol to the man's head and unloaded three rounds without even blinking.

Then the killer stood to begin his meticulous cleaning process.

Part 1

Innocence

Chapter 1

"Jus, come on son! We're gonna be late!" The voice echoed throughout the house taking Justus out of his trance. Justus was having a hard time deciding between the blue Levi's or the black True Religion jeans to wear to his cousin's party. He quickly chose the Levi's and met his father in the basement.

"Wassup Pop?" Justus greeted his father as he entered the basement.

"What I tell you about calling me that? I ain't no old man."

"A'ight, a'ight," Justus conceded, throwing up his hands in mock defense. His father was quicker.

Leader parried left, then swept Justus off his feet where he lay on the ground defeated.

"You're getting there, but you're not ready yet," his father scolded. "Now go get the car so we can ride out."

As they entered the garage, Leader stood by the passenger door of his cherished '79 Eldorado, surprising Justus. Leader never let anyone drive his precious Cadillac. Not even his wife. He tossed Justus the keys and Justus started the car with a smirk, thoroughly pleased that his father finally trusted him. He pulled the car out of the garage very carefully and eased into the street headed for Topeka Heights.

As they drifted down the highway, his father took the time to enlighten Justus to a few things.

"Jus, listen, I want to make sure you keep a close eye on things while I'm gone. Look after your mom and li'l sister," Leader instructed Justus. "Your sister's big for her age, and these little R. Kelly's running around here gon' make somebody hurt 'em. So, you keep an eye out. A'ight?"

"Yes sir."

"You can stop the *'yes sir'* shit now. You a man now. You turning eighteen in a few months."

"Yes—I mean—a'ight."

Leader turned on the radio and the sounds from Scarface's *The Fix* album filled the car. Justus was not shocked at all. He knew his father loved that raw gangsta music. Tupac, Geto Boys, Kool G. Rap. All the real music got repeated burn when Leader was in the 'Lac.

After nodding his head a few times, Leader turned the music down to address Justus some more, "Hey you still not worried about getting kicked off the team, are you?"

Justus shook his head.

"Good. Don't worry about it. It's good that you held on to your principles. The world needs more principled men."

Leader was referring to Justus not being allowed to play in his high school basketball championship game. He was suspended indefinitely for refusing to stand for the national anthem. In the past, when the national anthem was performed, he had found a convenient way to excuse himself. Unfortunately, in the game before the championship game the bathroom was full so he had no such luck. Unable to leave, he chose to remain seated amidst a gym full of people, sticking out like a grade-school erection. After much prodding from his coaches, Justus remained defiant. In a city like Fayetteville, home of Fort Bragg—home of the 82nd Airborne Division—refusing to stand for the national anthem was blasphemous. When Justus took the court to play ball, the crowd let their disapproval be known by salting the court with debris. Coach decided it would be best if Justus sat the game out, hence causing him to miss the most important game of his life. Justus, being a senior, would never get a chance to lace up for the hardwood and scorch a team for 21 and 10 again. Justus appeared unfazed, but only Leader, who sat in the audience observing the whole incident like an owl, knew the true extent of Justus's pain. Inwardly, Leader smiled. The incident could only be a catalyst to Justus becoming the person Leader was already training him to be.

Leader continued with the conversation. "When you graduate in a few weeks—"

"Six."

"Okay. In six weeks, you won't have to worry about any of that shit, because you'll be working with me in the family business."

Justus noted Leader was using profanity, which was something he seldom did in the presence of others. Leader was very articulate and extremely intelligent. Only a few people knew how gully he truly was. Justus was one of those people.

"Pop, what *is* our family business?" Justus asked, as he continued to smoothly maneuver the 'Lac down the highway.

Justus never knew exactly what his father did for a living. All he knew was his father's title on his business card read: *John Moore, Security Consultant.* Justus did know his father's job required him going out of town a lot. He also knew his father was well respected in the streets due to his reputation from back in the day. Again, Justus had no idea what exactly his father was known for. What he *did* know was that it wasn't drugs. Leader despised the fact that drug dealers got all the props.

"You'll see soon enough," Leader assured him, to which Justus chuckled. "What's so funny, son?"

"You. You remind me of Tommy on *Martin.* He always talking about his job, but nobody knew where he worked at. So, the joke was that he didn't have one."

Leader mulled this over for a second, then responded, "Oh, it's a job alright. Fact, it's more than a job; it's an adventure!" he joked.

"I won't have to cut my beard off, will I?" Justus asked, stroking his peach fuzz.

"Maybe. Why?"

"'Cause I notice every time you go out of town on business you cut off all your hair and trim your eyebrows."

This was true, of course. In fact, Leader trimmed the hair from his *entire* body. Ass crack and all. His eyebrows, he would shave completely off, then sketch new ones. He especially cut the hairs in his nose. This was an occupational precaution.

"Yeah, I know," Leader admitted, then added, "You're pretty observant."

Justus laughed. "It's obvious! You be looking like a black Mr. Clean!"

Leader nudged him. "Shut up. Laugh now, get laughed at later," Leader warned, before turning the music back up. Justus settled into a more comfortable position and drove on to their destination.

Topeka Heights was one of the many neighborhoods in Fayetteville that caused the city to be known as *Fayettenam*. The residents of Topeka Heights reveled in their status. To them, ghetto wasn't necessarily a bad thing. Ghetto produced strength. Ghetto produced camaraderie. After all, everyone knew that within the confines of the ghetto were some of the richest people. Some rich in heart, others in spirit. Some in actual monetary wealth. The latter were the people who were savvy and ambitious enough to hustle hope into something tangible. People like Terry "Pug" Daniels, Justus's maternal cousin.

Pug was just returning home from a three-year state bid. At just twenty-two, Pug was a major player in Fayettenam's comparatively small heroin trade. Prior to his incarceration at the age of nineteen, Pug had a few dope spots sprinkled all over the city. Pug was a dropout to the nth degree, leaving junior high at thirteen to provide for his sick mother, whose main ailment was being broke. He started out selling weed, then made the natural transition up the ladder to crack cocaine. However, through trial and error, he later found that nothing sold like that "P-Funk," as heroin was called in the streets. An old-head from the neighboring city of Lumberton, plugged Pug in with a sweet connect, and Pug never looked back. Riches and street fame came, followed by the requisite hate that bred drama.

One night while returning from the movies with his girl, some young enterprising jack-boys attempted to rob him. Pug, no stranger to gunplay, blazed one of them quicker than a California forest fire. He fled the scene in his girlfriend's Audi, but was captured by authorities a few days later. Turned out, one of the jack-boys moonlit as a rat. Pug dropped ten racks on a lawyer and managed to finagle a three-year plea for weapons possession. Now he was home to reclaim the streets that embraced him.

When Justus wheeled the Eldorado into the courtyard amidst a rambunctious crowd, all eyes were on him. He was smiling from ear to ear, happy to be seen whipping his father around. He quickly found a vacant spot and he and his father exited the vehicle. They walked side-by-side up to the apartment where everyone was gathered out front enjoying the sounds that emanated from inside. While Leader dipped inside to find his wife, Justus lingered outside to mingle with the crowd.

"What up, Jus?" Some of the older dudes greeted Justus. Most of them were Pug's partners. Justus was five years younger than Pug, but no one seemed to care because ever since Justus was able to walk, he hung with Pug. Pug was the big brother Justus never had, and everyone who was anyone knew it.

Besides, with Justus standing a stout six-feet tall, no one paid attention to the age disparity. Justus was one of their own as far as they were concerned.

"Chillin'," Justus responded coolly. "What's the bidness?"

"Ain't shit," replied Kenny. "Wanna hit the blunt?" He offered Justus the burning blunt.

"Hell naw. You know I don't smoke!" Justus reminded him.

"Ha-ha, I know. Your pops'll kick your ass. I was just fucking wit' cha. A, ah, pardon self, I need to holla at this broad real quick." Kenny passed the blunt to a comrade, then ran off across the courtyard to meet a thick, chocolate sista carrying a baby in her arms.

Justus took survey of the courtyard, observing all the goings-on. Five different smoke ciphers. Beautiful women, so jaded they didn't realize their worth. Numerous young hustlers still trying to grind during the festivities. A part of him envied them. A part of him pitied them.

Justus noticed that Pug was still a no-show so he asked the crew about his whereabouts.

"He'll be here soon," answered Rico, Pug's right-hand man. "You know he like to make an entrance. Him and Jackie 'posed to go shopping 'fo they come here."

Just then, Pug's Suburban crept into the neighborhood. "There he go right there," a short, pudgy dude named Greg stated. The truck didn't come to where the crowd was assembled. Instead, it bent the corner toward the adjacent complex. It was evident he didn't leave the neighborhood because the steady thump from the Digital Design subwoofers rumbled from a block over. As soon as the truck was out of sight, conversation resumed.

"Aye dawg, you know Nikki moving out the hood, right?" Rico informed everyone.

"Word?" Justus piped up a little too eagerly.

"Yep. She got kicked out when ole' boy got caught up in there with that dope on 'im," Rico explained. "Housing Authority people say she gotta go 'cause she had a convicted felon with dope up in her spot."

"Damn, that's fucked up," Justus whispered, unable to disguise his disappointment.

"Don't matter though," Rico stated matter-of-factly. "She already got a place 'cross town off Cliffdale road. Plushed out too. Bitch on da lake an' shit," Rico let them know. He stayed up on the happenings.

"Damn, she making money like that at that hospital? I thought she was a dietician or something?" Greg wondered.

Rico answered, "I believe her dad got it for her. Since she not fucking with ole' boy no more, I guess he gon' take care of her. Either that or he don't want to see his daughter out in the street," he reasoned. All Justus heard was one thing.

"When she stopped messing with that dude?" Justus asked.

"Sheeit, nigga, when he got her spot ran up in! You know Nikki don't play that shit!"

"So when she moving?" Rico asked, looking at his phone. "That might be where Pug and Jackie went at."

"Her and dude broke up?" Justus insisted.

"Aye nigga, you can stop dreaming. You too

young for Nikki, and you don't pump, so your pockets too short."

Before Justus could respond to Rico's character assassination, he was snatched up into a yoke from behind. A sharp blade appeared under his neck.

"Money or your life?!" The voice offered. Justus noticed everyone remained cool, so he figured it could only be one person.

"Pug, stop playing, cousin."

Pug released him. "Ah nigga, you still too cool to be scared, huh? I thought you was gonna try some of that Bruce Lee shit." Pug laughed, then hugged Justus. "What's the bidness, li'l cuz?!"

"Chillin' big nigga," Justus assured him. Outside of Leader, Pug was the only person Justus truly admired, so he wanted to be seen in the best light in his eyes.

Justus was released from Pug's tight embrace long enough for the elder cousin to size the young one up.

"Damn, li'l nigga, your ass is getting big!" Pug commented after noticing the few inches Justus had grown since he had been gone. "I gotta watch you. You might try me one day. You working on that temper or what?"

"Yeah." Justus nodded unconvincingly.

"A'ight, you betta tighten up," Pug warned. "Let's go inside. You uncouth Negroes stay y'all asses out here," Pug remarked to his gang. He wrapped his arm around Justus's shoulder and the two went inside.

The front room of Gloria's house was immaculate by any standard. Pug made it a rule to keep his mother laced. Gloria resided in the projects, but she wasn't just anybody, she was the queen bee! A ghetto superstar. Her son was the hood general so that automatically gave her rank by proxy. Gloria's home reflected her status. Her living room was decorated with bone-white leather furniture and gold carpet. The lamps at each end of the sofa were made of pure gold and glass. No plastic was to be found on the sofas. People simply knew, don't fuck up Gloria's shit!

The kitchen was done in the traditional fashion of the PJs. White floors. Cheap wooden countertops and a glass table, which was being slammed with cards from an ongoing Spades game. It seemed like a trophy and cash prize was being awarded by all the trash being talked, when Pug and Justus entered the room.

"What's the bidness?!" Pug yelled when he burst into the room.

"Heeeeey baybee!" Gloria jumped to hug her son. "You finally made it home." She kissed Pug on his strong jaw, but the salutations were brief, as Gloria didn't miss a beat telling Pug what was on her mind. "Now I hope you stay home. I swear these gotdamn kids are driving me crazy! That woman of yours keep dropping them bad-ass boys off every day, talkin 'bout she going to school. And them little fuckers? I swear, they be running up here and running up there and running every got-damn where! Chile, I'm so glad you home, I don't know what to do! I just—"

"Gloria!"

The room went silent at the sound of the familiar voice. All eyes darted to the door to see

Leader swagger into the room with his smooth, confident stride. "Chill out, Glo. Let the boy enjoy his first day home." Gloria started to protest, but when she saw the telling glaze in Leader's opaque eyes, she quickly relented.

"Come here, gangsta." Leader spread his arms for Pug. Pug was probably the only person in the family who knew that Leader's *really* gangsta. Exponentially. Everyone else thought Leader's crime days were behind him, alongside his days as a Green Beret. To the uninitiated, Leader was a good businessman who gifted to his wife a thriving real estate business, just so he could start a security consulting firm, which took off immediately. To Pug, Leader was a whole different animal—literally and figuratively.

"What's up, Unc?" Pug proudly asked.

"You the man," Leader told him, beaming with pride. They didn't make them like Pug anymore. He was a throwback to Leader's days in the trenches. Leader beckoned Pug outside. "Let me speak with you a second. Excuse us." Leader and Pug distanced themselves from everyone.

While Leader and Pug conversed, Justus stuffed his face with chicken and potato salad. By the time he was done, Leader was calling him in the corner with him and Pug.

"Why your husband always so secretive?" Gloria asked Glenda, Justus's mom, not realizing she was whispering herself. Her liquor was clearly taking its effect.

"Girl, you know how he is about his son."

"*His* son? Hmp."

"Now, Glo, don't start."

"You haven't seen me get started," Gloria promised.

"Well don't."

When Justus met with Leader and Pug they were finishing their conversation. "Jus, meet me over at Nikki's in a few minutes so we can help her move." Pug commanded. "Don't be long, 'cause I gotta get at you about something else too. A'ight?'

Justus nodded. Pug gave Leader a knowing look then exited, leaving Leader alone with Justus. "What's up, Dad?" Justus wondered.

"I've been checking you out a lot lately, man. And it seem like you fascinated with that drug shit." Leader's tone was dead serious. "Don't lose focus, son. That shit don't last. It's just a hustle, and a hustle is just that. A hustle! It ain't meant to last long. I got the perfect spot for you with me. Best thing is, you've been training for it all your life.

"I have?" Justus asked, unsure of what Leader was implying.

Leader patted him on his head. "I made sure of it. So, while I'm gone keep your nose clean and look after your mother and sister. When I come back, we'll get down to the details. Alright?"

Justus nodded. He wasn't slow by any standard, but Leader's comments had him baffled. He didn't recall Leader "training" him for anything.

"Now, go get with Pug. If I don't see you before I leave remember what I said. You got some money?"

"A little."

"What you call a little?"

"'Bout twenty dollars."

Leader sucked his teeth. "That ain't no money.

I thought I always told you to keep some money in your pocket."

"That is money," Justus insisted.

"For a boy! You're a man now."

"I know. That's why I ain't want to ask you for no money."

"Well, I applaud your independence, but don't be stupid. You're one of the few youngsters that can take advantage of asking their father for money. So, do it." To illustrate his point, Leader dipped deep into his pocket and gave Justus a wad of cash. "You'll know when it's time to make your money. Plus, you can't get a woman like Nikki if you go around her broke.

Justus smiled. His father knew the object of his childhood crush. "Thanks, Dad."

"Don't worry 'bout it. Just keep doing the right thing."

"And what's that?" Justus challenged.

When Leader answered, his tone was colder than Justus had ever heard it. Looking at Justus directly in the eyes, he told him, "Whatever I tell you to do. Now go see Pug."

As Justus crossed the courtyard, he could see Pug's Suburban from a mile away. The chrome crash bars glinted underneath the street lamps like diamonds. The truck sat off by itself at the edge of the parking lot. Apparently, someone was inside, because the music was on ever so slightly. Sounded like a Trey Songz CD, no doubt. *Probably Jackie and Pug cuddling*, thought Justus. Remembering what Pug did to him earlier, Justus decided to get him back.

Justus crept up on the rear side of the Suburban, but didn't see anyone inside. When he slipped around back of the truck and peered around, his breath got caught in is throat. Pug had Jackie bent over at the front of his truck, pounding her from the back! Jackie's pleated skirt was thrown recklessly over her back, while she alternated rocking back on the heels of her knee-high boots and grabbing the crash bars attached to the front of the truck.

Justus, caught in the moment, openly lusted. How could he look away when Jackie's glorious ass was exposed for all to see?

Pug sensed someone watching and opened his eyes long enough to see Justus watching them from the back of the truck. Instead of him getting vexed about it, he winked at Justus then held his index finger up signaling for Justus to wait a minute. Before Justus left, Pug cracked a smile, then gave Jackie two hard thrusts for good measure. Jackie moaned loudly, causing Justus to run away from the scene before the temptation to stroke himself overwhelmed him.

While Leader entertained his family, he was oblivious to someone watching his every move from a parked car tucked away in the cut. As Leader spoke to Pug, the observer cracked the tinted window of the sedan to glean some of the conversation floating on the wind. Unfortunately, when Leader spoke, he cupped his hand over his mouth, as if he knew someone was watching his every move. For a second, the spy thought the mission had been compromised. However, the spy knew that if Leader had been aware of his tail, he would have quickly resolved the situation. Confident that the position was secure, the spy held up an iPhone and captured more video.

Leader had no idea that he had made a costly mistake, and the spy on his tail planned to bring his mistake to his door.

Justus went to Nikki's apartment and found the screen door wide open, so he coasted on in. He could hear Nikki talking to someone in the kitchen, so that's where he went. When he entered the kitchen, Nikki was so busy on the phone, she didn't notice him.

"Girl, I am so glad to be leaving this place, I don't know what to do," Nikki was saying over the telephone. "I swear these niggas be—oh! Hey Jus. I thought you was Jackie," she apologized when she realized it was Justus inside her home.

Justus was speechless, in awe of Nikki's raw beauty. On any scale, Nikki was *Baaad!* She wasn't a dyme. She was a Susan B. Anthony! Too red to be considered brown. Too brown to be considered red. Her complexion met somewhere in the middle in a beautiful marriage all to itself. Although she possessed curves to spare, Nikki was not ghetto-thick. She was shaped like the hood thought a runway model should be: ample up top, small in the middle, and baby-making hips with a heart-shaped ass that broke hearts. Even in sweats with a silk scarf tied over her shoulder-length hair, Nikki could still show up the baddest broad.

"What's wrong wit' chu, Justus?" Nikki asked

with a smirk on her face. Her voice was a high-pitched note that would be downright irritating from anyone else. Coming from Nikki, it was murderous seduction.

"Nothing. Just checking you out."

Nikki giggled, "Mm-hmmm, I hear you. Standing there looking like a little man," she flirted.

"I am a man," Justus assured her.

"Well come on, Mr. Man. Help me with these boxes. Did you see Pug and Jackie?"

"Uhh . . . yeah."

"Where they at? I'm surprised they not somewhere getting their freak on." Nikki ended the phone call then turned to face Justus.

"Don't be," Justus mumbled.

"What?"

"Nothing."

"Oh. Is the truck out there yet?"

"Yeah. They out there."

"Good. Take that box out there, and that one too," Nikki ordered, pointing to two small boxes. Justus didn't move. "What's wrong, Jus?" Nikki asked, concerned.

"I wanna know why you didn't tell me you moving. Why I had to hear it from somewhere else?" Justus asked, looking at Nikki seriously.

"What? You tripping."

"Nah. I'm serious." Justus's face didn't have any hint of amusement. "I wanna know."

"Look at your little young ass trying to sound demanding." Nikki laughed, trying to throw Justus off. However, he refused to be denied.

"What's so young about me?"

"Just 'cause you grew a li'l bit, don't mean your ass ain't still young, nigga."

"Okay, you right. I am young," Justus conceded. "I know."

"I'm young enough to enjoy what I do . . . and old enough to know how to do it."

"Oh really?" Nikki blushed. She liked his smooth answer.

"Really. And it's time you stopped sleeping on me and let me show you," stated Justus confidently.

Nikki sucked her teeth. "Your little mannish self."

"Yo, grown is as grown does."

"True. You got a point," Nikki conceded.

"Plus, this the 21st century. Older women and younger men is common."

"For some people," Nikki agreed. "But I'm twenty-two years old, Justus, 'bout to be twenty-three."

"Okay. And?" Justus spread his hands like he really didn't get the point. "I'm confused."

"And you should be."

Justus sighed. "Why you giving me a hard time, Nikki. I just want to put you back on top and put a smile on your face."

"So, how you plan on doing that?" Nikki challenged, with her hands on her hips.

Justus didn't miss a beat, "By being there and providing for you and your little girl."

Big points! He acknowledged her daughter, Diamond.

"And how is a seventeen-year old going to do

that? Drugs? Shit, been there done that, and I'm tired of it. I am done playing that game."

Justus hopped on the countertop. "Good, 'cause I'm tired of playing games." Justus held his hand up and ticked off on his fingers. "First off, I never sold drugs. I'ma be working with my dad. Second, you keep dogging me for being young, but as long as I can handle my business, it shouldn't matter," he reasoned, then added, "Apparently, them *older* niggas ain't handling they business too good. Rollers running all up in your shit. Got you stressed out and shit." Justus had Nikki's undivided attention at this point. She couldn't deny his truths.

"Now if I didn't feel like I could change your situation, I wouldn't come at you like that. To me, you're a queen and I've always felt like that. I just want to put you back in your rightful place. With a king."

Nikki was feeling Justus's words, but she couldn't let him get off that easy. "Oh, so you a king?"

"No doubt."

"Whateva. How about get those royal hands on this box then," Nikki joked. "Come on."

Nikki grabbed a box from the counter and started towards the door. At first, Justus thought his macking attempts had failed, but as Nikki walked past him he saw her sizing him up.

Outside, Jackie and Pug had just completed their tryst when Justus and Nikki made it to the truck. Jackie was reapplying her cherry lipstick, while Pug was readjusting his Dickies suit. Justus popped the hatch and put the boxes in the back of the truck. Nikki stopped to speak with her best friend, while Pug came around to talk to Justus.

"Aye cuz, you gon' stop living your life through my eyes." Pug joked, referring to the incident from earlier.

Justus laughed, "Aye you crazy, dawg!"

"I was beating that pussy up, huh?" Pug laughed mimicking his pumps. "That pussy still blazing too! Shit, I ain't been up in there in a while. I had to get me!"

"True. True."

"But check this," Pug said, suddenly turning serious. "What I wanted to holla at you about." He pulled Justus in close. "Day after tomorrow I need you to go wit' me to handle something."

"Something like what?" Justus wondered.

"Something serious. Like, life and death serious. That's why I need *you* to go wit' me. I can't trust none of them other fools."

"Oh, it's like that?"

"Just like that."

"Well, you know I'm down, but I gotta watch my li'l sister. Pops leaving tonight and Moms got a couple of auctions to go to," Justus explained.

"Man don't worry 'bout that. Jackie'll watch her. So, you down or what?"

"Yeah."

"Good! Let's finish moving this shit so we can party. I'm home now nigga."

They both laughed heartily, then went to retrieve the other boxes.

Little did Justus know, the happiness would be short-lived. The countdown to the end of his innocence had just begun.

Chapter 2

Leader stepped into the pick-up area of O'Hare International Airport and spotted his ride immediately. He adjusted his shoulder bag then walked to the awaiting limo. By the time he reached the Rolls Royce, the back door popped open. Leader knew the routine well so he slid in back to meet his contact, Menes.

"'Ow are you, me friend?" Menes greeted Leader in his thick Nigerian accent. Leader accepted the extended hand before settling into the comfy confines of the soft leather. After he was sure Leader was settled, Menes tapped on the glass partition, and the heavy limo lurched into traffic.

"Drink?" Menes offered as he poured himself some cognac from the mini bar.

"No thanks."

Menes chuckled, "Ju' reely should loosen up, me friend." He drained the liquor then commented on Leader's appearance. "I see you still don't trust me after all dees time?"

He was referring to Leader's disguise. "Leader

was wearing a long beard, hazel contacts, and a brown Afro that covered his forehead and extended down to his jaw line. The wig made it impossible to determine his actual appearance. Each time Leader met Menes, he wore some type of disguise, sometimes even going so far as to dress like a woman. This was done to prevent Menes (or anyone else) an accurate depicting of his looks should something go awry.

"Never can tell what the future holds so this little precaution protects us both," Leader explained. Menes caught the hint.

"Always bout business," Menes noticed.

"Always."

"Very well then." Menes passed Leader the envelope containing the assignment. Leader opened it and perused the contents in silence as the limo drifted through the congested traffic. He grunted when he reached page three.

"I know what yur tinking, but trust, de' job is se'cure."

Inside the packet was Leader's mark, a Gary, Indiana police officer. According to the packet, the policeman had shot and killed a sixteen-year-old football star during a routine traffic stop. After pressure from the boy's family, the department reluctantly opened an investigation, but due to poor effort, charges were never filed. The family subsequently filed a civil suit, eventually settling out of court for a whopping three million dollars.

But the family wasn't satisfied.

They wanted the officer's job. When the department refused to take any action against him (they even promoted him) the family demanded

street justice. They sent some local goons to rough
him up, but they didn't do the job well enough.
The retaliation made the national news. Conse-
quently, the department began providing him with
additional off-duty security.

The additional security was what had Leader
spooked.

Leader completed the packet and addressed
his concerns to Menes.

Menes raised his soot-colored hand, silencing
Leader's thoughts. "The as'ault 'appened 'bout six
months ago," he explained. The early morning
sun burrowing through the dark tint made the diamonds in his pinky ring light up the car as he
continued to clarify the ramifications of the contract. "When de fam'a lee come to me, I tell dem it
be a while before I get de job done. Dey give half
the money upfront. So, now dey 'ave me word. Ya
undastand dat, yes?"

Leader understood quite well what Menes was
implying. He had given the family his word. In
their business, your word was gold. Your word was
equal to your life, sometimes more than your life,
for if the person you offended felt *your* life wasn't
sufficient, then anyone you held dear was in danger. Such was the nature of their business.

As the Rolls cruised the Magnificent Mile,
Leader looked at the early morning shoppers and
reflected on how he had gotten involved in the
business that was his life.

Leader was raised by his grandfather in Harlem,
New York for the first part of his life. Leader's grand-

father, Johnathan Moore (for whom he was named) took Leader away from his mother when he was an infant because he was dissatisfied with the fact his baby girl had been impregnated by a drop shot. Leader's grandfather possessed a strong work ethic and thought he had instilled the same ethic in his only daughter. John Mo, as he was called by everyone who knew him, was a real estate tycoon by day, and a pit boss by night. He ran numbers and illegal gambling houses from his numerous properties spread throughout Manhattan. He had met Leader's grandmother Annette in one of his gambling houses one night. She was in town from down south visiting relatives. John Mo laid eyes on her and refused to be denied. They engaged in a brief yet intense fling, and Leader's mother, Carmen, was born nine months later.

Carmen grew up between New York and North Carolina. She went to school in North Carolina while her summers were spent in New York. One day while walking home from school, she met Leader's father. He was a part-time construction worker and a full-time drunk. He was five years older than her, and full of game. He quickly swept Carmen off her feet. When reality brought her crashing down, it was too late. She was already three months pregnant. When John Mo received word that his precious daughter was knocked up by some drop shot, he rushed down south to pay his beloved a visit, and lay down the law on her baby daddy.

When John Mo arrived down south in his new Lincoln, surrounded by his big-city goons, all eyes were on him. John Mo waltzed into his one-time fling's home, noted the drab conditions, and immediately demanded she move to New York with him. He and Annette had their thing and kept in touch over the years on the strength of their child, and though he had his own type of love for her, he was a sporting man and not fit for settling down. Still, he didn't know she was living like *this*. A man of stature, he had to offer help to her. Of course, Annette accepted his offer. So while she gathered her affairs in order to move to New York, John Mo went to see Carmen. When he arrived at the mobile home, his anger intensified upon seeing what his daughter had selected for a mate. Leader's father, Slab, was planted in the love seat with one hand cupping a bottle of Gin, the other cupping his nuts.

John Mo was livid!

To Slab's detriment, the situation escalated when Carmen hobbled her swollen belly around the corner sporting a black eye. Without warning, John Mo snatched the scrawny Slab out of the chair and commenced to pummel him. After Slab lay on the floor bleeding, John Mo stuffed his knee into his chest, and his Derringer underneath his chin. Told him if he ever put his dirty hands on his daughter again, he'd tap dance on his liver. He then ordered Carmen to pack a bag and get in the car.

Leader was born the following month in Mount Sinai hospital in Manhattan. Carmen remained in New York long enough to breastfeed before being summoned down south by her *boy*friend. John Mo allowed her to go on one condition: she had to leave little John Mo with him. Carmen resisted initially, but after much pressure from her sick mother, she agreed, and fled to North Carolina. The following month, Annette lost her bout with cancer, leaving John Mo with his grandson as his only blood relative living with him in New York City.

John Mo doted on Leader, providing him with anything his young heart desired, and taught him all about life—real life—not the fairy tale presented to most children. He also schooled Leader about the real value of a dollar, and more importantly, how to earn one, honestly and otherwise. He taught him real estate tricks. He taught him how to study people to find out their weaknesses, then exploit them. John Mo gave his grandson the most valuable gift a parent could give a child. He gave him knowledge.

For Leader's part, he soaked everything in like cheap carpet. In fact, that was how he received his moniker. John Mo saw how quickly his grandson grasped things and realized he was destined to become a leader. He gave him the name Leader to remind and motivate him to be the best he could be so when the time came, he could be the best leader he could possibly be. Leader lived up to the name so much, that as a young boy everyone began calling him Leader, oblivious to the fact his grandfather had already given him the name.

When Leader was sixteen, his father killed his mother, then killed himself, in a bloody murder-suicide that haunted the city of Fayetteville for years to come. It was reported that so much blood was spilled, the police could smell it as soon as they hit the block. Sadly, six months later, John Mo died lying in his own blood.

A young Leader cradled John Mo's head in his

lap while awaiting the paramedics. Deep down inside he knew he wasn't going to make it. John Mo
was stabbed thirteen times by a gambler who had
lost his rent money in the card game the previous
night. The holes were so big Leader was able to
put his fingers clean through them. Which was exactly what he did to curb the bleeding. Unfortunately, he didn't have enough fingers.

When John Mo died, a part of Leader died
along with him. Leader became depressed with
the helpless feeling of not being able to save his
grandfather. The feeling consumed him to the
point that all he wanted to do was kill just to prove
himself worthy of living. His grandfather's death
occurred near the end of the first Gulf War, so
Leader knew exactly where to appease his hunger
to inflict pain. Leader joined the army with the
sole intention of learning how to kill. He refused
to let danger near any of his loved ones again, and
he not be prepared.

Leader joined a unit guaranteed to see action. True to his name. Leader rose through the
ranks to become a Non-Commissioned Officer in
no time. Much to his surprise (and his Comman-
der's pleasure) he was an efficient killing machine
with nine confirmed and countless unconfirmed
kills during his first tour. Leader was a natural because killing was his therapy. Every time he van-
quished a life, in his mind it was reciprocity for the
life of his grandfather. It didn't matter that his
grandfather never had any qualms with any Arabs.
Leader's mind had flipped. To him, the world had
killed his grandfather, therefore he held a grudge
against the world.

As a result of his stellar combat record, the Special Forces came calling, and Leader answered.

Leader began training at Fort Bragg, North Carolina, in June of 1994. From Bragg, he ventured to Fort Benning, Georgia for additional training before returning to Bragg for even more grueling training. By the time Leader was done, he had been turned into a fine-tuned machine, especially designed to build or destroy.

As a Green Beret, Leader learned all about nation building. They also taught other impoverished countries how to defend themselves, equipped them with weapons and training to use them. Over the course of two years, Leader bounced from country to country, training troops with his twelve-man team. At the age of twenty-one, he was transferred to Afghanistan to assist in training their army.

The Afghans were gearing up to fight the Taliban. Although the conflict would not explode on the world stage for quite a few years, U.S. troops were already in place. It was there that Leader discovered the dubiousness of his country. His CO's would order one thing, then do the opposite. Situations would occur one way, but the media would report a contrary story. When Leader began demanding answers, he was quickly shipped out of Afghanistan into North Africa.

His assignment? Assassinate Colonel Muammar Qaddafi.

Leader was selected because he was the lone black man in his twelve-man squad. He was also the best at what they wanted done, which essentially boiled down to murder without a trace.

Leader was educated on the languages and

customs of his AO (area of operations) in the Sudan and Morocco. Teaching him was none other than a Sudanese national with ties to a far-reaching crime syndicate. In addition to teaching Leader what was needed for his mission, he also opened Leader's eyes to limitless lucrative opportunities in the private sector. Every job from legal mercenary to illegal assassinations were discussed, ranging from locations as diverse as Timbuktu to the good ole' U.S. of A. Leader was blown away at the possibilities, but he was still indebted to the U.S. Army, so he was forced to decline, opting to revisit the particulars at a possible later date.

The hit on Colonel Qaddafi was eventually cancelled, but Leader continued to make his bones elsewhere. During the end of his enlistment, Leader grew disheartened with the whole bureaucratic process of the military and sought employment in numerous places for when he left the military. Much to his chagrin, no one was interested in hiring someone whose only skill was killing, therefore Leader was forced to leave the military without a viable job. New York was fraught with bad memories, so he opted to stay in Fayetteville, N.C.

Leader found a series of odd jobs, but found that he still possessed violent desires. His favorite pastime became frequenting a social club just off Bragg Boulevard. The club was rumored to be owned by one of Fayetteville's most well-known drug dealers, an O.G. name Sherlock.

One night while Leader was at the club, a man attempted to shoot another man, just feet away from where Leader was standing, enjoying his drink. Call it instinct. Call it survival. Call it thrill.

Regardless of the reason, the result was Leader dis-
arming the assailant before he could get a shot off.
When the assailant struck back with a wild blow,
Leader effortlessly blocked it, then issued a palm-
heel strike to his nose.

The man was dead before he hit the ground.

Leader knew he had fucked up big time! With
his training on record, he knew the state would
charge him with murder. Luckily for him, the man
whose life he had saved was the notorious Sherlock. Sherlock had Fayetteville on lock! Police on
the payroll. Crooked lawyers. Greedy judges. The
whole enchilada. When Leader killed the man inside Sherlock's club, Sherlock didn't flip out. Instead, he offered Leader support and a job. After
Sherlock ensured the body was disposed of properly, Leader began working as his personal bodyguard, with pay starting at $1,000 dollars a day.

For the next five years, Leader never left Sherlock's side. He eventually became more than just
Sherlock's bodyguard, he became his cleaner,
eliminating adversaries and competitors alike with
a brutal force never seen before on the streets of
Fayetteville. As a result, Sherlock became even
wealthier, and the riches trickled down to Leader.
Leader used the knowledge injected into him
from his grandfather to acquire real estate all over
the Carolinas. Because Sherlock put Leader into a
position to become financially secure, Leader was
fiercely loyal. Sherlock only had to think of a problem and Leader handled it, swiftly and violently.
Over time, in certain circles, Leader became more
feared than Sherlock, for it was known that Leader
was the crux of Sherlock's power.

Then it all suddenly came crashing down.

The Feds indicted Sherlock. True to O.G. form, Sherlock held his water, didn't implicate anyone else. He took his "elbow" like a man.

At first, Leader was on the verge of losing it. He held Sherlock in high regard. Sherlock reminded Leader of his grandfather in so many ways. Leader stayed in contact with Sherlock throughout his bid, putting thousands of dollars on his books. Sherlock became ill and the letters become more infrequent. One day, Leader received an important encrypted letter from Sherlock. According to the letter, Sherlock had been telling some old African about Leader's "skills." As it turned out, the African knew people in high places who could benefit from his service. Not that "ghetto-shit" (as the African eloquently put it.) Sherlock assured Leader anonymity, and all but ordered he accept the offer. He gave Leader the contact information and three weeks later Leader was meeting Menes for the first time in an underground parking garage in New Jersey.

Leader's first job was a female business executive whose husband would rather she die than give her a divorce. Leader shadowed her for two days before making his move. The next day, while she was out for her daily run, he slipped into her home, injected cyanide into her orange juice, and slipped out without being noticed. His only instruction was to make it look like a suicide, to which he followed in spades. Later, as he sat inside his hotel room removing his disguise, he saw the news report of a marketing executive found dead in her home. Cause of death? Suicide by poison. The reporter spoke of her going through a messy divorce, and even ran footage of her bereaved, estranged husband. Authorities made it quite clear that homicide was ruled out.

Leader collected $250,000 for his troubles.

From that point on, Menes provided Leader with a job bi-monthly. His jobs were as close as Charlotte, North Carolina and as far away as Beijing, China. Leader eventually had to create a security-consulting firm as a front, to justify his extensive travel and steadily growing bank account. He became knowledgeable of the world's major languages and religions to assist in facilitating his jobs. In time, he became a wealthy man without a care in the world, and only enough love for himself and the almighty dollar.

Then he met Glenda.

Leader's thoughts drifted back to the present. Menes had never steered him wrong on a mark in the past, and Leader didn't detect any hint of malice now, but you could never be too careful.

"Yeah, I understand your position," Leader answered, "But you understand mine, too. Right?"

"Absolutely." Menes reached into the humidor to extract a cigar, offered Leader one, which he declined. When he was done clipping the end, he lit it. "And like I tell you: ev'rything is ev'ry thing. You not ac'ting like dis because a de mark is a cop, are you?"

"Hell naw!" Leader responded, a little too enthused. "That's icing on the cake, far as I'm concerned." He meant every word of what he said. Leader despised cops with a passion. In fact, in the past, he had contemplated taking a page out of the book of South Americans. South Americans were notorious for assassinating authorities. Judges, lawyers, investigators . . . they all were cannon fodder for their criminal cartels. Leader thought about going straight vigilante numerous times, but he was a businessman. Businessmen never gave for free that which could be bought. Besides, vendettas didn't pay bills.

"Good, good. Well, your mo'ney will be de'posited as usual. Anything else?"

Leader shook his head. "Just watch the news. I'll be in touch."

With that, Leader popped out of the limo with his bag over his shoulder, disappearing into the Chi-town crowd.

Chapter 3

"Brrraaaaat!! Brrraaaat!! The clique affirmations echoed through the halls of the high school as two boys swerved around Justus and kept running to catch up with their comrades. Justus was finishing his last few weeks as a senior at 71st Senior High School, and was on top of the world. Oblivious to the affiliations surrounding him, he only had one thing on his mind: Panee.

Panee was Justus's pretty young thang, or P.Y.T. She was a senior also, but she was only sixteen. Panee was like most prodigies, extremely book smart, but life-illiterate, and Justus exploited her weakness to the fullest. Half Native, half black, Panee was one of the baddest chicks in school. Her mother was of the Lumbee tribe from Lumberton, North Carolina. Her father, though long gone, was a soldier. Justus had spotted her when she was a sophomore, and his slick, smooth ass swept the youngster right off her feet. She had been mobbed down with him ever since.

Justus had not seen or spoken with Panee

since the day of Pug's party, two days prior, and he wanted to know why. He bent the corner by the cafeteria and ran into an impromptu rap cipher. During the lunch hours, a rap cipher was guaranteed to be in session, and there were always women gathered around. As Justus made his way through the sea of bodies, he spotted his Panee, deeply enthralled in conversation with some no-neck football-playing brotha. Justus decided to size the scene up a bit before making himself known. The longer he stood and watched, the hotter he became underneath the collar. When he couldn't take anymore, he stepped over, pulling Panee away by the arm.

"Ouch Jus! What the hell is wrong with you?" Panee demanded in her proper speech.

"No, what the hell is wrong witchu?! All yakkety yakking with this nigga." Justus jerked his finger toward the dude, and saw that he was gritting on him. "What nigga?! I know you ain't beefing?" Jus challenged. Seeing that no-neck wasn't backing down, Justus released Panee's arm and stepped closer. Panee attempted to pull Justus back, but he snatched his arm away. Before Justus covered the short distance to his opponent, the rappers stopped their cipher and intervened to break them up. No-neck became overly belligerent, screaming obscenities and promises at Justus. This further infuriated Justus. When he saw his partner, Magi, standing behind the football player, he really got amped. Magi was a known brawler!

Not one to disappoint, Magi flailed a hooking overhand right and cuffed the dude in the top of the dome. Then all hell broke loose as other football players joined the fracas, beating on the innocent rappers. Soon, school security arrived, pulling bodies apart left and right. Once Justus ensured Magi was okay, he snatched Panee by the arm and dipped out before he was caught.

Justus and Panee stole away behind the staircase at the end of the hallway. Once they were alone, Justus slammed Panee against the wall.

"I can't believe you trying to play me, gurl!"

"Jus, what are you talking about? We were just talking."

"Talking my ass!" Justus exploded. "I stood there and watched you kee-keeing all up in that nigga face."

"You are really tripping," Panee mumbled angrily. "You just can't wait to fly off the handle like some Neanderthal." She tried to turn away, but Justus spun her back around.

"You see me fuckin' talking to you. Don't play wit' me dawg."

Panee had enough. "Oh, you mad now? Justus is upset. What's new?" She asked herself. "Do I get upset when all of those hood rats are in your face, Mr. Basketball? And I know for a fact that you are fucking them!"

"Don't try to change the subject."

"This *is* the subject!"

"No, it's not!!"

"Yes, it is!!!"

"A'ight gurl, I'm serious now," Justus warned.

"I'm for real too, Jus. You know what? Maybe we should take a break from each other because this is not going anywhere."

"What?" Damn, Justus did not expect this.

"Y-yo, what you saying? You wanna break up 'cause of a little argument? We've argued before."

Panee exhaled, "I know, but it's more than that. I mean, we're graduating soon. I'm going to college. You're going to be working with your dad. How could this work?" She asked, practically begging for a solution. Justus, finally realizing the seriousness of the situation, couldn't offer one. He couldn't believe his P.Y.T. was breaking up with *him*. Imagine that?

"So when were you going to tell me this?" Justus asked, stalling for time.

"I've been feeling this way for quite some time now. You're just always too busy to talk. If you want, we can talk some more tonight. I have to go to class now."

Justus slowly shook his head, "Nah, tonight's no good for me. I gotta help my cousin, Pug, with something."

"Pug? When he get out?"

"The other day."

"Well, can't he get somebody else to help him?" Panee snapped.

"I gave him my word."

"So now you a man of your word?"

"What?" He couldn't believe she was coming at him like that! "Look, I see you had your little moment of clarity or whatever. Even though I wasn't consulted, it's obvious your mind is made up so . . ."

"Jus wait! Don't walk away. Please?"

Justus spun around to face her. "Why? It's obvious there's nothing more to say here."

"It's not like that."

"What's it like then?"

Panee dropped her head. "We're just too different," she whispered. "We're going in two different directions."

This time when Justus walked away, he didn't turn back when Panee called out to him. Instead he focused on the future. Maybe this was for the best, he thought. 71st had no shortage of honies. Different nationalities too. Puerto Ricans, Vietnamese, Filipinas, Germans, Mexicans. And a heavy mixture of everything in between, courtesy of Fort Bragg. As a single man Justus was free to explore with his remaining time at 71st.

Also on Justus's mind was Nikki. He could tell he had struck a nerve with her that night. She had been the object of his affection since he was a child. Now he was finally beginning to convince her to see him as a man. Justus felt if he could bag Nikki, then fuck Panee! Nikki was a WOMAN.

Leader had always taught Justus that when one door closed another opened. Maybe this was for the best. Justus knew Pug could help put him in the car with Nikki, and he had every intention of approaching him with the idea later that night.

That was his intention anyway.

Chapter 4

Leader stared back at the bald-faced man in the mirror, pleased at what he saw. He had taken the liberty to shave his entire body again once he settled into his hotel room. Then he began the arduous task of applying electrical tape to his limbs, all the way from his hands up to his shoulders. Then from his knees down to his toes.

This was his way.

Law enforcement held a theory that proved true 99.9% of the time. This was that for every murder committed, two things held true for the crime scene: the assailant always brought something foreign to the scene, and the assailant always took something away from the scene. These "things" accounted for the majority of clues found in homicide cases.

Leader had full knowledge of this theory, so he sought to use it to his advantage, minimizing anything that could be left to implicate him. In most cases, hair or blood would be extracted from the crime scene, allowing investigators to draw a

DNA sample. To combat this, Leader shaved his entire body bald minutes before he went out on a job. He would then tape his limbs with thick electrical tape just in case a struggle ensued, the victim would not have any of his skin underneath their fingertips.

No hair deposited. No blood extracted. No DNA. The battle was halfway won.

For the second part of the theory, Leader would manipulate the crime scene. For instance, he would wear either bigger or smaller shoes to imprint the crime scene. He would walk extra heavy or light to simulate a different weight distribution on the ground. He would walk very erect or slouched over to appear taller or shorter. This would derail any would-be witnesses that he couldn't get to himself. Sometimes he would set the crime scene ablaze or simply blow it up. After a job was completed, he would find a remote location (sometimes in another state) to burn his clothing. He would then stuff the ashes in a bag and flush them down a toilet.

Whatever the situation called for, Leader would handle it in the most professional manner, for he was nothing if not swift and interchangeable.

Satisfied with his appearance, Leader pulled himself away from the mirror to get dressed. On the bed lay a Gary, Indiana police uniform replica, complete with badge, gun, and cap. The only thing different about his uniform was the long sleeves, but this would not pose a problem. Most people didn't give policemen the twice-over to critique their apparel. They were too busy trying to stay the hell out of their way, especially in Gary, Indiana.

Policemen in Gary had established their reputation over the years that they were not to be trifled with. This particular night, Leader had plans to shatter that myth.

All he had to do was wait for night to fall.

The music bumped at low volume in the old-school bucket as it drifted down the highway. Pug was slumped low in the driver's seat while Justus fiddled with the food in his lap as he rode shotgun. His heart was heavy with the situation with Panee, so he had been bending Pug's ear with is grievances for the better part of an hour. Finally, Pug grew tired.

"Man, cuz, fuck that bitch! If she don't want you no mo' then fuck her." Pug had been saying the same thing, in so many words, the entire trip. Finally, he grew disgusted, and had to make it plain. "That's what's wrong wit' dem seditty hoes anyway. They be thinking they betta than a nigga an' shit. All they want is a hen picked nigga fo' dem to run over anyway." Pug sat up briefly to get a better look at a road sign then slumped back into the seat and continued, "That li'l hoe young anyway. What-chu wetting that for'? She can't even take care of herself, more less, you. Don't be fucking these li'l broads for free. Make 'em bring sumthin' to the table, ya dig?"

"I dig."

"Good. Now check this out." Pug exited the road they were traveling, found the first gas station on the right, and backed the Cutlass in the cut on the side of the building. The gas station was still open, but only a clerk, who looked to be in her mid-twenties, was inside. The store was in the middle of the boonies so it was no surprise that the store had no customers.

Pug cut the engine, pulled his bucket hat lower on his face, and leaned even further back into the seat.

"What the fuck are you doing, dawg? You 'bout to rob the joint?" Justus wondered, looking around, scoping out the surroundings.

"Chill cousin. You'll see," answered Pug calmly. "Now back to what I was saying earlier . . ." He paused like he was about to tell Justus who killed Kennedy.

"What fool?"

"Ole' girl digging you."

"Who?"

"Nikki."

"Who?" Justus wasn't sure he heard him right.

"Nigga, you heard me! Nikki."

"Say word! How you figure?"

Pug shrugged his shoulders like he hadn't just told Justus the most important news of his life, "She told Jackie."

"What she told Jackie?" Justus wanted details. He wanted Pug to turn into Picasso.

"Calm down, nigga. Damn!" Pug swore as he looked around the lot suspiciously. "She told Jackie that you tried to holla at her on some ole' put-her-on-top shit."

Justus blushed.

"It was lame," Pug informed him. "but ole' girl said she was digging it though. She told Jackie she would turn your li'l young ass out. Wouldn't mind her trying to turn me out. I'll knock the bottom out that pussy! Shit look like it's blazing too," Pug thought aloud. "Anyway, me and J s'posed to be going to the movies Friday. Y'all wanna go? I can set it up an' shit."

"No doubt," Justus agreed.

"Shit, say no more. It's on then." Pug scoped the parking lot again. It appeared he was waiting on someone. A car traveled from the highway in the opposite direction from the way they were facing. Pug scrutinized it closely before relaxing in his seat.

"Yo, you think she really digging me?" Justus asked, snapping Pug out of his trance.

"What? Who?"

"Nikki."

"Oh, I guess so. Look, I put you in the car, you gotta drive yourself."

"True. You right," Justus smirked in the dark. The two men sat in silence for a while. Car after car came and went.

"Damn, where this muthafucka at!" Pug swore to himself, impatiently looking at his watch.

"Who man?" Justus was tired of playing in the dark, and not knowing why. Pug glanced at him from the side, sizing him up before he pulled on his coat. He finally decided it was time to let the cat out of the bag.

"This punk ass C.O., from when I was locked down," Pug relayed quietly. "The nigga kept fuckin' wit' me when I was down. I tried to warn him, but he kept acting like he couldn't get it or something."

"So, what you gon' do then?" Justus asked, a little concerned.

"Look, don't go bitchin' up on me!" Pug snapped. "You here now."

"Ain't nobody bitchin' up. I was just asking," Justus said.

Pug nodded his head. "Um-hmm. We 'bout to see right now." Justus raised his head and peeped a blue Eclipse pulling into the gas station. At the same time, Pug reached in the backseat and retrieved a shotgun from under the blanket. Upon closer inspection, Justus realized Pug didn't hold just any shotgun. He held an automatic shotgun, known on the streets as a "streetsweeper" for its ability to clear a whole block out. The weapon was equipped with a cylinder drum holding up to one hundred rounds of ammunition. Pug double-checked the weapon, chambered a round, and then focused his attention on the Eclipse. He watched the tall, lanky driver, still in his corrections uniform, pump gas then go inside to pay.

"Take the wheel!" Pug demanded, switching places with Justus. "When he come out, do exactly as I say!"

Leader waited patiently until Moose reached a two-lane highway before he planted his portable blue light onto the roof of the cruiser. Moose spotted the blue lights in his rearview, traveled a few more feet, then pulled to the shoulder of the road. Leader lingered inside the car a few extra moments for good measure then exited the vehicle.

As Leader approached the car, his mouth began to water unconsciously in anticipation of some action. On the sly, he surveyed his surroundings for anything out of the ordinary. No sooner than he arrived at the car window, Moose began pleading his case expecting leniency because he was a fellow officer of the law.

"Ah, was I speeding, Officer?" Moose asked, chuckling. As he searched for his I.D. inside of his wallet, he made sure to let his badge show. "You know how it is, get used to speeding around in those department cruisers, and it just becomes a habit." He continued to ramble, while Leader looked at him unfazed by his spiel. Leader's heart thumped in anticipation. He wanted to crack him in the face with his pistol until the blood stopped spurting. But this was business. "Surely, you can let this one slide, huh?" Moose pleaded.

"Maybe we can, but first I need to see some identification, sir."

Leader scanned the road as Moose reached inside his glove box to retrieve his papers. When Moose looked up, he was looking directly at the prongs of Leader's stun gun. The second he realized what it was, it flashed. A burst of hot pain seized Moose's upper chest. His body convulsed uncontrollably, then darkness enveloped him.

Leader moved with efficient precision, snatching open the door to remove Moose from the car. At the moment he extracted Moose, a motorist passed from the opposite direction, slowing down to be nosy. Leader waved a gloved hand to move the car on then returned to the task at hand.

He hoisted Moose over his shoulder, and carried him to the already open trunk. He dumped Moose into the trunk with a thud and slammed it shut. When he was done, he returned to the car, started the engine, and turned the cruiser in the opposite direction. With the engine still idling, he got out.

Leader walked back toward Moose's car, stopping mere feet away. He clenched the bottle in his right hand tightly, lit the hankie, and then tossed the Molotov cocktail through the air.

He was back at his car by the time he heard the minor explosion from the Molotov. He drove away slowly with his eyes riveted on the rearview mirror while mentally checking the next phase of his plan. Suddenly his mirror ignited with a flash, and the ground shook violently. Leader smiled, then floored the accelerator to his next destination.

The Corrections Officer paid for his gas then ventured back out into the unseasonably cool Carolina air, none-the-wiser that just a few feet away someone was planning to do him harm.

Inside the bucket, Pug passed Justus a hat to pull over his head, and instructed him to follow the Eclipse. When the C.O. pulled out, Justus was right behind him.

Justus was tripping. All he kept thinking was, *Damn!! I didn't know Pug wanted me to be an accomplice to murder!* When he agreed to help Pug he never dreamed it would entail this. Now he understood why Pug insisted *he* help him. Pug knew that Justus would never betray him. Justus was pissed that Pug didn't confide in him earlier, but now was not the time to address it.

"You a'ight?" Pug asked. Justus didn't answer. Instead, he mean-mugged Pug something vicious, however Pug didn't care. "Pull up beside the car," he instructed.

Pug leaned out the window, holding the shotgun in both hands, aiming at the window of the Eclipse. The wind whipped past his head nearly taking his bucket hat off. Pug gritted his teeth and smiled. He felt alive! He lived for the action, and teaching this arrogant wannabe cop a lesson was an unparalleled adrenaline rush.

Pug held the barrel trained on the window for what seemed like an eternity. Justus didn't know what was taking so long. He was ready to be gone already. Pug aimed the shotgun a little while longer then pulled the trigger.

BOOM! BOOM! BOOM!

Shots erupted in rapid succession, stealing the calm from the cool night air. Instinctively, Justus jerked the wheel to the left to avoid being sideswiped, then sped up with Pug hanging on to the window. They heard a loud hiss, then a flapping sound, as the Eclipse's two tires were blown out.

"Yeeah muthafucka!" Pug screamed, holding the street-sweeper up like a trophy. Pug ducked back into the vehicle with his energy on a thousand. "We got that muthafucka, Jus!"

Justus punched the throttle and put some distance between them and the unstable Eclipse. In his rearview, he witnessed the car continuing to slide and swerve perpendicularly in the road before it toppled over and flipped a dozen times. The roof of the car slammed into a tree violently, and the other halves of the vehicle wrapped around it.

Justus looked at Pug in bewilderment. He knew if Pug wanted to kill him, he could have just shot into the car. Instead he aimed at the tires and decided to leave it to fate. Justus was about to demand an explanation, but before he could, Pug stuck the shotgun out the window and unleashed the entire drum. Justus clamped his hands over his ears to deafen the lead orchestra. The strong stench of gunpowder drifted back into the car and singed Justus's nostrils.

"Yooo, what the fuck, Pug?" Justus barked.

Pug snickered and peered out the back window. "If the cocksucker lives through that, it's on him," he stated apathetically. "If he dies, he dies."

Leader pulled his cruiser to the shoulder of the dark road, looked both ways, and then exited when he was sure the coast was clear. He popped the trunk to retrieve his package.

Officer Moose was just beginning to regain consciousness. He attempted to say something, but due to the rag crammed inside his mouth, secured with tape, everything was muffled. Leader had Moose restrained with his own handcuffs behind his back. His feet were tied together extra tight with rope, and another rope ran from his feet to the handcuffs, connecting the two, causing Moose to resemble a triangle.

Leader double-checked his surroundings, before snatching Moose from the trunk by the rope. He made sure to inflict as much pain as possible. Moose's screams were barely audible through the gag, but they were enough to suffice Leader's lust. He knew time was of the essence, so he sped up the process. Leader slammed Moose on the ground face first then issued a swift kick in the ass. Moose's teeth scraped through the concrete.

"You remember this place, motherfucker?"

Normally, Leader wouldn't taunt his victims. He'd heard stories of victims turning the tables on their assassins because they didn't stick to the script. They waxed poetic seeking validation for their actions and ended up paying for their amateurish ways. Leader was far beyond seeking validation, but this was different. He was tired of cops gunning down young brothas and sistas in the streets of Amerikkka, only to be set free by their peers. He was tired of seeing the broken-hearted pleas of the have-nots crying out for justice. An opportunity that made sense to him had finally presented itself. He finally had a way to exact a slice of revenge on the overseers for the lives they'd squashed and killed with no retribution. Therefore, he couldn't resist the taunts.

"I said, do you remember this place?" Leader kicked him in the ass again. Leader had taken the officer to the exact location where he had murdered James Jenkins, the young football star.

Officer Moose mumbled something incoherently. Tears trickled down his face as he realized this was how his time on earth would end. He knew why Leader had come for him. He had done many men wrong during his tenure on the force, but the Jenkins case was one that haunted him. He instinctively knew this was about the Jenkins case.

"Turn your punk ass over!" Leader flipped Moose over. Due to the way he was tied, his body was inverted. The only parts of him touching the ground were his head and his feet. Leader raised his leg high in the air and came down hard on Moose's stomach. "This is for all my brothas and sistas you confined to misery just for being black!"

Leader aimed his silenced .357 right at Moose's head and fired.

After Leader unloaded the pistol, he removed the tape from the handle then tossed it beside the body to allow investigators to lift fingerprints from the handle. He laughed at the thought of police searching for a dead man. He had imprinted the fingerprints of a corpse from a previous job onto the handle before having the gun shipped up from the Carolinas. He chuckled at the irony of the investigators looking for a dead man to solve the murder of another dead man.

On his way back to his cruiser (which would later be found roasted) Leader rubbed the detached finger inside his satchel. He had liberated the digit from Moose while he was still alive. The trigger finger was to be a gift to the family.

If they wanted it.

Chapter 5

Honk! Honk!

Justus looked out the window and saw Pug's Suburban sitting pretty on 26-inch rims and tires.

"Dad! They here! I'm 'bout to go!" Justus yelled. He spared himself one last look in the mirror, adjusted his matching Akoo bucket and got ready to dip. "Damn, I forgot something," he muttered to himself, doubling back to his dresser to rub on the Egyptian Musk Oil.

When he galloped downstairs, Leader was waiting on him at the door in his velvet robe. "Whoa son, where you rushing to?"

"I got a date, remember?"

Leader snapped his fingers, "Oh yeah! With Pug and Jackie, right?"

"Pug, Jackie, and Nikki," Justus corrected, blushing.

"Alright. Here, take some money," suggested Leader, digging into his robe.

"I'm straight. Pug gave me some." Justus blurted out.

Leader looked at him speculatively, "What Pug give you money for?"

"Well, you know, I helped him, um, move that night so he let me hold a li'l something," Justus lied.

"Oh yeah?" Leader questioned, looking Justus in his eyes with that penetrating stare of his. Justus swore his father was looking at his soul. It felt like it anyway.

"Uh, yeah."

Leader narrowed his eyes, "How little something?"

"Couple yards," whispered Justus. Leader wasn't buying it.

"Tell Pug to come inside." Leader stepped aside to let his son pass.

"Dad, we already late as it is!" Justus objected. "What? You don't trust me or something?"

Leader weighed his next words carefully before responding, "Yeah, I trust you, but let me tell you something . . ." Leader placed both his hands on his son's shoulders and buried his gaze even deeper, "Don't you *ever* lie to me. Nothing is that bad that you have to lie. I don't care if you kill a nigga. Don't lie to me about it."

Justus gulped. Did Leader know about that night?

"You understand, Jus? Never! If anything, I'll help you bury the body. Got it?" Justus nodded. "Good. Now, get out of here. I got a date."

"With who?"

"Yo' mama, fool. We got the house to ourselves tonight," Leader announced with freaky implications.

"Awww Pop. Spare me! That's T.M.I."

"T.M. who?"

"Too much information," Justus laughed.

"Aww, Negro, please. When you ready to step up with Nikki, I'll show you how to lock it down," Leader joked.

"A'ight, a'ight."

Suddenly Leader turned serious, "Seriously though, be careful out there. And stay with Pug. I can trust Pug. He won't steer you wrong. He respects what I'm trying to do."

Sheeeeit! If you only knew, thought Justus.

Leader passed Justus a knot of money. "Take this. You can never have enough money with a woman like Nikki."

"Thanks."

Outside when Justus climbed in the back of the Suburban, he couldn't shake the feeling that Leader knew something. However, when he saw Nikki's hand extended, offering to help him climb up, all his previous thoughts vanished.

Nikki was wearing a black, sleeveless catsuit, made of a wool-linen blend. The fabric was stretched tight across her shapely hips, which were accented by her sitting down, with her legs crossed at the ankles. Her hair was swept up into a bun with a bang left hanging to cover her forehead. Her jewels were representing everywhere. Fingers. Wrist. Neck. Toes. Ears. Everything was dripping, showing the signs of a well-kept woman. Justus wondered if he was biting off more than he could chew.

"'Sup Jus?" Nikki greeted in her sexy squawk. Her sweet fragrance claimed the confines of the truck.

"What's up, peoples?"

"Cuz-o!" Pug responded with enthusiasm.

"Heey Jus," Jackie cooed, with a smirk on her face.

Pug turned the music up and pulled out of the driveway. The four 15-inch subwoofers and four separate component sets made the truck sound like Reggae Sunsplash! as Buju Banton's guttural drawl echoed through the truck's confines. Up front, Pug was putting fire to a stick of kind bud, when he saw bubblegum flash in his rearview.

"Shit!" Pug swore. He muted the sound system and dropped the blunt into the center console. When the security transporter passed them, Pug exhaled, expressing his displeasure. "Gotdamn man, why y'all gotta live way the fuck out here wit' these uppity mu'fuckas? Y'all too good for common folk? Damn, rent-a-cops 'bout to give me a heart attack."

Pug was referring to their upper middle-class neighborhood, of course. Justus's family lived in a subdivision off Ramsey Street. The homes started at half a million dollars. Because of a recent rash of break-ins, the community now boasted a series of security substations.

"Man, I ain't got no say in where we live," Justus said, looking through the back window for any sign of security. "But I'm glad I don't live in the hood. Who the fuck want to live bad?" Justus snapped. He was still a little vexed about Pug playing him. Since the incident had occurred, the two had only spoken once to confirm their date.

"Yeah nigga, whatever."

"Pug, leave Justus alone."

"Oh shit, look at that," Pug laughed, covering his mouth. To him, it was comical that Nikki was stepping in to defend Justus. "A'ight, Nikki, be warned: I'll put both y'all asses to kicking rocks. Cute or not."

Jackie turned around in her seat shaking her head. "No he won't, gurl. Pug just acting out. Don't pay him no mind."

"A'ight. Think I won't."

"Anyway. Y'all know what we going to see, right?" When no one answered, Jackie told them. "That new movie, *For the Love of the Beat*. Y'all remember? It's about the rapper dude, Qwess. It's telling all about how his crew came up. A lot of it was shot right here in Fayetteville," she informed them.

"You getting real excited over there, talking 'bout that nigga." Pug noticed. "Let me find out."

"Oh please. I got my Bookie." Jackie wrapped her arms around Pug and kissed him on his cheek while he drove. Pug blushed unabashedly and Jackie returned to her synopsis. "It's supposed to be shot by his new film company. The news say he supposed to be there tonight."

Pug scoffed, "Fuck he gon' do that. When I was in the clink, I read in a magazine he got knocked for conspiracy to commit murder. Some shit about he paid somebody to kill the broad that used to run his old record label. You remember she got murked, right Jus?"

Justus piped up from the backseat, "Yeah, I remember, but ole' boy beat that case. You know he got that bread. Nigga got old dope money, plus he married that broad, Lisa Ivory."

"No doubt," Pug agreed.

"And his partner King Reece was paid before he got killed. You know he ain't take all that dough wit' him," Justus added.

"Shit, the nigga tried. You know he got buried in a mosque or some shit."

"You mean put in a mausoleum?" Jackie corrected. "You don't get buried when you in a mausoleum."

"Well, what the fuck ever, bitch," Pug spat dismissively. Nikki gasped while looking at Justus to gauge his reaction. "Like I was saying, the nigga got put in a mausoleum. I saw that in the magazine too."

"Is that all you did was read magazines?" Jackie queried, obviously letting it be known that she had been offended by Pug's words.

But Pug was not about to concede power.

He noticed Jackie had been getting slick out the mouth lately any damn way. It was time to put her ass back in check, lest the balance of power be upset.

"Nah, that ain't all I read. I read them freaky ass letters you used to send. Jacked off on them mu'fuckas 'bout every night too. Right along wit' dem freaky ass pictures you sent wit' your shit all bust open too. Now!" Pug sneered at Jackie to drive his point home. Jackie pouted her lips then blasted the radio to drown out Pug's insolence.

In the backseat, Nikki was holding Justus's hand. She leaned over and whispered in his ear, "I hope that's not how you treat your women."

"Nah, I can be mean in the street. When I

come home, all I want is sweetness." Justus assured her, flashing his pearly whites.

"Hm-mmm. That's what they all say."

"You'll see."

"How will I see?" Nikki teased. Justus nudged closer to Nikki, draped his arm around her.

"Cause I'ma make you my woman," he stated confidently.

"What makes you so sure?"

"I told you, I'm an eternal optimist."

"Optimism is good," Nikki acknowledged. She snuggled further underneath Justus's arm. For the remainder of the ride, they exchanged small talk.

When they arrived at Omni Theaters, traffic was at a standstill. The movie was being shown as the dollar movie on opening night out of love for the city. The movie's executive producers, Qwess and Rolando, were hometown favorites. Fayette-ville embraced them for their contributions to the entertainment industry. Qwess, along with his slain comrade King Reece, was once at the helm of the notorious Crescent Crew, a gang of young, wealthy, ruthless drug-dealers that once controlled a substantial part of the southern drug trade. Upon Qwess's release from prison, he formed his own record label and sold 50,000 records independently. His label, *A.B.P.*, eventually became the envy of the industry. Qwess and his business manager, Doe, had started a film company to tell their stories and other stories of the street. Both Qwess and Rolando were married to R&B starlets. Judging by the long line dripping from inside the theater, the executive producers must have been present.

The movie wasn't expected to begin for another hour.

"Damn, this shit is thick!" Pug exclaimed, turning the music down to be heard. A plethora of new luxury vehicles flooded the parking lot along with rimmed out Cadillacs, and the Fayetteville staple, Oldsmobile Ninety-Eights.

Pug navigated his way through the parking lot, having to stop every few feet to let someone walk in front of the truck. A chick walked by with an ass so fat it was hanging out the bottom of her shorts. Pug had to feign a cough to keep his cool. When he lifted his head, a car in front of him was flicking its headlights repeatedly. At first, Pug didn't recognize the car. When he left the street, it was just a regular Olds Ninety-Eight. The car flagging him down now was coated with a beautiful, shiny purple paint job, and sitting on them thangs: Trues and vogues. However, Pug still recognized the vanity plate attached to the front. It read A.B.

When Pug drew next to the car, he rolled down his window, "What up, Dawg?"

"What's the bidness, P-U-Gee?!" A.B. yelled. "I heard yo' ass was home. Fuck you ain't holla at me?"

Pug leaned down out of the truck to give A.B. some dap. "You know how it is. I wanted to get back on my feet first."

"Sheeit, nigga, look like you still standing tall to me," commented A.B., sizing up the big rims on Pug's Suburban.

"Oh, I am now. I'm standing like a giant now," Pug informed him in the discreet way that let him know that if he wanted to cop some work, everything was everything. "What up wit' chu? Look like you done came up."

A.B. seemed a little uncomfortable answering, "Yeah no doubt," he admitted, cutting his eye at the beauty seated in his passenger seat. "So, you know I need to see you."

"A'ight, just hit me up later. What's up in there. You seen the movie?'

"Yeah, shit blazing, dawg. Huh babe?" A.B. tapped his date on the leg. She agreed with him. "That nigga Qwess in there with his boy, Doe. They in there signing autographs. Niggas wives wit' em too. Broads fine as hell." A.B. couldn't pass up the observation. Pug smirked and was in the process of offering a comment of his own until the trailing car blew its horn for him to move. Pug swore under his breath, but moved nonetheless.

In the backseat, Justus was still laying his mack game down with Nikki. So far everything was going well.

"Ooh, I like that," Nikki pointed across the parking lot to an arrest-me red Porsche GT parked beside a black McLaren 720S. Both cars were backed into their spaces in V.I.P. fashion. Sitting still, both cars looked fast.

"Yeah, it's hot. I've always liked Porsches. I'ma get me one. If you play your cards right, I'll let you drive it." Justus told Nikki.

"Damn, Daddy, if you digging me like you say you are, you should buy me my own," Nikki said, spitting game. It was obvious how she had amassed the precious stones she wore that were still lighting up the truck's interior.

"You should think bigger, Babygirl. You ride with

me I'm going to give you the world. To put you in a
Porsche is nothing."

"Um-hmmm. Promises, promises."

As they exited the vehicle, Nikki was in deep
thought reflecting on Justus. It turned out he was
very mature for his age, and his confidence was refreshing to see in a man. He really felt that he
could take on the world. Nikki was convinced also.
She couldn't deny that she was really feeling him.
With a little training, he could be a good man, she
thought. There was something about molding a
man to her exact requirements that appealed to
her.

Justus was in deep thought as well. He meant
every word he had told Nikki. He had adored her
from afar, and lusted up close for most of his life.
If given the chance, he planned to spoil her rot-
ten. Fuck her boyfriend in the clink! She was out
with him now, and he was going to do everything
in his power to ensure there were many dates to
come. Justus had learned a long time ago, when
one man's away, another man steps in to play
daddy. That's just what he intended to do.

Leader looked at himself in the mirror, scruti-
nizing every inch of his body. At forty-seven, Leader
could easily pass for ten to fifteen years younger. His
wonderful physique was attributed to his rigorous
workout regimen. Leader had a home gym installed
in the attic, which he visited five days a week. He
also adhered to Eastern arts, from yoga to several
different forms of martial arts. Leader took great
pains not to bulk up. In his profession, one had to

be able to maintain an unassuming and anonymous look. You could always add more clothing to appear bigger, but once you were so big, it was next to impossible to appear considerably slimmer. This was why Leader maintained himself at an even two hundred pounds, which fit perfectly on his six-foot-one-inch frame.

Leader heard someone come in downstairs. After slipping on a pair of silk boxers, he rushed down to investigate. His wife was coming through the door.

Glenda was wearing a snazzy royal blue skirt suit with a white silk blouse. Blue heels with a silver spike set the ensemble off. She wore no stockings, putting her shapely legs on display. Even though she had not run track in over twenty years, her round calves still looked like they belonged on a track. Glenda was an age-defying beauty. If forty was the new thirty for the millennium woman, Glenda was twenty. She followed a strict diet and exercise routine, and she benefited tremendously from it.

Leader absolutely adored his wife. He lived to please Glenda. Anything she wished for was his command. From the first day he set eyes on her, he had to have her by any means. If life was a game, Glenda was the prize.

"Hey baby, you scared me," said Glenda when she noticed Leader camped out by the steps. Upon closer observation, Glenda asked, "What are you up to?"

"Come see," Leader challenged.

"I think I will." Glenda sauntered over toward the steps where Leader wrapped her into his embrace with a kiss. After savoring Glenda's taste, he ordered her to remove her clothes.

"What?" Glenda asked, unsure. "Where's Justus?"

"Out. It's just us."

After hearing this, Glenda complied with the request. She began a seductive dance, stripping off layer after layer. When she was done, Leader loaded her into his powerful arms and carried her upstairs where he proceeded to gift to her one of his special massages. Leader was so versed in massage therapy, he could have been a masseuse. This was one of the many things he learned during his world travels. Glenda looked forward to his massages because he always provided a "full release." When Glenda rolled over on her back to accommodate Leader, her hard nipples pierced the air like missiles. Leader noticed, and a part of him hardened as well, however it would be the better part of an hour before he consummated his lust. For Leader, Glenda was the music that soothed the beast in him. As he stroked his wife, he recalled how they met.

Leader had just returned from a business trip in South America via Chicago. It was one of the few times he actually decided to attend a nightclub. Wanting to mingle amongst his former comrades, he was dressed to impress when he stepped inside the NCO club on Fort Bragg. Glenda and her sister Gloria were already there. They were the envy of the club and the life of the party. Gloria, in all her ghetto fabulousness, and Glenda in her hood chic. They both wore sexy dresses. Gloria's was strapless, short, and sheer. Glenda's, spaghetti, silk, and tight. After observing them both for a while, Leader decided he would pursue Glenda. She seemed a bit more humble. Leader hated loud women.

He stepped to her, bought her a few drinks, chatted the night away. Everything was fine until Glenda informed him she had a man. Unfazed and undaunted, Leader continued to pursue her relentlessly. Eventually, he won her over in true Gladiator fashion, and they'd been inseparable ever since. On their road to bliss, Leader committed crimes against nature and his fellow man just to put stones that glittered upon her hand. If he had to do it all over again, he would.

Pug, Justus, Nikki, and Jackie had left Omni theaters in good spirits. The movie was good, the conversation better. Justus and Nikki were bonding, and Pug and Jackie were back to normal.

"What you wanna do, gurl?" Jackie asked Nikki as they drove down McPherson Church Road.

"While I would love to chill, I got a long day ahead of me. I'm still moving, ya know," Nikki explained. "But we'll hang later, Justus." Nikki promised, stroking his chin.

"Well, we'll drop you off at your place," Pug decided, eager to be alone with Jackie so they could engage in make-up sex.

After dropping Nikki off at her place off Cliffdale Road, Pug made Jackie drive while he sat in back to talk to Justus.

"You a'ight?" Pug asked Justus, a little concerned.

"What ch'mean."

"You been acting real salty lately. You mad about the other night? You got scared or something?"

"Nah, I wasn't scared," Justus insisted. "Not about dude getting hit up anyway."

"Word?' Justus nodded. "So, what were you scared of then?" Pug asked.

Justus mumbled, "Getting caught."

Pug stared at Justus for a long time, waiting on him to elaborate, but he never did. He just returned Pug's stare. After a moment, Pug said, "Get the fuck outta here!" He hit the remote, turned the music up louder, and puffed his blunt.

Pug may have thought Justus was putting on, but in actuality he wasn't. Justus was dead serious. He couldn't care less about the man getting hurt. He was only worried about getting caught. How would he explain something like that to his father? Justus knew his father was sacrificing a lot, bringing him into their business, and he didn't want to fuck that up. He respected his father, so much so, that as a child Leader never had to beat him. All it took for him to get in line was a hard stare, and a good talking to. Justus never wanted to disappoint his father. This was why he didn't want to get caught.

Justus's answer not only surprised Pug. It surprised him too. He was surprised he had such little regard for a person's life. Surprised he could feel so cold. Surprised he felt absolutely nothing. Yet that was exactly what he felt.

Nothing.

It was what it was.

Chapter 6

"What do you mean, you're going to be gone longer than anticipated?" Glenda asked. "We don't spend time together as it is."

"What are you talking about? We spent the entire night together a week ago," Leader reminded her. "I still shake just thinking about it."

"Don't try to butter me up. Last week was fine, but that's not what I'm talking about. We're supposed to be raising a family together," Glenda stated, clearly not buying it.

"Baby, just trust me. Now is not the time to talk about it." The telephone rang.

"Why is there a phone ringing?" Glenda asked, suspiciously, "John Mo, why are you talking to me on a cell phone if you're in the hotel? What's going on?"

"Damnit, Glenda, nothing! We'll talk later." Leader ended the call and answered the hotel phone.

Minutes later, he and Menes sat in the back of a limo discussing business.

"I saw the news. I am very pleased. Very." Menes reached into his jacket pocket and handed Leader an envelope stuffed with cash. "A bonus. As always, you came through again," Menes noted in his thick accent.

Leader accepted his compliment with a smile, then reached into his pocket to retrieve his own bonus. He passed the package to Menes.

"What's this?"

"A gift for the family."

Menes opened the box and jumped back in surprise when he saw the detached finger with the red ribbon wrapped around it. He tried to chuckle to appear calm, but it was obvious he was shook. "You don't know 'ow you make'a me feel some'a-time," Menes told Leader, his accent thickening by the syllable. When Menes was excited, his accent grew to indecipherable proportions. "Some'atime I wish I had two of you."

"Be careful what you wish for," Leader warned. "That could be costly."

"No, I am serious," Menes assured him. "Neva mind a cost. I am reech."

The limo took a U-turn and headed for the south side. Leader and Menes sipped cognac and chatted for an hour like they were old friends, despite the fact Leader still wore his disguise. In a sense, they were old friends, but both remained wary of each other. They both understood that the man next to them possessed the power to bring the other to his knees. Farfetched. Yet very possible.

Leader decided to turn down two very lucrative contracts Menes had scheduled for him in order to spend some Q.T. with his wife. Menes was disappointed, but he understood. Leader was his own man.

Menes dropped Leader off at his hotel just past midnight. Leader removed his first costume, and applied a fake goatee to this face before venturing downstairs to the bar for a drink. Grabbing a spot at the bar, he breathed a heavy sigh of relief at a job well done. He glanced down the long bar.

That's when he saw her.

"Uh-oh Jus, keep up if you can!" Nikki called out as she rolled backwards on her skates. Justus pumped his legs harder and easily caught up with Nikki, grabbing her hand.

"Ha! Told you you can't outdo me," Justus challenged.

"Well, let me go then."

"Can't!" Justus screamed over the loud music and huge crowd. Skate Sunday in Bordeaux Plaza was a staple in Fayetteville so on any Sunday night, the rink would be packed with people. Justus and Nikki had already received a few harsh stares from a few comrades of Nikki's incarcerated boyfriend, Jock. Here she was out enjoying their favorite Sunday pastime with another dude when the ink had not even dried on Jock's fingerprints yet.

Oblivious to the stares, Justus continued to hold Nikki's hand while they skated around the rink until they came upon a roadblock on the floor. They attempted to roll around the spilled skaters, but ended up spilling themselves. Nikki fell hard. Justus fell on top of her, right between her legs. They shared a huge laugh before the chemistry between them birthed silence. Their eyes locked and before they knew it, they were kissing.

Ever since the night they had double-dated with Pug and Jackie, they had been inseparable. Justus had always told himself that if Nikki ever gave him any light, he would run toward it like the sun. He did that in spades. When Nikki awoke, he was there. On her lunch break, he was there. Before she went to sleep at night, he made sure his voice was the last thing she heard. He provided her fresh flowers, going from white carnations, to pink carnations, to red, long-stemmed roses. Nikki loved the attention Justus lavished on her. It had been quite some time since she felt appreciated by a man. And yes, Justus was a man! He was confident, intelligent, strong, and sincere. All the things she desired in a man. So, what if it came in a younger package! So far they had only kissed, but she was planning something real big for his graduation the following week.

Real big.

Leader had been sipping his drink for the better part of an hour, quietly observing the woman at the end of the bar. Her mannerisms, clothes, and demeanor all spelled class. He entertained the thought of sending her a drink, but didn't want to become familiar. After all, this was the one place he could come to relax while remaining anonymous. Not to mention he was happily married. Still, he couldn't resist the urge to stare. His decision was made for him when the bartender issued him another Crown on the rocks.

"It's from the lady," the bartender said. Leader looked in her direction once again and went weak in the knees. She was smiling a smile so bright it could replace the sun! She waved before leaving the stool, headed in his direction.

Oh shit! Leader thought to himself.

The woman was wearing high-waist slacks up to her midriff. Grey blouse two shades lighter than her pants. Killer black boots with spike heels that had to be at least four inches. Leader likened her strut to a runway model's, all hips and swagger, with her eyes locked on him like he was the cameraman. He placed her in her late twenties, early thirties at the most.

She brought her powerful swagger to a halt directly in front of Leader. She stared at him with her pouty lips pursed, saying nothing for a few seconds. Then she leaned over in his ear, her long, curly hair sweeping his shoulder. "Enjoy your drink," she whispered seductively. Then, she spun on her tall heels and strutted back to her stool.

Leader could not tear his eyes from the woman. Her sensual scent lingered in his nose as he watched her perform for him. There was something about her that intrigued him. Her aura drew him in like an insect into a spider's web. For a second, he forgot he was married. Actually, he was very aware of his marital status. He just didn't give a fuck.

*   *   *

Nikki and Justus emerged from the skating rink arm-in-arm, headed to Nikki's Cadillac, when gunshots erupted from behind them. Justus stuffed Nikki under his arm, crouched low, and ran to the car. Placing his back against the Cadillac door, he thrust Nikki to the ground.

"Get down! Stay the fuck down!" Justus roared. He deactivated the car alarm before stealing a peek in the direction from whence the shots came. When there was an interruption of fire, he tossed Nikki in the backseat and took the wheel. He barreled out of the parking lot at breakneck speed, dodging other escaping motorists with calculated precision. Justus was amazed himself at how well he maneuvered the big 'Lac. From behind him, he heard more shots from an automatic weapon of some sort.

"Stupid mu'fuckas!" Justus swore under his breath once they were free of the melee. "Can't even hit nothing. I bet they ain't hit nothing. You a'ight, baby?"

Nikki poked her head up from the safety of the backseat. "Yeah."

"Did you see who it was? I saw you peeking out the back window. Get your damn head shot off," Justus joked.

"No. I didn't see who it was?" She lied. Nikki knew exactly who was doing the shooting.

"Niggas stupid, man." Justus sucked his teeth. "I bet I can out shoot any of them with one eye closed."

"Jus, what you know about guns? You better not be shooting guns all crazy."

Justus looked through the rearview at Nikki like she was crazy. "Girl, I been shooting guns since I was able to stand up. Whatchu talking 'bout?"

"For real?"

"Yeah, my daddy taught me. Shit, that's how I learned how to count—counting bullets," Justus stated matter-of-factly. "It's six rounds in a standard revolver, but some .22's have eight rounds. Standard pump shotguns carry six rounds, but they can be modified. The first Glocks carried sixteen shots with the capability to hold one in the head. Rugers, the same thing. Browning 9mm's carry nine rounds along with Colt .45's. AR-15's can carry thirty, fifty, and a hundred round magazines, but the barrel will melt if you don't be careful."

Nikki sat in amazement as Justus rattled off spec after spec about guns she had only heard about in movies. When he was done, she was compelled to ask.

"Justus, you ever shot somebody? And don't lie, 'cause I know how you and Pug get when you two are together."

"Somebody?"

"Yeah."

"No."

Nikki caught Justus's apprehension so she asked, "What have you shot then?" She had her arm draped over the back of Justus's seat, her mouth inches from his neck.

"Deer," he answered. "Me and my dad used to go hunting all the time when I was younger. Shit, for most of my teens, if I wasn't hunting or fucking, I was hunting something to fuck. My dad used to make me field dress the deer and everything."

"What's that?" Nikki asked, stroking his neck lightly with one finger.

"Field dressing is when you hang a deer upside down by his feet, peel the skin off, and cut his stomach open so the guts can fall out," Justus explained.

"Eww, never mind. That's nasty," Nikki said. "Sorry I asked."

"No, you not."

"Yes, I am."

"No. You're not sorry. You may apologize, but you're not sorry. Words have power. If you say you sorry, that's what you'll be. So, don't ever say that."

Nikki loved the way Justus stood his ground. He was full of maxims too.

"Justus, you're different than your peers. You know that, right?" Nikki reached around to caress his chin.

"I hear you."

Nikki continued, "You're different because you have a father. So many brothas don't. That's why they act like they do. So, please don't take that for granted."

"Um-hmm. We going home or what?" Justus asked, exiting the highway.

"We? I'm not taking you home with me!" Nikki said incredulously.

"Come on, gurl."

"Come on what? Boy please! I'll turn your little young ass out, I ain't had any in a while, either. Hell nah!"

Justus chuckled. "Alright, keep running, I'ma have you fiendin' for this dick."

Nikki smacked the back of his head. "You so nasty! Anyway, what kind of work you going to be doing with your father?"

"I'm not sure, but he's a security consultant so I'll probably be doing that. Long as I don't have to pump no dope or shovel no shit, it don't matter. He told me I'll be able to afford anything I want. For that, I'll follow him to the moon and back."

Young Justus didn't know that his words were soon to be put to the test. He was filled with the arrogance of youth and the promise of prosperity. Add to that the fact that he was on the verge of tackling his childhood goal, and he was feeling invincible. He proudly took the exit to his home. He wanted to go home with Nikki, but he wasn't pressed. He knew that in due time, he would smash. When he did, he planned on breaking her back for making him wait. Patience was his strong suit, and he would come to live by it or die by it.

Literally.

Chapter 7

Glenda was busy doing laundry. She was feeling good about herself as she rifled her way through the dirty clothes. Her husband had been a permanent fixture in the home for the past week, and they had spent countless hours of Q.T. together. She could hear Leader in the backyard practicing martial arts moves with Justus. They were grunting perversely as they went through their routines. Basically, it was just another day, until she stumbled upon something in one of Leader's jacket pockets.

Unfolding the piece of paper, Glenda saw that it was a crumpled business card with a number scrawled on it. She gasped audibly when she noted a woman's name accompanied with a Chicago area code. She sniffled the card as if that would tell her more about what was going on. She recognized the White Diamond perfume. She'd know that anywhere, as it was the same fragrance she wore daily, however this was not her card.

Glenda stormed to the back door. "John Mo!"

"What?" Leader was snatched out of his routine. He saw Glenda standing at the glass door, hands on her hips, mean-mugging him. She eyed him maliciously for a few seconds before storming off in the opposite direction.

"Uh-oh, somebody's in trouble again," Justus joked. "Damn, Pop, you stay in the doghouse."

"Alright boy, watch your mouth."

"All I said was damn," Justus complained.

"I'm talking 'bout that Pop shit."

Justus chuckled a bit, "Oh."

"Anyway, I'll worry about that later. What you doing tonight?"

"Pug and them throwing a graduation party at their crib."

"Pug and who?' Leader queried.

"Pug and Nikki." Leader raised his eyes. "I told you I'm on my game, Pop."

"Anyway, if you won't be coming in tonight, let me know. Call me, not your mother."

"A'ight."

"Now let me go handle this."

Leader left Justus alone, practicing katas until he could barely stand. When he was done, he went inside to prepare for his party. He had every intention of making this night one to remember.

Topeka Heights was packed with people in a festive mood. Even people who didn't normally associate with each other were partying together. All came to pay respect to Pug. Sure, it was Justus's party, but Pug was throwing it. Thus, Pug was doing the invitations. To refuse was tantamount to disrespect.

In a matter of months, Pug had returned home and reclaimed his throne. He may not have been the biggest dopeboy in Fayettenam, but he was definitely amongst its ranks. To the streets, Pug was a throwback soldier. No snitching. No compromising. No "whipped-up" product. Pug didn't suffer from delusions. He knew his place in society and he embraced it. Pug was 100% NIGGA and proud of it! A young black male in a racist society with limited book smarts and limited opportunities, he had pulled himself up by his boot straps to become the king of his concrete palace.

"Here, grab another drink, cuz!" Pug forced the Hennessey down Justus's throat, spilling a little onto his linen suit. The suit was a present from Nikki. "You a fuckin' man, now!" Pug bellowed.

"Damn, Pug, you gonna kill him!" Nikki protested. From the moment Justus walked in the door, Nikki had been by his side, staking her claim.

"Naw, he alright," responded Pug, drunker than all get out. "This my nigga here."

"Whateva. Come on Jus." Nikki grabbed Justus's arm, pulling him into the kitchen where they ran into Gloria.

"Heeeey baabaay!!" Gloria reached to hug Justus. Justus caught the strong whiff of every alcohol at the party. "You having fun?"

"Yeah Auntie."

"Good," she slurred. "Where y'all going?" Gloria asked when she noticed Nikki leading Justus by the arm. Justus shrugged his shoulders, but kept following Nikki.

"We going home, Ms. Gloria." Nikki answered

for the both of them. Gloria stalled for a moment then released a loud cackle.

"Nikki, what you 'bout to do to my nephew gurl?"

"Everything he can handle, Ms. Gloria."

"Ooh chile! Don't you go fuckin' my nephew to death. He graduating tomorrow. Now Justus, don't let this old heifer drain your youth. You be safe for your graduation tomorrow 'cause I'ma be there standing proud when my baby walk across that stage, ya hear?" Gloria smiled brightly, revealing her gold bicuspid teeth. Pug entered the kitchen, observed what was going on and got on his mother.

"Ma, leave 'em alone so they can go. It's getting late."

"Whateva," Gloria sucked her teeth before walking off. Nikki excused herself to the car while Pug collared Justus and offered him weed, ecstasy, and some shit Justus had never heard of. Justus declined, but settled for extra condoms before joining Nikki in the car.

The whole ride over to Nikki's place, Justus was silent as R. Kelly's classic album, *TP2*, bumped from the speakers. All he kept thinking was, *this is it. This is it.* He silently prayed that his dick wouldn't go limp from anticipation, or that he wouldn't bust early from excitement, though he did have a remedy for that. He tried to telepathically send Nikki the same request R. Kelly was making on the radio: "Don't you say no tonight . . ."

Justus would not be disappointed this night, for as soon as they crossed Nikki's threshold, she thrust her tongue into Justus's mouth hungrily. Justus reciprocated as best he could, but Nikki passion was intensified by the alcohol she had consumed at the party. The more he matched her desire, the hungrier she grew. Nikki suddenly clutched Justus's erect penis in her hand through his trousers and eyed him sternly. She practically demanded he look at her. "I want you so bad," she whispered to him through kisses. Justus almost lost his load right there on the spot, but he held strong.

Nikki stepped out of her skirt and walked into the bedroom in nothing but her heels and a G-sting. She paused at the door and curled her finger for Justus to follow.

Justus followed in Nikki's footsteps, mesmerized by her beauty. Nikki's body was everything he dreamed it to be. He filed away the visual of Nikki's heart-shaped ass for later and entered the bedroom.

Nikki stripped him of his clothes and kissed his chest while stroking him at the same time. Justus pushed her on the bed and began an exploration of his own. Nikki's skin was so soft, it seemed to melt in his mouth. When Justus slid her G-string down her legs unimpeded he was met with an adrenaline rush like he had conquered the world. He stared in silent admiration at her flawless body. Not a single blemish was on her skin. NO stretch marks, or nothing. Just beautiful light skin with red nipples and a perfectly manicured landing strip below. Justus had never eaten pussy in his life, and he had never even had an inclination to do so, but upon seeing Nikki's beauty sprawled across the bed, he knew he had to go above and beyond to please her.

But first he had to do one thing.

Justus quickly leaped from the bed and sprinted to the adjoining bathroom, leaving Nikki's squirming on the bed. Once inside the bathroom he conjured up the image of Nikki walking in front of him and used it to work himself to a climax, just as Pug had instructed him to. According to Pug, the first nut always came fast, especially if you were anxious. To combat this, and not be called a minuteman, you put the first one in the toilet, automatically giving you staying power. Then you could focus on foreplay while waiting for your dick to get back hard. If it worked, women would say that you were unselfish in bed and you had staying power. A win-win. With Nikki, Justus wanted to win-win-win so he did as he was told. Unbeknownst to Justus, his plan worked better than expected. His brief exit allowed Nikki's temperature to rise and fall, prolonging the experience.

When Justus emerged from the bathroom, Nikki was more than ready. Her sweet aroma filled the whole room. Justus wasted no time picking up where he left off. He kissed and sucked all the requisite places before venturing down south. After softly kissing Nikki's inner thigh, he plunged his tongue directly into her center. He didn't know any techniques. He just mimicked what he saw the men do on Pornhub. Nikki's shrill cry let him know he was onto something, and before long, he caught a rhythm. He quickly learned he couldn't hesitate when it came to oral sex. He had to go

hard or go home. Justus was quickly rewarded for
his revelation for the more he got into it, the more
Nikki screeched his name and grabbed his big
ears. Justus couldn't believe it! He had never gotten a response from a female like this. He almost
wanted to continue eating her all night.

Almost.

Justus removed his face from Nikki's pleasure
center and tried to stealth her but Nikki checked
him quick.

"Unh-unh. You better strap up."

"Word?"

"Word nigga."

"A'ight, a'ight."

Justus slid a condom on and entered Nikki real
slow. The moment he touched the inside of her
flesh it felt as if he had been born again. For years
he had fantasized about this moment. Nikki had
been his unicorn, a mythical creature that only ex-
isted in his dreams. Now, he was achieving his
dream.

Justus sank himself in slowly inch by inch until
all of his thick member was embedded inside of
Nikki. He remained dead-man still, savoring every
moment of ecstasy. Nikki was tighter, hotter, and
wetter than his best dream. Each stroke was a slice
of disbelief. He couldn't believe he was actually
plunging his manhood inside of Nikki. He couldn't
believe she was really scratching his back, calling
his name. He couldn't believe he was really about
to . . .

Oh shit.

He felt it, but he wasn't sure so he didn't stop.
He kept pumping into that magical place where

worries ceased to exist. The magical place where a man realized his true power. Young Justus continued his journey from a boy to a man, not stopping until he released his whole load right night inside of Nikki.

"Shit Jus!" Nikki moaned, kicking him off her. "The rubber bust!"

"Say word?"

"WORD nigga!" Nikki stormed into the bathroom and slammed the door behind her. Justus heard water running, the toilet flushing, then silence. He walked to the door with his semi-flaccid penis swinging in the wind. He knocked gently then pushed the door slightly ajar. Nikki was sitting on the toilet with her head in her hands.

"What's wrong, Nikki?"

"What's wrong? Didn't you just hear what I said, Justus? The rubber bust. You bust a whole fuckin' nut inside of me." Nikki looked at Justus with contempt. She shook her head, "I can't have no more kids right now. It's hard enough taking care of the one I got now."

Justus said nothing.

"I knew it. I fuckin' knew it!" She slapped her head in frustration. "It'll be just my luck, your li'l young ass will knock me up." Nikki looked at Justus's dick with contempt before burying her head back into her palms.

Justus grabbed Nikki by the hand, "Come 'ere."

"What?" Nikki stood.

Justus grabbed her hands, pulling her to him. He locked eye contact and promised, "As long as I have breath in my body, you'll never have to worry about anything. You hear me?" He clasped her chin into his thumb and forefinger. "I mean it, Nikki. I love you, gurl."

"Well, love don't pay no bills, buy no diapers—" Justus shushed her with is index finger.

"What? You don't believe in me?"

"Jus, you don't even have a job." Nikki whined.

"Look, let's cut the bullshit. I got a spot guaranteed with my father. If that's not enough, I'll mob down with Pug and get paid. Bottom line: you won't want for anything. Money is the least of our worries."

Justus's sincerity impressed Nikki, but she didn't think he realized how serious having a child could be. She laid her head on Justus's chest. "Jus, I don't want another drug-dealer for a boyfriend," she whispered.

"I know baby, and that's not my M.O." Justus admitted. "But I will do whatever it takes to make sure the world is placed at your feet."

Nikki looked at Justus thoughtfully, "That's so sweet, Justus."

"I mean it too."

Nikki kissed his cheek. "We getting all worked up over nothing. I may not even be pregnant. This was supposed to be a celebration."

"I know. I just want you to know I got you."

Nikki smiled. "I know. I believe you."

Justus ended up taking Nikki in the bathroom, then again on the bed. As they lay in each other's arms, Nikki feeling secure, Justus feeling like he had climbed Mount Everest, the house phone rang.

The machine picked up the call and wrecked their night. It was Jock, and he was pissed.

"Nikki?! Nikki?! Bitch, pick up the phone! I know you hear me. That's a'ight. You got that young nigga riding around in my shit?! I ain't gon' be in here forever. I'ma see both you mu'fuckas when I get out. Watch!"

Chapter 8

Cumberland County Civic Center was crowded with graduates from four area high schools. 71st Senior High, Pine Forest, E.E. Smith, and Douglas Byrd all held their graduation ceremonies on the same day. 71st was late in the order so Justus was forced to sit through three graduations. The graduates were seated in a separate section from the audience so Justus did not see either of his parents. He was able to locate his Aunt Gloria in the middle of the crowd, seated with Nikki, Jackie, and his little sister Keisha, looking impatient. Pug was not present. He did not do the high school scene. His gift was the party the previous night, therefore Nikki had taken his ticket.

Justus spotted Nikki seated beside his Aunt and his heart skipped a beat. Nikki was clearly the baddest chick in the building. He caught a woody admiring her regal look. Her hair was pinned up and she wore a satin dress the color of her skin. Her wide hips spilled out of the tight seat. Justus couldn't determine if he was in love or in an intense state of infatuation. Whatever it was, it warmed his soul.

As irony would have it, Panee was seated next to Justus because their names fell behind each other on the senior roster. Justus Moore and Panee Locklear. Justus hadn't seen much of Panee since the day she had broken off their relationship. He had been so upset about it that he really didn't care if he saw her or not. Besides he had been with a *woman* now. Everything else paled in comparison. Nikki was five years older than him, and almost seven years older than Panee. What did he need with a little girl now?

Panee was having a difficult time dealing with Justus's cold shoulder routine. She knew she had broken off what they shared, but thought he could at least be civil. As it stood, Justus had only said one word to her all night: Congratulations.

Douglas Byrd's graduates were finishing up, so Justus's class was being summoned backstage to prepare. Surveying the crowd once again, Justus still failed to locate his parents. He consulted his watch and noted they should've been there an hour ago.

Backstage, Justus adjusted his red gown in preparation to walk across the stage. He planned on acting a fool when he received his diploma. No more bullshit teachers. No more hating-ass-wannabe-thugs. No more sleeping in class due to lack of interest. Justus couldn't wait to cross the stage a graduate. The sooner this was over, the sooner he could dig Nikki out again.

Justus's turn across the stage seemed to come quicker than expected. It seemed in no time, his name was announced. He swaggered across the stage to Principal Patterson with his arms raised triumphantly. Catcalls and shouts rang out from the crowd as Justus's associates and admirers gave him his props. Justus accepted his diploma (along with a stern look) from Principal Patterson, then pimped backstage to join his crew, where Magi was the first to greet him. Justus felt proud, but his mind was in another place. While he did see Aunt Glo and Nikki cutting up when he crossed the stage, he still hadn't located his parents.

Now he was worried. His mother would never miss seeing her only son graduate. The video Gloria was shooting would not suffice. His mother wanted to see this in person. Justus milled about backstage until the ceremony was completed, then met his family in the auxiliary room.

"Congratulations baby!" Nikki planted a juicy kiss on Justus's lips while his classmates looked on in awe.

Gloria hugged Justus then handed him a neatly wrapped package. "This is from us. Oh, and Pug told me to give you this," she added, giving Justus a sealed envelope. Justus knew the envelope contained cash, but he wasn't concerned about that right now.

"Thanks Auntie. Where's my mom and dad though?"

Gloria shrugged her shoulders, "Honey, I don't know. They dropped Keisha off and were supposed to meet us here."

"So, you haven't heard from them since?"

"Nope. Not since this morning. Why?"

"Nothing," Justus lied, disappointment evident on his face. He recalled his parents arguing, but he didn't think it was that serious to warrant them missing the most important day of his life.

"Honey, don't worry, she ain't miss nothing. I got it all right here," Gloria tapped her Galaxy phone for proof.

"That's right, Jus. I'm sure they're proud of you," Nikki interjected, stroking his back.

"I know I am," Keisha punched him in the arm.

After taking pictures on the lawn, Justus ventured to the car to remove his gown.

It was then he saw him.

Leader was standing in front of a car that he had used to block Gloria's car off with. The first thing Justus noticed was Leader's attire. He was clad in all black with his pants tucked inside of his combat boots. Clearly not ceremonial clothing. The next thing Justus noticed was that Leader was alone.

Justus ran over to Leader. "'Sup Dad? Where's Mom?"

Leader briefly dropped his head then looked at Justus with sad eyes. Before he could answer, Gloria joined them.

"Hey John, where is my sister at? How come y'all late?" Gloria had a thousand questions, but Leader was not ready to entertain any of them. He was obviously carrying a heavy load.

"Hello everyone. Sorry I'm late," Leader offered, showing his discomfort. "I don't mean any disrespect, but I need to speak with my son for a second. Alone."

"What's happening, John?" Gloria demanded.

"Not now, Glo. We'll talk when I get back," Leader promised, pulling Justus away.

Leader climbed behind the wheel of the car while Justus fell into the passenger seat. Leader peeled off, leaving Nikki, Gloria, and Keisha dumbfounded.

Inside the car, Leader was silent. Justus could smell the wheels turning inside his head. Something was not right. Justus's curiosity was expelled when Leader finally revealed what had happened.

"So, I have some bad news and some worse news," Leader said.

"What is it, Dad? What's going on?"

Leader sighed. "I've lived all my life so that the things I had to do to provide for my family wouldn't affect my family. You understand that, right?"

"Yeah, Dad, I know. Why are you reminding me of this?"

Leader wiped his face with his open palms and sighed again. "I fucked up, son. I let *my* shit become *our* shit, and now someone has taken your mom."

"What?! What do you mean 'took' her?"

Leader turned onto Highway 301 and checked the rearview mirror. "This guy I had a beef with years ago just came home and decided to reignite things with me. He made a move on me before I knew he was home. He kidnapped your mom this morning when she was leaving the salon, and now he's demanding a ransom," Leader explained.

Justus's mind was blown. He couldn't fathom his mother, his world, the woman that lit up his life being abducted and in harm's way. "How much is the ransom?" Justus asked. His voice cracked a little but he caught himself.

"There is no amount of money that is worth your mother's life, so the money is not the issue," Leader assured his son. "However, there is no amount of money that can fix this situation," he added.

Justus imagined his mother being tortured and abused. The vision was enough to send his stomach into somersaults. "So, where is she? Do you know where she is? Are we going to get her now?" he asked.

Leader rode in silence for a full minute before he responded to Justus's questions. "I'm not going to lie to you, son. This is going to get ugly. There are a lot of things you don't know about me, but after tonight you will," he promised. "Now I have $250,000 in that knapsack on the backseat, money that I gathered to get your mom back. But first, I need to know how you feel about this?"

Justus looked at his father. "Whatchu mean?"

"I mean, how do you feel about some punk-ass muthafucka having the nerve to take your mother—on your graduation day no less—and demand money for her?!"

"I'm pissed off!" Justus spat, feeding off his father's anger.

"Me too! So what you wanna do about it?"

"I would hurt him if I could."

"You would?"

"Yeah!" Justus's mind was going a mile a minute. The images made his blood boil, and his infamous temper surfaced—just as Leader wanted.

"Okay." Leader nodded his head and pulled

the car into a parking lot off of Owen Drive. He shifted the car into park and looked at Justus. "I know where she is, and I have a plan to get her back," Leader shared. "Are you in?"

"Of course, Dad."

"Justus, this is a different kind of help though. This is the kind of help that has to stay between me and you. Nobody can know about what happens from this point on. Nobody. Not Gloria, Pug, Nikki—nobody. This is *family* business."

"I understand Dad."

Leader sized his son up. "You sure? Because after this you can't go back. You are the only person I trust."

Justus recalled the incident with Pug and the C.O. This felt eerily similar. The help his father was requesting felt similar to the help Pug requested. Like before, Justus was down to do whatever, especially to rescue his mother. The difference was Justus held no fear this time.

"I'm positive Dad. You can count on me," Justus assured him. "I won't let you down and this is strictly between us."

Leader nodded. "Good. Now, let's go get your mother."

An hour later, Justus pulled his Domino's Pizza hat down over his eyes and rang the doorbell. He heard someone rustling around from inside then someone called out to him from the behind the door, "Who is it?"

"Domino's! I have a delivery," Justus said in a fake nasal twang.

"Ain't no-damn-body order no pizza!"

Justus was persistent in his charade, "Sir, the address says 22 Wendy Lane. This is 22 Wendy Lane, isn't it?"

"This is 22 Wendy Lane, but ain't nobody order no goddamn pizza!" The voice yelled. "Now ride the fuck out 'fo you regret it!"

Justus began to get worried. Things weren't going as good as Leader suggested they would. The man was getting belligerent, and Justus feared for his mother's life. Still, he had to stick to the script. Leader told him to keep the guy occupied until he gave him the signal.

"Okay sir, if you can just sign this refusal, then I'll be on my way." Justus improvised. There was no slip and no pizza. Just a cardboard box.

Justus heard the lock clicking. Seconds later the door snatched open only partway because of the chain.

A voice snarled through the dark space of the door, "Give me the damn paper."

The man reached through the space for a pen and Justus saw the burnt fingertips of a smoker. Just when Justus was thinking about taking the man out, he saw a glint of metal fly through the air behind the man and crash down on his head. The man yelped then crumpled to the ground. Justus heard footsteps, then the door snatched open. There, Leader stood with a silenced pistol clutched tightly in his hand. He yanked Justus inside then slammed the door.

Once inside, Justus saw the kidnapper lying on the floor with blood gushing from his head. He seemed to be drifting in and out of consciousness.

"Gag him while I get your mother," Leader ordered.

Justus gagged him with a dirty sock he found on the floor. The man attempted to say something, but Justus crammed the sock in his mouth then punched him in his face. Moments later, Leader returned with his wife thrown over his shoulder.

"Son-of-a-bitch drugged her," Leader answered Justus's questioning look before leaving the room with her. He returned with a chair and rope in hand. He strapped the kidnapper to the chair with the rope while Justus looked on. After Leader had him situated, he removed the gag.

"Please man. This wasn't part of the plan," he panted.

"I know," Leader stated flatly. "You fucked up."

"N-NO, I did everything you ask—" Leader stuffed the sock back into the man's mouth.

"Shut up! You tried. You failed. Time to pay the piper muthafucka!"

Leader walked around to the back of the chair and placed the barrel of the weapon against the man's head. His finger rested on the trigger. He slowly applied pressure while looking at Justus. He expected Justus to cringe, or close his eyes, or even dismiss himself. Much to his surprise, Justus stood tall and defiant, as if he *wanted* to see the man's brains explode from his cranium.

Justus was unfamiliar with himself. Mysterious feelings overwhelmed him. He had never seen such paralyzing fear in a man. Justus could smell the fear emanating from his pores! So much was going through his young mind. He was sure he was about to witness a murder. A murder at the hands of his father. He would've thought that he would be afraid or timid. Instead he felt powerful witnessing this moment. A weird energy surged through the room and Justus allowed himself to bask in it.

"Justus?" Justus looked at his father. Leader appeared to be handing him the revolver. "Here son. Handle your business."

"H-huh?"

"I said, handle your business," Leader repeated.

Justus was dumbfounded. What was he saying? *Did he actually want him to kill somebody?*

"You said you would hurt him if you could. Well, here is your chance."

"Yeah but I meant, like, *hurt him* hurt him. Not like this."

Leader walked over to Justus and placed his hands on his shoulders. He whispered in his ear. "Listen son, either way it goes, he's never leaving this room. You're looking at a dead man. You understand? He violated us in the worst way. For that, he has to pay.

"Now, I'm giving you a chance to prove yourself. Defend your honor. I can't have any cowards carrying on my legacy. This nigga violated us in the worst way! Now you have to handle your business."

It was crystal clear now. His father was asking—no, telling—him to kill a man. His father was giving him permission to commit the ultimate sin to preserve their family honor. From this point on, nothing would ever be the same again. If Justus obeyed, his innocence would be lost. If he disobeyed, his trust would be lost. In his father's eyes, he would be the coward that was afraid to defend the family's honor.

What was he to do?

He wrestled with indecision. To be a murderer or a coward. Which was worse?

In a daze, Justus took the gun from his father and walked over to the kidnapper. He raised the pistol to the back of the man's head and paused.

"NO!" Leader yelled. Justus was so startled he almost pulled the trigger. "Always look a man in the eye before you kill him."

Justus walked around to the front of his victim and raised the pistol center mass with his forehand. Again, he paused. Looking a man in his eyes was different. More personal. Justus was unsure if he could carry out his mission this way. He looked to his father for support.

"Jus, if you want to work with me, prove yourself. Ice this low-life so we can roll," Leader ordered.

Justus wasn't sure he heard him correctly. "If I wanna work with you? What's this gotta do with my job wit' chu? I thought you were a consultant."

"In a sense," Leader admitted. "Truth is, I'm a cleaner. I kill people for a living."

Justus's mouth fell open.

Leader nodded, "It's true son. I'm a hitman. So are you if you can prove yourself. This *is* the family business. This is what I've been training you for. This is your destiny." As Leader spoke, he was trying to get a read on Justus, but Justus's expression never changed from one of shock, so he continued to make his case. "There's no one better to carry on my legacy than you. You're my son. You're a soldier. Stop looking crazy!"

Justus straightened his face, "I don't know nothing 'bout being no hitman," he admitted.

"That's what I'm here for, Jus. If I can do it, so can you. Now stop bullshitting and finish the job!" Leader looked at his watch.

Justus was overcome with a plethora of emotions. Too many things were happening at one time, but one thing was clear: he could not leave until the job was completed. This was clear.

Justus turned again to his victim who had shit his pants watching the exchange before him. Tears rained down his face, and he was panting heavily. He knew his fate was sealed.

Justus shut his eyes, and with them all emotions. He held his breath and pulled the trigger twice.

BOMP! BOMP!

A warm, wet substance coated Justus' face. He opened his eyes, and wiped his face. Seeing the blood on his hands, he began to shake. He eyed the .357 in his hand like it was foreign to this world. He was amazed at the rush it had given him. He felt omnipotent. A euphoric feeling gripped him and soon the shaking stopped. After a while, he was able to look at his casualty straight up without wincing. Two holes punctured his forehead. Justus reached out to close the man's eyes.

Leader observed Justus carefully. He understood the transformation Justus was going through. From fear to certainty to power. The first few minutes of a kill determined if a person was cut out for the life. When the cold reality set in, most men hurled up their guts. Those were the weak ones. Others stared in amazement at the travesty brought forth by their own hands. Those were the stronger ones. Still, others reveled in the pure supremacy over another human being. Those were the real assassins. As Leader observed Justus, he surmised he was hovering between the middle and the last phase. However, by the end of the night he would most assuredly know where he stood.

"Help me wrap him up," Leader told Justus. "We have a lot to do before the night is out."

As Leader negotiated the long dark road, Justus was deep in thought about the night's events. They had dropped Glenda off at home, and after issuing her another sedative, journeyed back out into the night, presumably to dispose of their quarry that was still inside the trunk. As they rode along, Leader used the downtime to orient Justus. He had informed him that his "training" would begin the following morning at an undisclosed location. As part of his assimilation, he would have no contact with the outside world for the duration of his training, which was estimated to be no less than three months. Ultimately, it would depend on how fast Justus grasped what was to be given to him. Leader promised him he would learn every aspect of his profession so thoroughly that things would become second nature.

For his part, Justus didn't approve of being thrust into the situation without any say, but after Leader broke everything down to its simplest form, how could he disagree? Justus quickly con-

ceded Leader was right when he told him the only
way for a black man to get rich in America was by
either selling out or selling his soul. Justus also
conceded the best crimes are the ones felt but not
seen. Justus definitely had to agree when Leader
told him a person received more time in jail for
drugs than murder. In the drug game, you had to
win every day. The police only had to win once,
and with snitching being all too prevalent in the
dope game nowadays, they would eventually win. By
contrast, their transactions were done anonymously,
forcing all parties involved to remain honest.

As Leader explained all of this to Justus, he
agreed totally. In actuality, it didn't matter if he
agreed or not because the damage was already
done. He had already killed a man, therefore they
were truly bound by blood. True, he had reacted
because of his mother, but surprisingly he felt no
remorse. In fact, he felt exhilarated! *Maybe I am cut
out for this*, he thought.

Leader turned the car down another road,
drove down a little more, and came upon a farm.
He pulled around back, where they were immediately assaulted by the stench of hog. As they exited
the vehicle, Justus covered his nose and mouth.

"Man up!" Leader ordered, not bothering to
cover up at all. "This is nothing. Trust me."

When they opened the trunk to retrieve the
body, Leader's point was made, as the smell of blood
and burnt flesh singed their nostrils.

"Damn!" Justus turned his head and spat.

"Don't worry, you'll get used to it," Leader
chuckled. He heaved the tarp-wrapped body over
his shoulder. Oblivious to the blood spattering his

coveralls, he humped around to the back of the barn with Justus hot on his tail.

After unwrapping the body Leader pointed to a dirty saw for Justus to retrieve. Justus attempted to pass Leader the saw, but instead Leader instructed him to saw the limbs from the body.

"Do *what*?" Justus was flabbergasted.

"Saw the limbs off," Leader repeated. "What you looking at me like that for? It ain't no different than field-dressing a deer," he stated matter-of-factly.

"Sure it is Dad. This is a human being!"

"Not anymore," Leader joked. "In any event, it's the same difference. Now cut him."

Justus didn't like this side of his father. He seemed so cold and detached from reality, like he didn't realize he was telling his son to cut up a fucking body. Nonetheless, he did as he was told. When he was done, Leader piled each limb into a plastic bag then ordered Justus to follow him to another location on the farm.

Before they arrived at the pig sty, Justus could smell the odor of the hogs. The closer they got to the actual gates themselves, the more Justus could hear the pigs grunting and squealing. It was too dark for Justus to see inside the pen, which was good because Leader's next instructions made Justus's stomach lurch.

"Toss the limbs inside, son," Leader ordered, throwing the first arm into the pen like it was daily trash. As each body part hit the pen, the hogs went into a feeding frenzy, squealing, grunting, and fighting each other over the flesh. Leader crossed his arms, taking the whole scene in with aplomb. He glanced at his son to his side to gauge his reaction. Justus was breathing hard, shivering a little from the cold, but he looked like he was going to be alright. Leader offered him a smile.

"Now you see why I tell you not to eat pork?"

Justus grimaced.

Part 2

The Making of a Murderer

Chapter 9

Justus's training location was a fifty-acre plot sprinkled with various degrees of landscape and terrain. The grounds were situated between Fort Bragg and Pineville, North Carolina. A secret location where the U.S. military trained its Special Operations Groups, the property was actually owned by the government. However, since Leader had greased the palm of the head groundskeeper many times in the past, he was afforded free access to the compound at any time he desired. The compound consisted of any and everything needed to whip the human body into its highest form of natural perfection, including numerous obstacle courses, shooting ranges, and miles of forestry. The property contained a modern log cabin, complete with an armory, Jacuzzi, and three spacious bedrooms. Behind the cabin were four-wheelers and fishing equipment, to allow one to travel over the land expeditiously, and to pluck fish from the lake in back to fry on the flat oven inside. This was the only building on the premises that allowed a person modern creature comforts. Anyone else who stayed literally lived on the land.

This was the place Leader and Justus arrived at bright and early the morning following their assassination. This was the place Justus was to be confined to for three months of rigorous training.

The first day started out with a hike around the perimeter of the grounds to familiarize Justus with the area. Unfortunately, all of Justus's attention was focused on the eighty-pound rucksack strapped to his back and the AR-15 assault rifle he carried in his arms. Leader carried the same thing as well, leading the way the entire time, throwing potshots at Justus's youth. He made sure not to allow Justus any rest or time to think about the previous night's transgressions. He planned to penetrate Justus's young mind with his own powerful psychology. This was the purpose of the march into the woods. Once they settled into their trek, Leader began his spiel.

"Anybody can kill someone. That's easy. A stray bullet. An errant traffic stop. Too much to drink. A well-placed punch. Just like that. BOOM! A life is lost. Just that easy. But, it takes a special kind of person to be an assassin. The type of person who kills for a living. Over and over again, getting away each time. Surviving the assignment physically is one thing, but the most important thing is surviving each assignment mentally and morally. Each time you take a life, you must do a battle with your conscience. Was I wrong? Did the person deserve it? Am I a bad person? Am I going to hell? Some of the same questions I'm sure you are asking yourself right now." Almost out of breath, Justus nodded. "You have to be stronger than that though. Your mind is yours. You control that. Claim it. Own it.

"Usually tough conditions, harsh environments, or bad upbringings produce the type of psyche needed for an individual to win in this field of work. Sometimes, combinations of all of the above breed the type of man that can snuff out a life and feel no remorse. Other times this lifestyle is inherited. A brother, cousin, or even a parent excelled in it, and had the connections to make things happen. It becomes a natural journey. Though there are some exceptions, usually a successor is already genetically inclined, either physically or mentally, to become an efficient killing machine."

Leader paused to see if Justus was soaking it all in.

"There are rules to this just like any other trade. Rule number one: never allow your emotions to cloud your decisions. Your emotions will cause you to second-guess, and second-guessing will kill you quicker than any bullet. Rule two: never, ever look back at the past. Not for validation, rationalization, justification. Nothing. The past is the past. Leave it. And don't overanalyze the future because it's filled with uncertainty, except for that which you plan. Rule number three: If you fail to plan then you plan to fail. Any crime is only as good as its escape route. You wouldn't plan a robbery without an escape plan, would you? Well, it's the same thing with this. That's the main problem I have with drug dealers. They commit crimes every day, but neglect to form an escape route."

Justus was finding it difficult to grasp all that
Leader was spitting at him, although the words
were a welcome distraction from the burning sensation in his legs caused by their constant hiking.
Consulting his tactical watch, he realized they had
been marching for the better part of an hour. He
was tired, short of breath, and hungry as hell, but
he sucked it up and drove on.

"Don't be fooled by the shit-stem," Leader continued. "They'll tell you killing is wrong, killing is
against the law. Yet if you kill for your country
you're a hero. They'll give you a medal for it. Hell,
the so-called founders of this country were mass
murders and they got a whole damn monument
for them. Why you think they call it Mount Rush-
more? 'Cause they kept rushing more troops over
from England to kill off the Indians. Shit, the
whole way they got this country was through bloodshed. Now you want to tell me I can't shed blood
to provide for me and mine? Fuck 'em!"

Justus could tell just discussing the government made Leader amped because he had quickened his pace so much he had to slow down for
Justus to catch up. While Leader waited for Justus,
thinking if he had covered all the bases, he realized he had left a major stone unturned. When he
and Justus resumed their trek through the bushy
trails Leader addressed this pertinent issue.

"Most people think killing goes against the
laws of God, but wasn't it God himself who insti-
tuted killing? Wasn't it God who brought death to
the world as life's twin brother? It's widely believed
that the penalty for disobeying God is an early

death. That's what they say anyway. But then they'll tell you that no one goes before their time. Moses is known as the lawgiver. He brought the Ten Commandments, one of which is Thou Shalt Not Kill. Yet Moses himself killed a man. Even Abraham was told to kill his own son. Even Jesus had to face death. So, see my son, killing is as natural as living. Ultimately, we're born to die. We're just assisting in the natural process. All scripture says there will be a judgement day. If you're not dead already, on that day God will kill you himself then judge you. Dying is inevitable. In a way, we're walking dead." Leader chuckled at the thought.

The remainder of the first day went the same way. Leader spoon feeding Justus from his book of maxims as they familiarized themselves with the grounds. At the end of the day, one lesson was clear: Ninety percent of being an assassin was mental, ten percent was physical.

For the next two weeks, Leader took Justus's young body to unparalleled heights. They did aerobics, yoga, and hard-core kung fu. Leader expanded Justus's knowledge of martial arts even further, teaching him about Iron Hand and Poison Hand. Iron hand was the act of utilizing your hands as different weapons like steel, stone, blades, claws, etc. To train his hands for this method, Leader had Justus punch walls, slap trees, and knead buckets of wet sand. The test was being able to knock bark off a tree without feeling a thing. It would take years to accomplish this feat, but Justus was well on his way.

Poison Hand (also called Dim Mak) consisted
of hitting certain parts of the body in a way to cause
instantaneous death. Some people never mastered
this art as it was extremely difficult, and fraught with
responsibility. Leader took years to master Poison
Hand, and still brushed up regularly to retain his
skills. To prepare Justus, Leader made a dummy
filled with water. He marked certain spots on the
dummy that, when struck correctly, caused the
water to burst out. It took three days of constant,
repeated instruction before Justus was able to
strike the dummy well enough to draw a drop of
water. When he did, he felt he had conquered the
world. No one was more shocked and surprised
than Leader.

It took Leader a full week before he achieved
his first burst of water from the dummy.

The following week found Justus brushing up
on weapons training. Having been trained since
he was a baby, Justus knew firearms like he knew
his name, but Leader introduced him to a whole
new way of using them. Natural, manmade silencers,
interchangeable calibers, homemade bullets with
higher velocities; all these things and more, Justus
learned that second week.

By the end of that first month Justus could see
noticeable changes in his body. His mind was
more alert than ever and he felt more comfortable
with himself than he'd ever felt in his life. His
thought process produced the biggest change.
When he'd killed a man the previous month, he
was filled with regret. Now, he felt nonchalant. It
was what it was. He only had two regrets: he couldn't

check up on his mother to see how she was handling things, and he couldn't see Nikki.

He hadn't seen or talked to her since graduation night.

Nikki hurried about the house, gathering things for her two-year-old daughter, Diamond. After months of prodding from Diamond's father, Jock, Nikki was finally taking their daughter to see him.

Jock was being held downtown at the Cumberland County Detention Center. He had pled guilty to drug possession charges and had been sentenced to one year in the County Jail. The whole incident put a strain on his and Nikki's relationship, but in actuality, the relationship had been over since long before the incident occurred. Nikki was simply fed up with being a hustler's wifey and all that it entailed. Jock had been more in love with the streets than her, and Nikki felt she deserved better. She was only bringing their daughter to visit out of respect for the father-daughter bond, not because he deserved it.

When Nikki arrived at the detention center, she was met with resistance because of her skirt being too short. After much pleading, and a fake-number pass off with a promise to call, they were allowed entry. Working men were nothing new to Nikki, a testament to her pedigree of a top-notch game girl.

As Nikki ascended to the fifth floor, she couldn't help but think why she elected to wear the skirt in

114 *Shaun Sinclair*

the first place. All her jeans were fitting *too* tight.
She had gained a considerable amount of weight
in the past month. She brushed it off as stress attributed to Justus's abrupt departure. However,
she was aware of the fact that her "Aunt Flo" had
pulled a disappearing act for the month. She
planned to make a stop after seeing Jock that
would put all her worries to bed.

Nikki stepped off the elevator into the visiting
area looking fabulous, strutting hard on the six-
inch heels of her thigh-high D&G boots. Diamond
was dressed exquisitely as well, in a jean ensemble.
Together, they strolled to the officer station in the
center of the room and passed the C.O. the visitation
slip. Surrounding them were numerous cubicles
equipped with two-way telephones and Plexiglas
windows. The C.O. directed Nikki to one of the
booths. After waiting a few minutes, Jock appeared. As he sat down on the stool, Nikki noticed
his face had filled out, making him look bigger
than she remembered. Nikki thought the extra
weight looked good on him.

"'Sup, Babygurl?" Jock drawled through the receiver. Nikki scowled at him and passed the phone
to Diamond. Jock greeted his little angel, said a few
words with enthusiasm, then ordered her to give
the phone back to Nikki.

"What, Jock?"

"What's wrong witchu, I was calling you
Babygurl, and you gon' go give the phone to Diamond," Jock chastised. "Shit, I musta called you
dat too much since you done fucked around and
got a baby boy," he leered.

Nikki sucked her teeth, "What is you talking 'bout?

"You know what the fuck I'm talking 'bout!" Jock stuck his face closer to the glass, and sneered through clenched teeth. "Why is you playing wit' me, dawg? You don't wanna answer the phone when I call and shit? That's my muthafucking phone! I paid that bill. You riding this li'l nigga around in the car I bought? You done lost yo' god-damn mind. Got mu'fuckas laughing at me like I'm some joke. And you *know* I get down fa mines." Finished with his spiel, Jock returned to his stool.

"Yeah, I know you get down for yours," Nikki retorted. "You beat women—after you fuck around on them. You bring dope around your own daughter. Then you leave us both to fend for ourselves!"

Jock couldn't believe Nikki was talking to him all reckless, but he had to admit she was right. Nikki had hit a nerve with the mention of his daughter so he calmed his tone down to assuage the situation. "Yo, I swear that shit was an accident, Babygirl. I was only keeping it in there for one night. Somebody dropped dimes on me. That's word!"

"That's what you don't understand, Jock," Nikki whined, allowing a glimpse of her feelings to surface. "It only takes one time. You gotta win every day. They only gotta win once. And I can't have my daughter around that. I need some stability. I need a man that's gonna be there."

"Like who? That li'l nigga, Justus?" Jock shot back. His expression let on that he knew something. Nikki's expression told him that she was sorry he knew. "Yeah that li'l nigga played yo' ass. Damn near twenty-three, getting played by a teenager." Jock laughed.

"You don't know what the fuck you talking 'bout!"

"Oh, I don't?" Jock asked rhetorically, laughing between words. "Gave that young nigga dat good-ass pussy and he dipped on you. Bet you feel stupid as fuck now. Bet you feel real stable, huh?"

Nikki looked at Jock with pure disgust, "You make me sick."

"Oh, and you don't think it make me sick to hear of a nigga playing you like that. You my mu'fucking wifey, Nikki!"

"Jock, please. You exaggerating."

"Oh? Where he at then?"

"Pug say he off at school." Nikki answered unconvincingly.

"And you believe it? Fuck outta here!" Jock scoffed. "Before I forget though. Tell dat nigga Pug, that's some fucked up shit. I used to see dis nigga daily and he gon' hook my bitch up wit' another nigga." He stated. He was getting heated just thinking about it.

"Jock, I'm not your bitch."

"What?"

"You heard me. I don't belong to you no more."

"Bitch, you betta stop tripping. I only got a year. I'll be home before that pussy get cold. Now, I forgive you for fucking li'l dude once. Don't let that shit happen again."

Nikki sucked her teeth, muttering, "What-ever."

"For the rest of the time I'm here, you need to play your position. Keep that bread on my books. Send them letters, and come up here. A'ight?"

"Maybe you didn't hear me, Jock," Nikki responded. Looking at Jock like he had lost his mind. "I said it's over."

"Yo, li'l dude ain't coming back. He shitted on you, now, you betta tighten up 'fo I ex yo' ass out."

"It ain't got nothing to do with him!" Nikki shouted through the phone, virtually in tears. "It's about you and your lifestyle. I'm done with it. I'm going back to school to be the doctor I always wanted to be," she vowed. Although she was fed up with the way Jock carried on, that was only part of the reason she was leaving. The truth was, she secretly awaited Justus's return eagerly. She longed for any sign telling her what Jock said wasn't true. That Justus had not abandoned her. She'd had enough of Jock's smug teasing. Gathering herself, she looked Jock in his eyes defiantly.

"Look, I didn't come for this. I brought your daughter to see you out of respect. If you can't act any better than that, you better get a good look at her now because I won't be bringing her again."

As Jock was about to respond, the guard tapped him on the shoulder, "McNeil, time's up."

"A'ight," Jock told the guard. Before he left, he gave Nikki some parting words: "Yo, if I find out you fucking wit' dat young nigga again, I'ma dumb out and kill both you mu'fuckas. Watch!" he slammed the phone down and blew a kiss to Diamond.

Nikki stormed out of the visiting area silently cursing under her breath. She was determined to show Jock she meant business. As she entered the elevator, she caught a sharp cramp in her side. She buckled briefly, recovered, and then walked out of the building nonstop. She did not request additional visiting privileges. She did not leave any money on his books.

She headed straight to the doctor.

Chapter 10

Leader pulled into his driveway directly behind a shiny maroon Cadillac with vanity plates that read "Jesus."

"What the fuck?" Leader thought aloud.

He exited the bucket and walked around the Cadillac inspecting it. When he got to the rear of the car, Leader took one look at the window and knew who the car belonged to. The window was decorated like a trophy case. All types of squares, compasses, stars, swords, and fish etched on different platforms were sprawled across the rear glass.

"Oh, HELL NAW!!"

Leader stormed inside his home and found Reverend Butkus Bucks cocked to the side in a recliner with his legs crossed. Glenda was sitting across from him. A bible lay open between them on the glass table.

"Hey Daddy," Glenda greeted, but failed to stand for Leader.

Leader looked Reverend Bucks up and down, from his conked hair, to his expensive tailor-made suit and big diamonds, all the way to his alligator shoes. In fact, Leader did it twice just in case he missed something the first time. He peered through Reverend Bucks' gold framed glasses to his beady eyes and told him, "You got until the time I go downstairs and back to be gone."

Reverend Bucks raised his hands in surrender, "Oh brother, don't be that way. Sister Glenda was just telling me that you all were having some marital problems. Now that you're here we can discuss them together. Just us and the Lord, of course." He looked up to the sky.

"What part don't you understand?" Leader asked. "I said you need to go NOW. Whatever goes on in my house stays in my house. What happens between my wife and I is between us!" Leader jabbed his chest. "Now, I'm dead-ass serious. I'm about to send you to your maker if you don't get the hell outta my house. The place you sing about all the time? You about to go there."

"My brother, if you'll just—"

Leader never heard him. He was already half-way downstairs to retrieve his pistol. By the time he returned upstairs, Reverend Buck was practically tearing the door off his precious Cadillac. Leader glanced at Glenda seated on the sofa, her face in her hands, her head dropped between her legs, and kept on moving. He was determined to make his point.

When Leader made it outside, Reverend Bucks was peeling out in reverse. Leader aimed his weapon at the windshield and the red beam danced across the glass. He thought about licking a couple of shots over the Cadillac for motivation. Reverend

Bucks straightened the car out and left rubber on the pavement as he made his getaway.

"That'll teach him," Leader said to himself. "Slimy bastard."

Leader knew the old adage was true: No one got more pussy than a trucker, a sailor, and a preacher. He was not about to let his crown-jewel fall victim to the smooth-talking, bible-toting, gigolo.

When Leader went back inside he found his wife sobbing uncontrollably in the kitchen. He held her inside his tight embrace and listened as she confided in him all that she had been feeling lately. Her nightmares from the kidnapping. The emptiness felt from Justus leaving their house. The hassles of their daughter feeling herself because she was negotiating the hills of puberty. And her feelings about the card she had found in his pocket when he returned from his business trip.

Leader listened carefully, empathized, and then fished Glenda's head from his chest. "Listen, baby, the guy who did that to you, trust me when I tell you that he will never do anything to anyone again. Ever! The kidnapping was about money, that's all. It wasn't personal."

"But why?" Glenda cried.

"He was a fiend, baby! A fiend who is smoking that shit with his God now." Leader left out the fact that Justus had executed the honors. He placed her head back on his chest. "And Justus is a man now. He is under my tutelage. When he returns from his training, he will be living on his own."

"But he's my baby!" Glenda protested.

Leader chuckled. "He will always be your baby,

but he is a man now. It's time for us to let him be a man."

Glenda sighed. "I know," she whispered.

"And Keisha is growing up too. Soon, she will be a woman. The quicker we accept it, the happier we will be. Right?"

Glenda wasn't too convinced, but her husband had spoken, and she still believed in him. "I guess," she said.

"Look at it like this," Leader suggested. "At least we will have our home to ourselves real soon."

Leader continued to console his wife and wrapped all of her concerns up in a pretty little bow. However, he could not so easily dismiss Glenda's concerns about the woman on the card. Oh, he had contacted her alright. Her name was Carmen, and he definitely intended to see her soon. For now, he was hell bent on make-up sex.

Leader scooped Glenda in his arms to carry her upstairs. They were on their way upstairs when the buzzer to the front door rang. Leader discarded Glenda on the bed then went to answer the door. When he looked through the peephole he knew make-up sex was out the window.

Nikki was at the door, and she was crying hysterically.

Chapter 11

Justus was in deep mediation, recalling all the things he had learned over the past three and a half months. With each breath inhaled, he felt stronger. The only weak point in his training was foreign languages. His German was a little suspect, but he could speak enough Spanish, Italian, and Arabic to make up for it. *Hell, the Germans don't even speak German so I'll be cool,* Justus thought. His training was so intense, Justus learned in three months what most people would take years to learn. He was even shocked by his progress. Guess his father was correct; he was a natural. His results were visible whenever he looked at himself in the mirror. He was now built like a warrior. Not brolic, but chiseled like a Greek statue. Even his thoughts had changed. When he encountered a tree on their nature walks, his first thought was how to scale the tree quickly without being seen. When they encountered wild animals, his first thought was how to use the animal to his advantage, or at the very least, how to kill the animal as expediently as possible without a sound. In fact, Justus used every opportunity as a learning experience, a chance to hone his new craft.

Justus heard someone, or rather felt someone enter the room. He opened his eyes to find Leader with yet more clothes in his hand, and a wicked smile plastered across his face.

Each week, Leader would leave for a day with explicit instructions for Justus to review what he learned. When he returned, Leader would always have something different with him, pieces of clothing mostly. Over the course of three months, Leader had refurbished Justus's whole wardrobe, replacing Akoo with Armani, True Religion with Yves Saint Laurent, and Timberland with Ferragamo. Justus was now a businessman, therefore it was imperative that his wardrobe reflected that.

"What's up, son?" Leader greeted.

"Hey, what's up?" Justus returned, getting up from the floor in his linen drawstring pants and shirtless torso.

"What's up, is I have some good news. That's what's up?" Leader said cheerfully, walking over to the fireplace.

"What kind of good news?" Justus wondered. He used a towel to wipe sweat from his brow.

"One, we have a job in New York, day after tomorrow. The job pays two-hundred and fifty."

"Two-hundred fifty what?"

"Two-hundred fifty K."

"K, as in thousand?" Justus wondered in amazement.

"Absolutely." Leader answered nonchalantly.

Justus initially thought he was bluffing, but when he didn't crack a smile, Justus knew he was serious. Of course, he should've known all along. When it came to business, Leader didn't joke.

"Two-hundred and fifty thousand!? What could be better than that?" Justus wondered aloud, more to himself than to Leader.

"Oh, I can think of a couple of things."

"Name one," Justus challenged. He couldn't think of anything better than going from broke to hood rich overnight.

"Twins," Leader offered.

"Twins?" Justus repeated, confused.

"Yeah. Twins. Nikki dropped by the house. You gon' be a daddy, boy!" Leader gushed excitedly. He stuck his hand out to Justus on his good fortune. "Congratulations. Nikki is pregnant . . . with twins."

All of the breathing techniques Justus had learned went out the window. He began to hyperventilate. "Pregnant?" He couldn't believe his ears.

"Yup. Three months."

Leader relayed to Justus how Nikki had come by the house three months pregnant with twins, crying hysterically, and scared as shit. She thought Justus had abandoned her in the classic smash-and-dash fashion, because even Pug didn't know of Justus's whereabouts (at least he wasn't telling her). Nikki had patiently waited and waited until she couldn't bear the prospect of disappointment any longer. She stormed over to Justus's parents' house with evidence of their son's transgressions protruding from her belly. Much to her satisfac-

tion, Leader calmed her down and informed her
that Justus had not abandoned her. That he was, in
fact, in strict classes that required he not have any
contact with the outside world. Leader further explained to her that these classes were imperative
for his career, the career that will allow him to take
care of a woman with twins, and that he would be
home soon. Nikki took the news like it was a respi-
rator. It replenished her breath. She bid Leader
farewell, making him promise to tell Justus that
she missed him, and that she would be eagerly
awaiting his return.

When Leader finished telling Justus the news,
Justus walked outside for some fresh air to clear his
head. *Damn. Twins?* Justus thought. He had always
wanted Nikki and now he had her . . . *forever.* Justus's reflection was short-lived for as soon as he
sank into deep thought, Leader yanked him out.

"Come on, son. No time to focus on that now.
You have your whole life to deal with that. We got
work to do. We got a job, and we gotta get that
paper."

For Leader, it was business as usual. Nikki's
news couldn't have come at a better time. Justus
now had a real sense of purpose, a reason to chase
that bag. Aside from the fear of poverty propelling
him to make moves, he now had a family to provide for. If there were any previous doubts about
Justus following through on the training he received, they were now dispelled. The prospect of
obtaining money in mass amounts, coupled with
being a provider, was too much of a compelling
blend to refuse. Justus was now inducted into "the

life." His first official hit would determine how deep he would delve.

"Come on, we got a lot of planning to do," Leader informed him. Justus followed his daddy back inside.

He was now ready.

Chapter 12

One thing Leader loved about New York City
was the hustle and bustle. Seven million people
moving about, recklessly striving to attain lofty
goals, or stay on top. Living in this type of space, a
person had to adopt a mantra to survive, the most
common mantra being "only the strong survive."
Next in line to this mantra was the mantra of "see
nothing, hear nothing." New York's citizens lived
the latter mantra to a T. A person could live in the
same building with another person for a year and
never know it. A year!

This was why Leader loved jobs in New York.
They were by far easy money in the bank. And did
they have money to burn! New Yorkers were
loaded with money and didn't mind spending it to
keep it.

Justus's first mark was a high-ranking labor official who had pissed off the wrong people. Justus
was carrying out the job, but Leader was supervis-
ing to ensure everything went as planned.

The labor official lived in a high-rise condo on

the east side of Manhattan. The building boasted its own sublevel parking garage, a glass-enclosed elevator, valet, and doorman. The doorman is what Leader became after the original doorman met with an unfortunate accident. From that vantage point, he could see everything he needed to see. Plus, he could guide Justus, who was already staked out in the labor official's condo. After waiting in the brisk, autumn night for hours, Leader finally spotted their mark walking up the street. Leader opened the door for the short, pudgy, balding man as he stumbled into the lobby, then notified Justus.

Justus was camped out inside the opulent home, passing time by gazing out at the Manhattan skyline. He had shed his bellhop outfit and now wore a full-body nylon suit complete with balaclava. When Leader radioed that the mark was en route, Justus took his position by the front door.

As Justus waited to commit cold-blooded murder, his thoughts centered on what he was about to do. He was about to commit *murder*. Strangely enough, he had no qualms. When he had killed before, it was personal. This was *business*! His heart raced so rapidly that it felt like it was in his ear, his breathing was ragged, and his hands were shaking, but this was attributed to anticipation, not fear. Adrenaline was good, for it produced another reserve of energy from which to pull from. Justus channeled that energy to do his bidding and waited. He closed his eyes, visualized his mission, and waited.

He didn't have long to wait. Justus heard the door beep twice then he saw his mark stagger in, breathing heavily. The man exhaled loudly as he dropped his keys on the glass table by the door. The man was so drunk he didn't realize he had an intruder.

That would be his final mistake.

Justus acted quickly, seizing the element of surprise. He slipped his garrote over the heavy man's neck before the man could react. He spun around, put his back against the old man's, and bent over as far as possible, lifting the man off the floor. The man kicked his feet and flailed his arms, desperately trying to escape. He reached back and attempted to grab Justus's head. Justus bent over further and suspended him even higher in the air, until all his weight fell on the thin wire. Justus rocked back and forth to drive the wire deeper into his neck.

Soon, the man began to struggle less. Justus knew that meant he was growing weak. He squeezed harder and bent deeper, so deep his head nearly scraped the marble floor. The man gurgled in his attempts to scream, while desperately trying to grab Justus.

All to no avail.

In under a minute, the man ceased kicking, gurgling, or anything. In under a minute, he was dead. Justus held him in the air a few seconds longer to ensure that he was dead before he dropped him to the ground with a thud.

Justus bent over to catch his breath. He wheezed hard and clutched his chest. Everything happened so fast! The old man was a lot stronger than he anticipated. His adrenaline was on a thousand, but he kept his focus until the first half of the job was done.

Justus eyed his wristwatch to confirm he was keeping schedule. He dragged the limp body over to the window of the balcony overlooking the streets below. He opened the glass door and slid the body over to the balcony. Justus hoisted the limp body up and flipped it over the ledge, where it fell sixty stories down to the street and burst.

On the street, Leader was checking his watch every few seconds. He was beginning to get worried, until he heard a woman scream from a few feet away. He looked in the direction of the scream just in time to see the body smack the street and burst open like a piñata. A throng of people gathered around the mess. Leader blended in with the crowd to see the carnage. Satisfied, he made a clean exit.

An hour later, he linked back up with Justus at their rendezvous point. Shortly after, the two were on a train headed back to North Carolina.

Chapter 13

Nikki was celebrating her twenty-third birthday with family and friends at a local restaurant called On the Lake. Just as the name suggested, the restaurant was on the lake and offered the finest dishes from the Middle East. Nikki's father had reserved a private table in the back for this occasion. Although he was striving to remain positive, it was hard. His baby girl had just dropped a bombshell in his lap.

"Nikki darling, I hope this pregnancy business won't interfere with your studies," Darlene whined in her southern twang. "I can see your mother just rolling over in her grave right now," Darlene carried on. Nikki's other mother died in a tragic car accident when Nikki was ten years old. Since that time, Darlene had assumed the motherly role for Nikki. Nikki's family all came from bougie roots, all doctors, lawyers, and politicians. Darlene was no different. She was a surgeon at Cape Fear Valley hospital.

"No Auntie, I'm still going to school. Nothing

has changed." Nikki was tired of the complaints. This was supposed to be a celebration.

"Well, when darling? You're twenty-three years old." Darlene reminded her. The she dropped her voice an octave. "Is the father still in jail?" Darlene gasped, clutching the pearls that hung from her neck.

Jackie giggled, "Uh-oh."

"No ma'am, he's not." Nikki answered defiantly. "Jock is not the father."

"He's not?! Aww lord, Nikki baby," Darlene clutched her pearls again. "You're twenty-three years old with two baby fathers. This can't be good. Who is the father?"

Nikki hesitated a moment. "Justus."

"Justus!" her father spat, suddenly interested in the conversation. "The young boy?"

"Who is Justus?" Darlene asked, dumbfounded.

"How could he possibly help you take care of twins? He's a baby himself!"

"Who is Justus?" Darlene repeated, a little louder this time.

"Some seventeen-year-old kid."

"Actually, he's eighteen now, Dad, and I'd appreciate it if you'd lay off of him. He is a good person, despite his age," Nikki countered, indignantly.

"Yeah, Mr. Harrison, Justus is a great guy," Jackie piped in, aiding her best friend. "And he cares a great deal for your daughter. Even if he is a little . . . young . . . he's very mature. In fact, he's an entrepreneur."

"Oh?" Darlene was interested now. "In what capacity?"

"He's a Security Consultant," Jackie proudly informed her. "I've known him for quite a while, and he's very ambitious. Nikki is my best friend so I wouldn't want nothing but the best for her. I can honestly say that Justus is a step up for her." As Jackie sold Justus to Nikki's family, Nikki was listening intently. Hell, the way Jackie was telling it, she had Nikki thinking Justus was the best thing since sliced bread.

Aunt Darlene was suddenly on Nikki's side. "Well, William, how bad could he be. We were young once and had children. Anybody is better than that guy that Nikki was dating. At least this guy has an honest living. And from what I can tell, he cares for Nikki."

Nikki smiled at her aunt, "Thank you Auntie." Darlene smiled back.

Nikki's father took it all in then asked, "Just tell me one thing." He threw down his napkin about to make a point when he was suddenly interrupted by the waiter. The waiter whispered in his ear, and William's light face turned red, then contorted into a frown. He nodded to the waiter, "Very well."

The waiter disappeared. A few minutes later, in walked Justus wearing a black two-piece Armani suit, with a purple button-down silk shirt.

"Justus!" Nikki shrieked. She jumped from the table into Justus's arms. "Ohmigod baby! Where have you been? I missed you so much." Nikki hugged Justus around his neck, holding him so tight he thought she was going to pull his neck off.

Nikki rubbed Justus's low Caesar, and caressed his hard chest. "You look so different," she whispered. Nikki was so caught up in their reunion that she forgot all about her family members. One by one, Justus shook their hands. When he got to Jackie, he playfully nuggied her head. When he shook Darlene's hand, she allowed her hand to linger a bit while she sized him up. When she noticed his expensive alligator shoes, she shot Nikki a look of approval.

Apparently, he did have money.

Justus took his seat, and commenced to shoot down question after question with maturity and class. Nikki's father was particularly hard on Justus initially, but after just a few questions, Justus had won him over. As for Darlene, she was smitten from the moment Justus complimented her on her hair. She continued to smile through the remainder of the meal.

Nikki silently observed Justus work the table and felt a sense of pride. This was a different Justus. He was more polished than she remembered, and supremely confident. He now possessed a magnetism that oozed from his pores like mist, enslaving everyone under his will. When he spoke to William, his tone was that of an equal. It was like he knew something the rest of the world did not know. Nikki searched for the words to describe the difference in Justus's character. The only word that came to mind was power. Justus seemed powerful, like he ruled the world.

Nikki was pleased with the new Justus. Sure, he had temporarily abandoned her. But if his leaving was necessary for him to come back like this, necessary for him to matriculate, then she applauded his absence. All that mattered to her was that he was home now.

While Justus was solidifying his position with Nikki and her family, Leader was engaged in a conversation of his own with Carmen.

Leader had boarded a flight to Chicago to discuss more jobs with Menes. He thought, why not kill two birds with one stone, since he definitely needed to address the situation with Carmen.

To Leader's disappointment, Carmen refused to meet with him unless it was over dinner, her treat. He reluctantly agreed, and that's how they found themselves over a fabulous meal with a breathtaking view of Chicago from eighty stories up.

Carmen had spared no expense to impress Leader. She had sent a Mercedes Maybach to Leader's Lakeshore Drive hotel to drive him to the restaurant. In the cooler bisecting the backseat was a bottle of Dom Pérignon. In the adjacent seat sat a bouquet of flowers. When the car arrived at the restaurant, which was located atop one of the tallest buildings in the world, the driver discarded Leader at the entrance, where another assistant led him to Carmen.

Leader hadn't expected any of this treatment. He had agreed to meet with her to tell her that he was a married man. A loyal married man. He didn't have any intention of betraying his vows. He wanted nothing to do with her.

However, when he took in the sight of Carmen in her clingy, wine-colored, satin dress, with the plunging neckline and jewels dripping from every place possible, he caught amnesia. When the fog cleared, he was seated over a lobster talking world politics with a very engaging woman.

As the night waned, the conversation shifted toward love and relationships.

"So, you're telling me that there could not be two women if a man is really in love with one?" Carmen asked Leader disbelievingly.

"Of course not," boomed Leader dismissively.

Carmen chuckled lightly and her eyes lit up brighter than the candles that burned between them. "I submit to you that all kings loved their women in one way or another, yet they still had numerous concubines at their beck and call."

"That may be true for that day, but today things are more complicated. Society has bred that wild side out of most men."

"Well, if that were true, then the divorce rate wouldn't be so high," Carmen reasoned. "I submit to you that men still have a wild side, they just found new ways to explore it."

"Interesting," Leader admitted.

"That's what vacations are for." Carmen quipped. "By the way, what did you say you did again?"

"I didn't."

"Well?"

"I'm a security consultant."

"Really?"

"Yes. And yourself?"

"I'm a private investigator, emphasis on *private*."

"Hmm, I see." Leader was done playing games. "Well, you should already know that I'm a happily married man that doesn't stray on his wife. So, while this evening has been pleasant, it's time for it to end." Leader pushed his chair from the table to leave, but Carmen's penetrating gaze stopped him. "What? Did you not hear me?" Leader asked, irritated as hell.

"There's something in your eyes . . . you don't look happy," she suddenly concluded.

"You're wrong!" Leader stood. "I'm very happy."

"Well, why do you travel so much?"

"Excuse me?"

"You come to Chicago at least twice a month," Carmen revealed in a low tone, gazing at Leader.

"Alright goddammit! You're playing in dangerous territory!" Leader warned. He leaned across the table inches from Carmen's face. "I don't like nobody spying on me, got that?"

Carmen didn't even flinch. "Relax. No one is spying on you. I know what I know because I'm in the same hotel as you. Month after month, feeling just as lonely as you. Every time you come, I see you. So, I decided to make my move. Can't blame a sister, can you?"

Carmen's tone had softened considerably. A long curl fell across her face. Leader knew he was treading on thin ice, but there was something about Carmen that magnetized him.

"I won't pull your arm though. If you say you're happily married, then I must respect that," Carmen said. "Can we at least finish this wonderful meal?"

Against his better judgment, Leader agreed to finish the meal.

As they conversed, Leader found that Carmen was highly intelligent and world traveled. She spoke multiple languages, and was skilled in martial arts. In addition to her dazzling mind, Leader couldn't tear his eyes away from her. Her cinnamon-colored skin was as smooth as satin. Her cheekbones were high and round. Her hazel-hued eyes sparkled like diamonds reflecting the candle light. When the meal was over, both of them were reluctant to leave. Yet their time had come to an end.

Carmen stood and led Leader to the balcony. Outside the autumn air was brisk as it clipped their ears. Leader removed his suit jacket and draped it over Carmen's shoulders. Carmen smiled and backed into him, demanding that he hold her.

"It's beautiful, isn't it?" Carmen purred, referring to the Chicago skyline.

"Yeah," Leader confessed.

"Listen to me," Carmen turned her head to look Leader in his eyes. "I'm not trying to interfere with your happy home. I just think we have a lot in common, and a lot to offer each other. No one deserves to be lonely. I see the same look in your eye that I see when I look in the mirror. I'm just thinking maybe I can show you a good time whenever you're here—strictly platonic," she added.

Leader was feeling the proposal. But he knew that every big thing started small first. He was not up for any drama at home.

"Why me?"

"Other than the fact that you're attractive as hell? I sense that there is a part of you just dying to be released. I want to be the one to bring that out. Be your escape. Maybe we can free each other from our chains of loneliness."

The game Carmen spit was like music to Leader's ears. He knew he was flirting with betrayal. But the possibilities were too pleasing to pass up.

"I'll consider it."

Even as Leader mumbled his response, Carmen already knew she had him. If he wasn't interested, he simply would have said no. But he didn't. With the right amount of patience and perseverance, she knew she could weigh him down eventually and execute her plan. Then the real fun would begin.

Chapter 14

After Justus dispatched his first victim, he experienced a rush of guilt as his mind did battle with his heart. Leader had infused his brain with a new psychology of Objectivism and although Justus bought into it, like an updated computer program, his mind still had its glitches. To keep him in game mode, Leader had taken Justus hunting shortly after their return from New York. Over hunting they bonded, and Leader was able to correct the glitches in his mind.

Over the course of months following Justus's return, he and Nikki were inseparable. He had been accepted by her family so much that Aunt Darlene had become his personal spokesperson. Justus took it all in stride. Using tricks that Leader had schooled him about real estate, Justus was able to purchase land in Hope Mills, a small town bordering Fayetteville, at a cheap price. Justus arranged to have the land cleared then set up vacant lots for modular homes. Through a contract with HUD, Justus was guaranteed to lease at least half of his 25 plots out for $250 a month. It wasn't much compared to what he would clear for a job, but it was constant cash flow that legitimized his money. More importantly, it established a residual income so when he did make major purchases, his capital could be accounted for.

In conjunction with the real estate purchase, Justus acquired five acres to build his own home on. He even allowed Nikki to add input on the house plans. When the house was completed, it would consist of a three-car garage, a glass cylindrical bedroom with a Jacuzzi inside the master bath, a swimming pool in the shape of a J, and five bedrooms. Since it was being built from scratch, the house would cost only $300,000. Justus only received $150,000 from his first job, and his initial investment put a substantial dent in that cache. So, he was looking forward to going on more jobs.

Reenergized, Justus was ready to go hard. With the two of them together, their efficiency doubled and their reputation grew. As a result of this, they began pulling in no less than four jobs a month, for no less than $100K per job. Just as fast as transportation would get them to a job, they were there. As fast as transportation would allow, they were whisked away to the next job.

With each job, Justus's experience grew. In the real world, he received real world experience. Where his conscience used to bother him before, it was nonexistent now. He simply rationalized murder as work. He became methodical. He was meticulous.

He became a professional.

Leader assisted in Justus's transition every step

of the way. He was constantly critiquing him, always showing him better ways of doing things. He was always digging inside of Justus's mental soil to plant more wisdom. Pretty soon, he began trusting Justus enough for him to go on jobs by himself. While Justus was putting in work, Leader met with Menes in Chicago to receive new contracts. Menes had his suspicions about the speed and efficiency with which Leader was carrying out these jobs. However, in this business, the less you knew, the more insulated you were. As long as the jobs were being carried out, Menes would continue to be pleased.

Unfortunately for Leader, he began something else while in Chicago.

Every moment that wasn't spent handling business with Menes was spent with Carmen. She turned out to be cool peoples. She and Leader went everywhere together. They went to the theater, Bears and Bulls games, and every restaurant imaginable. One night in particular, Carmen took Leader gambling on the Majestic Star, a casino gambling boat owned by a black entrepreneur. They both got dolled up, Carmen in a red strapless gown, Leader in a black tux. Leader was in between jobs so of course his bald head was glistening like an 8-ball under the bright lights. He and Carmen spent the night gambling away thousands of dollars, tossing back drinks, and having fun. Leader felt like a kid again. He found himself really enjoying Carmen's company. The best part was that their boundaries were respected. Their relationship was purely platonic. Carmen found herself sorely missing Leader when he was away. Against her will, she was becoming attached, but in a different way.

Chapter 15

It was nearing time for Nikki to drop her load. Justus had promised Nikki he would be right by her side when she gave birth, so he only had time for one more job before he went into hiatus. Leader already had the job lined up. The payoff would be enormous, enough for the them both to ride off into the sunset for a while.

But they had to earn it.

Their mark was a highly-trained general that worked on the Joint Chiefs of Staff. Over his years of service, he had accumulated a body of evidence against the government. He knew of secret pacts with the Chinese, election tampering from the Russians, foreign assassinations. He knew it all! Disillusioned with the Trump Administration, he was ready to go bird against the very institution that made him. An attempt had already been made on the general's life, but the general managed to reverse the tables and kill the assassin. The incident spooked a lot of cleaners in the community, and drove the price up on the job. Despite the hefty tag on the contract, other cleaners were reluctant to accept the job.

Leader took the job because unlike most cleaners he had two wild cards. One, he had intimate knowledge of the general's location. Two, he had a duplicate of himself. Leader was banking on these two cards to give him the edge. If they pulled this job off, not only would he be set for retirement, he would also solidify his position in the community as a living legend.

He hoped.

Leader and Justus sat in the hotel room combing over their plan one last time before they embarked on their journey. They were doing things differently this time. Normally, they preferred to dispatch their marks close up because it allowed them greater control over the variables of the job. Because of the heightened security of this quarry, they were arranging a long-distance hit. Long shots were always tricky. The mark had to be in the right place at just the right time, the potential for witnesses was greater, even the wind conditions had to be just right for the perfect shot. To help their cause Leader had purchased a new toy for this assignment.

The Barret .50 caliber rifle was a state-of-the-art rifle designed for only one thing: killing at a distance. At nearly four-feet long, with a ten-round magazine, the Barret's killing range was just under a mile. If the shooter was accurate, anything within a mile was a guaranteed kill. For this assignment, Justus had been designated the shooter. He had trained with the weapon for the past month, taking at least a hundred shots a day. He was hitting his target at a rate of 98% before it was deemed he was ready.

Leader tossed the heavy case on the bed and popped it open. In the case lay the .50 broken down into fragments.

"Man, I remember the first time I fired one of these babies," Leader said. He exhaled a deep breath as if recalling the memory. "This thing will destroy anything it touches. You know it will penetrate metal?"

"Really?" Justus asked.

"Damn right. I saw one shoot clean through a Humvee before."

"Wow!"

Leader placed another case on the bed and pulled out a metal object as long and wide as a two-liter bottle. "This is the suppressor," he explained to Justus. "You need to make sure it's one shot, one kill because every time a round goes through this thing it changes the accuracy of your weapon. Got it?"

"Got it." Justus was ready for this contract to be over. The anticipation was killing him, and he found it hard to remain focused. Aside from the stress of this job, he was on the verge of becoming a father. The thought terrified and exhilarated him simultaneously. He took in a deep breath to reign in his thoughts as his father's words echoed in his ear.

A distracted soldier is a dead soldier.

* * *

Nikki stuffed the clothes inside the box and taped it shut. This was her second time moving in a year. The last time she was forced to move. This time she was happy to be moving. The contractors were nearly done with her and Justus's new home in Hope Mills, and she couldn't wait to get her new life started. Justus may have been younger than her, but he was adept at taking care of business. As far along as she was into her pregnancy, she knew she shouldn't have been working so hard, but if she didn't do it then it wasn't going to get done. Her twins were showing her who was boss as they kicked inside her belly like they were fighting in the UFC. Just as she was about to sit down to take a break, her phone shrilled to life. A private number.

"Hello?"

No one responded, just heavy breathing.

"Hello?" Nikki repeated. Still, no reply. "Look, why the hell did you call my phone if you didn't want anything?"

"Bitch, you think you can cross me and get away with it?" Jock snarled.

"Jock?"

"That's right, bitch! Didn't I tell you that I was going to fuck you and that nigga up if you shit on me?"

Nikki hadn't heard from Jock since the day she left him in jail. "Jock, don't call my phone no more. I've moved on. Now, if you call me again I'm going to go down to the jail and tell them people you got a cell phone and you using it to harass me," she promised.

Jock shrieked in laughter. "Go ahead and tell

them. I don't give a fuck. I got pull in this mother-fucker. I'll have two more phones by the time they take this one. Don't get it twisted, I'm still that nigga."

"Exactly. You still a nigga."

"Oh bitch, you wanna get smart now because the li'l nigga done knocked you up? Don't forget it was me who took care of your ass when you ain't have shit! Your parents disowned you after you got your father's Benz impounded when they found that dope under the seat."

"But it was your dope, Jock!"

"It don't fucking matter! The point is, they abandoned your ass and kicked you out. *I* took you in and put you back on your feet. *I* took care of all your needs and made you a queen in this city. *Me!* Don't bite the hand that fed you. Fuck with me and I'll kill both them little bastards in your stomach, and they daddy."

That threat really pissed Nikki off. "Yeah, yeah, say that shit, say that shit. You Mr. Bad Ass behind them bars. Why don't you tell him that to his face when you get home."

Jock laughed hysterically. "You know, I just might do that."

"What the fuck is so funny, Jock?"

"You funny. Bitch."

"Look, I ain't gonna be too many more of your bitches."

"You gonna be that one."

"I'm hanging up," Nikki announced.

"Wait! Hold up."

"Hold up for what, Jock?"

"I need you to do me a favor."

"What? After all that shit you talked? Fuck you!"

"Look out your door."

"What?"

"I said, look out your front door?"

"For what?"

"You'll see."

"Whatever Jock. I'm not playing games with you."

Even though she dismissed Jock, her curiosity overwhelmed her. She hobbled over to the door with the phone to her ear and snatched it open. To her astonishment, she saw Jock leaning behind the wheel of a Cadillac smoking a blunt. He rolled his window down and stuck his arm out. A red beam appeared just beside Nikki's head. A split second later, a shot crackled through the air.

Nikki jumped to the floor facedown and excruciating pain exploded through her entire body. Another shot crackled through the air but Nikki never heard it. She didn't hear Jock howl in laughter either. She never saw him peel out of her neighborhood in a cloud of smoke. Never heard him call her a dirty bitch.

Nikki was unaware of those things because when she hit the ground on her swollen belly her body went numb. Blood flowed freely between her legs and contractions wracked her body.

The last thing she was able to do was call Jackie.

Justus peered through the scope of his rifle down onto the Washington D.C. street. He was tucked safely in the back of a nondescript van parked at the top of a parking garage. The back window of the van was removed, giving him open access to the world outside the van. He spotted Leader in his peddler's disguise right away. Although Leader was nearly a mile away from his location, with the HD lens on the scope Justus could count the hairs in his nose.

The general was scheduled to meet with reporters in the Penthouse suite of a hotel to give a recorded deposition. The meeting was supposed to be top secret, but the location was leaked to Menes, who in turn passed the info on to Leader. It was rumored that after this meeting, the general was going underground. This would be the ideal time and place to strike because the general would be briefly exposed for the short walk from the parking garage to the hotel. The route would take him past a corridor of open buildings, right into Justus's sight line.

Justus swung the rifle in a wide arc once again, sweeping the street in search of his target. Still, no sign of the general. To pass time, Justus drew random targets into his sight picture and practiced taking the shot. He marveled at the efficiency of the weapons system. Each time he placed his crosshairs on a pedestrian his red dot landed centermass. Justus was beginning to believe the hype that his father lauded upon him. Maybe he was a natural.

Justus's earpiece squawked to life. "Get ready. I think I see him," Leader relayed.

Justus tightened his grip on the weapon and allowed his vision to go slack. His heartbeat quickened, and a lump rose in his throat. His hands began to sweat inside his leather gloves. This was the moment he was slowly starting to crave. The adrenaline rush, the surge of power as he stalked his target. The omnipotence of it all excited him more than it should have. This was what his father had warned him about. *Keep it professional,* Leader had schooled. *Don't let the job get into you.* Justus now understood the advice.

"It's him! It's him! We're hot." Leader said.

Justus scanned the street with the scope and saw the general bend the corner. He wasn't alone though. Two guards flanked him, one in front, one in the back.

"Don't worry about the guards," Leader coached. "One shot, one kill. Remember: one shot, one kill."

Justus drew the general's bulky chest into his sight picture. He steadied the weapon and his finger tapped the trigger. A red beam appeared at the center of the general's chest. Justus raised the beam until it danced at the base of the general's neck.

One shot, one kill . . .

Nikki blacked in and out of consciousness, as she felt herself rolling beneath bright lights. Her eyes flitted open and in those flashes she saw Jackie by her side. The pain in her stomach was unending, and her body was drenched from her navel to her toes.

"Come on, Nikki. Stay with us. I'm right here," Jackie said. "You're gonna be fine."

"Jus . . ." Nikki gasped. "Where is Justus?"

Jackie frowned. "Pug is on the way to get him right now," she lied.

"My babies, Jackie. What's happening to my babies?"

"You're going to be fine, Nikki. The babies are going to be fine," Jackie assured her. She hoped that she was telling the truth.

A pain ripped through Nikki's midsection. She bit her bottom lip to stifle the pain. "Justus, where are you???"

Justus laid his crosshairs on the general's neck and the red beam danced on his Adam's apple. He slowly reduced his breath to next to nothing and zoned out. He tightened his grip on the handle and prepared to take his shot.

But the general kept moving erratically. It was as if he knew he was under surveillance. Every few seconds he would speed up his pace, then slow down. Then he would walk in step with his guard in the front, before falling in step with the guard in the back. Justus also noted the general kept touching his waist. Justus deduced the general was packing heat.

"Do NOT engage him at all," Justus relayed to Leader. "He is spooked and he is holding."

The plan was for Leader to stop the group as they walked by and beg for spare change. The diversion would give Justus the opening he needed to take the shot. That was the original plan. With the general being so paranoid they had to go to plan B. Paranoid people were dangerous. They didn't think. They only reacted.

"Ten-four."

Justus refocused his sight picture. He would

take his shot right after they passed Leader, just in case something went wrong he could complete the job.

The group was now just a block away from the hotel, about fifty yards from Leader. Justus drew the general's head into his sight picture. The red dot appeared in the center of his head. Justus steeled his nerves, slowed his breath and began the meticulous process it took for the perfect shot.

The Barret required four pounds of pressure to the trigger to expel a round. Four pounds of steady pressure. Justus held his breath and began slowly squeezing the trigger . . .

Before he felt the recoil that confirmed a round had been released, he saw the general's head explode in a crimson burst. Justus detached his eye from the scope to clear his vision. When he peered through the scope again he saw the general's guards laying on top of his dead body, their heads aired out also.

"What the fuck?" Justus whispered.

"Good shooting!" Leader barked. "You took two down with one shot."

"That wasn't me! The shots came from somewhere else!"

Justus swung his weapon in a wide arc, scanning the surrounding rooftops for other shooters. Nothing.

He peered through his scope, observing the melee that had ensued nearly a mile away. People were stampeding over each other in all directions, getting as far away from the disaster as possible. One woman was drenched in blood and brain matter. She fell to her knees hysterically, wiping the substance from her face. Sirens wailed in the distance.

"What happened?" Leader demanded.

Justus scanned the rooftops again for shooters. "I don't know. Wait! I think I see somebody." On a rooftop about a half a mile away Justus saw a figure sprinting away. He attempted to bring a sight picture up into his scope but before he could get a good picture the figure jumped from the roof.

"What do you see?" Leader asked.

Justus didn't know how to answer that. He *thought* he just saw someone do a swan dive off a twenty-story roof. Surely his mind was playing tricks on him.

"Nothing. I thought I saw something," Justus replied.

"Let's go. Meet me at the R.P."

Justus spared one last look at his target to confirm the kill. The general and his security team were definitely dead. The only question was how?

Chapter 16

Justus and Pug stormed through the doors of Cape Fear Valley Hospital. Pug had contacted him with news of Nikki's early delivery while he and Leader were fleeing D.C. Jackie met them the second they stepped off the elevator. She helped Justus get prepped then ushered him into the delivery room to see his twins.

Justus walked into the room and saw Nikki laying in the bed with the twins on her chest, wailing. The sight of new life snatched him to the dark place of death. Instantly, he caught a flashback of the general's head exploding. He paused as his heartbeat quickened. He shook off the vision and went to the aid of his woman.

"Hey babe, you alright?" Justus asked Nikki, rubbing her hand. Nikki was so doped up on sedatives she could barely move. Due to her injuries, they had to perform an emergency C-section to bring their twins into the world.

"Jus . . . you're here," Nikki whispered.

"Of course, I'm here." Justus rubbed Nikki's

damp hair. "You had to do it all alone without me though," Justus lamented. "I thought they were coming a month from now."

Nikki offered a weak smile. "You can't predict nature, Justus."

Justus posted up beside the bed, phone in hand, and videoed his children as they began to doze quietly. He picked up and held one of his newborns in his arms with pride, a feeling of pride spreading in his chest as he took it all in. *A father. He was a father of twins at just nineteen.* The moment was surreal. The arc his life had taken in the past year was unbelievable. He went from being a broke star athlete with an immature girlfriend, to being a contract killer, living with the woman of his dreams with more money in the bank than he could have ever imagined. Tonight, he held a new life in his arms. Less than four hours ago, he witnessed a brutal murder.

Life sure had a wicked sense of humor.

Justus thought about names and chuckled at his first thought. Smith and Wesson. After all, that is how he would provide for them. Just as quickly as the thought came to mind he dismissed it. Nikki would never go for it.

Nikki and Justus exchanged tender looks while their babies familiarized themselves with the world. Their tender moment was short. News had spread that the twins were here and the family bombarded the room. Nikki's father, her aunt Darlene, and Keisha came in, followed by Pug and Jackie.

"Congratulations!" Everyone squealed.

Pug passed Justus a cigar, "Congrats, cuz-o!"

"Thanks fam." Justus passed the baby to Nikki's father and put the stogie in his mouth.

"Yo, you a'ight fam?" Pug asked. "You don't look like yourself."

"I mean, I just became a dad, cousin."

Pug eyed Justus closely. "Nah, it's something else. Everything a'ight?"

Pug was right. It was more than just the birth of his children. He was still spooked about Washington D.C. He kept seeing the general's head explode. By far, this was the most violent murder he had witnessed.

"I'm a'ight, dawg," Justus said. He coughed. "Just thinking . . . just thinking."

Pug put his hand on Justus's shoulder. "Listen up li'l cuz, nothing is more important than this moment so soak it all in. Don't let nothing stop you from enjoying this moment 'cause you can never get it back."

"Thanks cousin. I appreciate it."

Even as Justus said it, his mind was wandering. He couldn't shake the feeling that someone was onto them. Someone was out there watching them. They had been meticulous. They had been careful. Calculated. Yet, someone was onto them.

Although watching his children being born was supposed to be one of the happiest days in a man's life, Justus couldn't enjoy the moment because he was daydreaming about a death.

Leader and Glenda had just completed a tremendous lovemaking session. Each time Leader returned from a business trip their lovemaking was intensified. Absence definitely made the heart grow fonder in their life. Unbeknownst to Glenda, there was another reason their lovemaking was so intense.

Carmen.

Leader had allowed the other woman to penetrate deep into his psyche. Although he had never touched Carmen inappropriately during their dealings, he sure wanted to. Carmen was feminine perfection personified. Her body was sculpted like an Egyptian goddess. She was fluent in four languages, politically savvy, and a business owner. She was smart, world traveled, and classy. Yeah, Leader was really digging her, but he had pledged his allegiance to Glenda and his family. Besides, Glenda was still fine in her old age. Like wine, she got better with time. She had been a loyal wife, and a great mother. He owed her his loyalty.

Leader's heart remained true to his pledge, but his mind and penis sang a tune of their own.

When Leader plunged inside his wife, he imagined it was Carmen. When Glenda moaned inside his ears, it was Carmen's voice he heard. When he cupped Glenda's soft ass, he imagined he was palming Carmen's perfect rear. Fortunately, his wife couldn't read his mind.

"Aww honey, that was fantastic!" Glenda gushed. She snuggled underneath Leader's arms. "Something about going out of town brings the best out of you. You sure you don't have a sweet young thing tucked away somewhere recharging your battery?"

Glenda was joking, but the irony was not lost on Leader. "You think so?" he asked.

"Hmm-mmm," Glenda purred. She propped herself up on her elbow and gazed intently at her husband. "Honey, I'm tired of you leaving so much. I thought you said that when Justus started working with you, you wouldn't have to work so much?"

Leader exhaled. "I know baby. That was the plan but I had to make sure he would be okay out there by himself."

"Well?"

"Well, I think we have both earned a break for a bit. We'll be around home for a little while now."

Glenda hugged her husband deeply. "Thank you, baby."

Leader only told his wife half of the truth. All their operations had been suspended until they could get a grasp of what occurred in Washington D.C. Someone other than Justus had taken the fatal shot that got them paid. Someone who was as skilled a marksman as he had ever seen. Whomever had taken that shot had been nearly a mile away. There couldn't have been that many snipers in their community capable of that type of work. It would take some time, but he would get to the bottom of things.

Chapter 17

Nikki was released a week after delivering the twins with Justus and Diamond right by her side. Justus pushed Power and Supreme in their twin stroller while Diamond helped Nikki with the door. They looked like the perfect blended family.

Justus whipped his new Suburban into the circular driveway of their new home. In the driveway, another vehicle was sitting pretty with a large bow wrapped around the hood. It was a brand-new Porsche Panamera. The candy-apple red color sparkled under the sun.

Justus passed Nikki the keys with a peck on the cheek. "Congratulations baby!"

Nikki squirmed in her seat like a kid on Christmas. "Ohmigod Justus!"

"I know I promised you a coupe, but with the new additions to the family I thought this would be more practical."

"Justus, you didn't . . ."

"I did. Come on, let's check it out."

The family hopped out and inspected the sports sedan from all angles. Justus pointed out all of the special features, from the honey leather seats with red accents to the red-bottomed rims. As Justus ticked off each feature Nikki listened attentively. When he was done, Nikki gave him a big, wet kiss on his lips.

"Jus, I love you, baby. I really do," Nikki promised.

"And I love you too," Justus returned. "I told you a long time ago that I was going to take care of you."

"True, you did."

"And I always will."

"Thank you, Justus."

Justus grabbed Nikki by the arm. "Nikki, I will do anything for you, but I only ask one thing in return."

"What's that, Justus?"

"Don't ever cross me, Nikki."

The way he said it sent chills down her spine. Was that a veiled threat? It didn't matter, because Nikki had no intention of ever betraying Justus. He took care of her every need. He laid the pipe like a champion lover. And he respected her. Why mess that up?

Those were Nikki's thoughts on that day she brought her family home to begin their new life. However, over the next few months, she betrayed her intellect and allowed Jock to scurry back into her life. She had known Jock for most of her life. He was familiar to her. Although he had shown his true colors when he shot at her, Nikki still loved

Jock, and in her young lovestruck naiveté, Nikki partly blamed herself for the incident. She felt obligated to allow Jock to continue to hang around in her life.

Jock began sending flowers to her job with sweet salutations and profuse apologies. He kept up his campaign until one day Nikki agreed to meet him for lunch. Over lunch, Jock swore on everything that he was a changed man. Nikki wasn't convinced or impressed. She told Jock the truth. She was in love with Justus. Jock grudgingly accepted Nikki's answer but he vowed to win her heart back piece by piece, by doing all the things he should have done in the first place.

Nikki attempted to avoid Jock at all costs while she and Justus moved into their new home, more so for Jock's safety than her own. She couldn't put her finger on it, but something was different about Justus. He seemed hardened. Dangerous. Nikki couldn't forget how Jackie implored her not to tell Justus about how Jock induced her labor. Jackie seemed afraid of Justus.

Nikki soon found out why Justus was to be feared.

One night while the family was having dinner, loud music erupted from outside, interrupting their calm moment. Justus got up from the table and checked the camera monitors. Pug's Suburban sat idling by the wrought iron gates. Justus buzzed him in, and moments later Pug rushed in with a scowl on his face.

"I need to holla at you, cuz," Pug snarled. Justus took him into the game room so they could talk in private.

"What's up?" Justus asked once they were alone.

"Some niggas violated me!" Pug spat with tears in his eyes. "I'm so fucking mad right now."

"Wait. What happened? Who violated you?"

"Some lame ass niggas ran up in my spot," Pug informed him.

"What, one of your dope spots?"

"Nah nigga, my mu'fuckin' crib dawg!" Pug roared. "Tied babygirl up and shit."

"You bullshitting!"

"Nigga, would I play about something like that?"

Both men went silent while the incident soaked in. Someone had violated Pug in the worst way.

"How much they take?" Justus asked.

"'Bout ten bands, but fuck the bread. These niggas took my dignity, my safety. They violated me, cuz!" Pug clenched his fist so hard Justus thought he was going to draw blood.

"Facts."

"And then I know who did it but I can't even touch these niggas up."

"What? Why the fuck not?" Justus asked.

"Because one of them is ole' boy I touched up back in the day. The police still got files on it. If something happen to him I'll be the first person they look for. I can't stand the heat because I'm still on paperwork," Pug explained. "Plus po-po tagging my moves."

"What?" Justus ran to his window, paranoid.

"Calm yo ass down. I shook them hours ago," Pug laughed. "Anyway, I got a proposition for ya."

"What kind of proposition?"

Pug reached into his True Religion jeans and extracted a knot of money about four inches thick. He rifled through the stack to reveal nothing but fifties and blue hundreds. He placed the money on the pool table. "I got close to ten racks here. It's not much, but it's yours if you handle this for me."

Justus cocked his head. "Fuck is you saying? I look like one of them Fort Bragg niggas to you or something?"

Pug dropped his head in silence for a moment. He slowly raised his puppy dog eyes to Justus. "Cuz, I know everything," he whispered.

"Know everything like what?" Justus challenged.

Pug hopped on the smooth velvet lining of the red-topped pool table and stared at the picture of Jay-Z on the wall. "Remember the night I took you with me to handle the thing with the C.O.? Well, that was Leader's doing. He wanted to see if you were ready or not. He wanted to test you to see if you were cut out for the life. If you bitched up on me, then he wasn't going to teach you."

"Muthafucka . . . So you knew the whole time?" Justus couldn't believe what he was hearing.

Pug continued. "Yeah man, your pops set that up for you." Pug shook his head. "You don't get it huh? Your pops is a legend in certain circles. He used to hold Sherlock down back in the day. Shit, you should consider it an honor that he teaching you.

"I know it seems fucked up that he made moves behind your back but trust me it was worth it. And hell, from the looks of things it paid off." Pug gestured to the house.

Justus didn't like the fact that he had been played, but he understood. It's not like his father could have just come out and told him. He had to be tested first. "Yeah, I don't like it, but I understand," Justus reasoned aloud.

"Damn right," Pug agreed. He spread his hands open. "Now that you know that I know what you do, can you handle this for me? I got your bread because I respect the game. If it's not enough, let me know and I'll get more."

Justus stroked his chin, mulling things over. He was supposed to be on a hiatus while Leader investigated the Washington D.C. situation. Also, on numerous occasions, Leader had cautioned him to *never* do business in Fayetteville. Home was a sanctuary, and one never shit where he slept. However, this was different. Pug was family. Blood. If the roles were reversed, he knew Pug wouldn't have hesitated.

Justus walked to the pool table where Pug had thrown the wad of cash and picked it up. He straightened the bills up and pushed the money back into Pug's hand. Justus looked his cousin directly in the eyes. "Your money is no good here," he said. "Your violation is my violation. I got you fam. Consider it handled."

Inside the dining room, Nikki's mouth was agape. She had been watching the security camera from the game room on her phone. She was stunned by what had happened to her best friend, and her heart wept for her. She was more concerned with Pug offering Justus money to handle his beef. And what kind of test did Leader give Justus? *What the fuck was that about?*

Loyalty to her friend beating out her curiosity, she dialed Jackie's number to check on her. Unfortunately, that decision forced her to miss out on the last part of the conversation.

Pug told Justus that Nikki had been seeing Jock.

Chapter 18

"I want to see you."

Leader couldn't believe who the voice on the other end of his home phone belonged to.

"Carmen, what are you doing calling my home?" Leader hissed. He slipped into his office to talk in private.

"I haven't seen you in a while. I presume that's because you haven't been in the area lately on business?" Carmen's voice was articulate. Raspy. Sexy. It was as if she blew her words through the receiver.

Leader sighed. "I presume you're right."

"I understand that, but I thought we were friends. You could have at least kept in touch," Carmen cooed.

Leader closed his eyes and recalled how beautiful Carmen looked the last time he saw her. He could've sworn her scent was wafting through the receiver. He struggled to push back the feeling gripping his loins. "We are friends, Carmen," Leader replied.

"Friends keep in touch!" Carmen snapped.

"Whoa, whoa, check yourself," he advised Carmen.

"You're right. I apologize," Carmen conceded. "But listen, if I didn't need to speak with you about something important, I would have never encroached on your personal space. You understand that, don't you?"

"Ok. I'm listening."

Carmen paused. "I hear you're having problems at work."

Pause.

"What. Are. You. Talking. About."

"I hear you are having some problems at work," Carmen repeated.

"Carmen, if you know something I don't, you need to spit it out. I don't have much time to play games."

"How valuable is what I know?"

"Are you serious?"

"Very."

"Look, cut the shit Carmen."

"Oh, that's not very friendly. I thought we were friends."

"I'm about to hang up. Thanks for checking on me, friend."

"Washington D.C."

"Excuse me?" Leader froze. "What. Did. You. Say."

"I said, Washington D.C.," Carmen repeated. "You had a problem in Washington D.C."

Leader spoke in measured tones. "What do you know about D.C.?"

"It doesn't matter how I know. Just know that I may be able to help you solve your dilemma."

"I'm listening."

"Meet me?"

"Where? When?"

"Can you meet me in Mexico during Spring Break?"

Leader was wary but he really didn't have a choice. Carmen knew something about D.C. The only way to determine how much was to meet her.

"I'll be there," Leader promised. Oh, he would meet her alright, and if she knew too much, only one of them would be coming back from Mexico.

Leader ended the call. He walked out of his office into the kitchen and found Justus standing at the counter drinking a tall glass of milk.

"Dad, I need to holla at you about something," Justus said.

"Oh yeah? What's that?" Leader took a seat at the table.

"Something we never discussed in training."

Leader surfed the web on his phone. "Shoot."

"How do you feel about trust?" Justus laid the last word out like a foul odor.

"Hmm . . . trust huh? Where is this coming from?"

"Just been thinking lately."

"That's some pretty deep thinking."

"Let me ask you something? What would you do if you found out Mom was creeping on you?"

The question took Leader aback. How long had Justus been inside? Had he heard the conversation with Carmen? "Whoa . . . Uhhh, that's a hard one. I wouldn't even want to think about that one. Why? Is everything okay with you and Nikki?"

Justus hesitated. "I'm not sure," he admitted.

"I mean, I think we're happy. I try my best to do right by her. You know? But with a woman you just never know."

Leader placed his hand under his chin and cradled his elbow in his palm. After some contemplation, he gave it to his son raw and uncut. "Let me tell you something son, never put all your trust in anyone, especially your woman. When it comes to women, where trust goes, betrayal soon follows. If you're not doing the betrayal, then you are probably the one being betrayed."

Justus mulled the jewel over. "But does it have to be this way though?"

"Nah, it doesn't have to be, but it is. It's the way of the world."

"Ok. So what if you found out you were betrayed? What would you do?"

Leader answered the question in his cryptic manner by posing a question of his own. "Would you rather be feared or respected?"

"Respected." Justus answered almost immediately.

Leader smirked. "See, now you're showing your youth."

"How so?"

"Well, as to that question, it depends on who you're dealing with. See, some people only respect fear. You understand?"

"I'm not sure I do, Dad."

"Ok, let me break it down." Leader placed his phone on the table and stood to act out his point. "You could have a dude who is the coolest cat. You know, speaking to everyone, easygoing fella. Take care of his business and keep it moving. The young wolves see him, take his kindness for weakness, and make a move on him. Why? Lack of respect. Got it?"

Justus nodded.

"Now you could have that same guy. Every time somebody speaks, he gritting on 'em. Every time he step out the car, he flashing the heat. He still dress fly, still drive the same car. Only this time, he letting everybody who see him know he with the shits. They wouldn't dare make a move on him because they know he a wolf too. They would fear him. Understand?"

"I think so."

Leader held up his palm. "Always remember this, where fear goes, respect will follow."

Justus definitely understood that. He nodded his head vigorously. "Word."

Leader chuckled. "That's it?"

Justus stood and pushed his chair in to the table. "Yeah Dad, thanks."

"No problem, son." As Leader walked Justus out, he reminded him they had training later that week.

Outside, Justus sat in his Hellcat Challenger and weighed his father's words carefully. Based on what Leader said, there was only one way to handle Nikki's transgressions. He unlocked his phone and dialed Pug.

"Yoooo, what's good cousin?" Pug greeted.

"About that thing you told me about? Scratch my back and I'll scratch yours," Justus bargained.

"Done."

Chapter 19

It didn't take Justus long to track down the guys who had ran up in Pug's home. True to form, they were out scouting their next victim.

Justus spotted the two jack-boys in their neighborhood, Savoy Heights, a neighborhood at the bottom of Haymount Hill. He observed them from where he sat slumped inside of his bucket while they sat puffing weed. Justus waited until just the right time then he exited his vehicle. He stumbled toward their truck like a drunken man, bumbling around the parking lot of the rec center aimlessly, until one of the guys emerged from their truck and approached him.

"Yo, what up, dawg? You lost or something?" he asked Justus. His partner emerged from the truck and backed him up.

"Yeah, nigga. You lost?"

The park was dark and deserted this time of night. The men were only able to make out Justus's silhouette.

"You can't hear motherfucker?" The man tapped Justus on his shoulder.

Justus spun in one smooth motion. Like a cobra, his hand lashed out and struck. The man stumbled back clutching his throat. Blood spurted between his fingers from the gaping wound in his neck. His comrade saw the move and decided he didn't want any of that smoke. He stumbled backwards in a panic and bolted towards the edge of the parking lot. Justus let him gain a little distance then capped him in the leg with his silenced pistol.

Justus calmly walked over to the first man and put him out of his misery with one shot to the dome. Next, he walked over to the second victim who was desperately trying to crawl away to safety with his good leg.

"H-hey brother, let's talk about this. I don't even know that nigga, maaan!" he pleaded.

Justus retrieved his tranquilizer gun and shot a dart into his neck. While waiting on the dart to take effect, he dragged the first victim to their truck and sat him in upright in the driver's seat. Then he returned to the second victim and tossed him in the trunk of his bucket.

Before he left the scene, he made sure to leave his mark. Using the victim's blood he scrawled a message on the windshield of the truck: ROBBERY IS HAZARDOUS TO YOUR HEALTH.

While Justus was busy dispatching Pug's transgressors, Nikki was holed up in Jock's Dodge Charger inhaling second-hand marijuana smoke as he poured his heart out for the second time in as many months. They were parked on the side of a gas station on Cumberland Road. It was well past eleven o'clock so the gas station was closed.

"For real, Nikki baby, leave that li'l nigga alone and it's going to be us again. Only better this time. When I was locked up I got some counseling for my anger issues, and I'm going to give the game up after I make this one last move," Jock promised. He was laying it on thick. He had bought Nikki fresh roses and everything. "Oh yeah, I got something for you too." Jock reached over in the glove box and produced a long thin box. He placed the box on Nikki's lap. "Open it."

"Jock."

"Come on Nik, open it."

With a heavy sigh, Nikki opened the box. A beautiful three-carat tennis bracelet lay in the box. "Jock, I can't take this."

"Baby it's yours! I can't take it back," Jock insisted.

Nikki fingered the bracelet. "Jock it really is nice, but I can't take this home. How can I explain this?"

Jock twisted his mouth in disgust. "Damn, that li'l nigga got you shook like that?"

Nikki placed the bracelet in Jock's lap. "It's about respect, Jock. How would you feel if I was your woman and I came in the house with jewelry from another man?"

Jock nodded his head vigorously. "See, that's what I'm talking about! You loyal." He shook his head. "I know I fucked up Nik, but you got to give me another chance. You got to!"

A roller crept by the gas station and shined his light into the Charger.

"Shit! Police," Jock mumbled. He put the blunt out and began spraying Smoke Out.

Nikki craned her neck to look at the police. "Damn Jock, we got to go. That's just what I need, to get arrested in a car with you."

"Nah chill, we good. They kept going."

Nikki watched the cruiser pass them by and drive out of sight. Still, she felt uneasy. "Ok, but can you take me back to my car? Something just don't feel right."

"Nonsense. You forgot who I am?" Jock beat his chest. "You good! Trust me."

Nikki relaxed a bit and gave Jock another round. He lit his blunt and rolled the window down to let the smoke out.

Suddenly, bright lights beamed inside the Charger from a black truck on Nikki's side of the car.

"Damn, Jock, they came back," Nikki hissed. "I told you!"

Jock stuck his arm out the window to drop the blunt on the pavement. Someone grabbed his arm and snatched him clean through the open window. Jock's scrawny body went flailing through the air and slammed into the pavement mercilessly. A masked man racked a round into a pump shotgun and jammed the barrel into Jock's mouth.

"Jock!" Nikki screamed so loud her lungs hurt.

The passenger door opened and another masked man snatched Nikki from the vehicle and hemmed her up in a yolk from behind. He dragged her around to the other side of the Charger and

gave her a front row seat as his comrades pum-
meled Jock with lead pipes and baseball bats. They
raised their weapons high into the air and brought
them crashing down on Jock from all angles. Jock
managed to tuck himself into a fetal position to
protect his head but everything that was exposed
was abused. One man slipped through Jock's de-
fenses with his pipe and landed a good one right
on the top of his head. Blood leapt into the air
about a foot high from the lick.

"Ohmigod!" Nikki cried. She attempted to
turn away but the masked man wrenched her head
back to face the gruesome beating. She had never
been so scared in her life! This was exactly why she
didn't want to deal with him and his street shit any
more. Jock was a cutthroat hustler, so he had enemies far and wide. Just her luck that they would
track him down while she was with him. Nikki
openly wept as she thought about her family. Diamond. Power. Supreme. Justus. What would happen to them if she never made it home? What if
these men didn't allow her to leave.

She began to panic. "Please don't kill me," she
pleaded. Her captor placed a gloved hand over
her mouth to silence her pleas.

Inside the truck, Pug watched the beating with
a satisfied smirk tugging at the corners of his
mouth. He felt no remorse for Jock. Nada. He
should have known better than playing in another
man's yard. Nikki belonged to Justus now, and Jock
had to respect that or learn the hard way. Besides,
Pug had caught wind of Jock's big-shit talking
around town, saying what he was going to do to Pug
when he saw him. Well, Pug was seeing him first.

If it wasn't for Justus, Pug would've let his comrades finish Jock off right there while Nikki watched, but he had given his word that he would let him live on the strength of Diamond.

Pug flashed the lights and his goons stopped the beating and released Nikki. They rolled Jock's unconscious body over on his back and piled back into the truck. One man—the man that was holding Nikki captive—remained behind. He stood over Jock, whipped his dick out, and pissed all in his face while Nikki watched on in horror. Jock sputtered to consciousness, groaning and moaning. He clutched his side and the man punted his head like he was trying out for the Panthers.

Nikki screamed. "That's enough. You gonna kill him!"

The man chuckled through his mask. "You did this."

As the man climbed into the truck, Pug took the scene all in. He decided he couldn't stand the sight of his cousin's wifey shedding tears over the next man. He borrowed the shotgun from his comrade and fired a shot into the air through the moonroof. As expected, Nikki bolted into the night, leaving Jock to wallow in his own misery.

The following morning, Nikki hobbled downstairs on swollen ankles. She found Justus cooking breakfast in a wife-beater and sweats. Power and Supreme were in their car seats on the dining table. Between scrambling eggs and frying sausages, Justus sang to his sons. Diamond sat at the head of the table doing math problems.

"Morning babe!" Justus practically yelled. "How you feeling this morning?"

"Tired," Nikki grumbled. She plopped down at the table and placed her face inside her palms.

"Yeah, you should be. You got in kinda late last night," Justus remarked as he sat a plate of grits in front of her. "How was the concert?"

"Huh?" Nikki had lied and told Justus she was going to a concert with Jackie. "Oh . . . uhm . . . it was okay. A little overrated."

"Is that why Jackie left early?" Justus probed.

"Umm, I guess so."

Justus placed eggs on Nikki's plate. "SOOO, if Jackie left early, how did you get home?"

What was it with the questions? Did he know something? "Why? Is something wrong? Justus, I took an Uber, okay?" That wasn't exactly a lie. She did call an Uber—after she walked a few miles from Cumberland Road up to Hope Mills Road in heels.

"Nothing wrong, Babygirl. I was just asking," Justus replied casually. He turned around and finished tending to breakfast.

"You're in a mighty good mood this morning," Nikki said. "What's gotten into you?"

"Oh nothing. Just happy to be with my family on this glorious day."

"Right," Nikki quipped.

"There was something I had to tell you, but it slipped my mind," Justus claimed.

Supreme threw up. Without missing a beat, Justus scooped Supreme up and cleaned him off with a paper towel while Nikki ate her breakfast. Between bites Nikki stole glances at Justus. He was acting very weird this morning.

Suddenly, Justus snapped his fingers. "Oh yeah, I know what I meant to tell you!" He bent over and whispered in her ear. "Somebody told me your boy Jock in the hospital."

Justus dropped the bomb then walked away into the den. Nikki followed him, just as he expected. "They said somebody took a pipe to him pretty bad," Justus continued, looking out the window into the woods. "Something about him creeping with somebody's girl. I don't know." Justus shrugged his shoulders. "You heard anything about that?"

Nikki was speechless. Jock's attack had just happened a few hours ago. There was no way the word was in the streets already. The only way Justus could have known is if he was in on it.

"Anyway, being that he's Diamond's father, I think we should go pay him a visit and wish him well. Maybe take him some flowers."

"Justus, my baby is not going to see her daddy all bandaged and crippled like an invalid!" Nikki spat, her emotions a wreck.

"Well, he should've thought about that before he decided to play in another man's garden."

"You are crazy," Nikki whispered as the picture became clear.

Justus chuckled. "Nah, I ain't crazy about nothing but you and my family. I just hope that's clear now—to everyone." Justus slowly turned around and fixed Nikki with a psychotic stare. "We clear?"

Nikki gulped down a mouthful of fear. "Crystal."

* * *

Later that night, Justus did pay Jock a visit in his hospital room. When he walked into Jock's room he could see Jock's leg suspended in the air, encased in a cast. As he stepped closer to the bed, he saw that Jock's entire body was heavily bandaged. An IV was crammed in his arm, and his head was wrapped in bloody gauze.

Justus smiled at the handiwork. He tilted his fedora up in the front, adjusted his black leather sheath, then sat in the chair beside the bed.

Justus tapped Jock on the arm. "Yo, you up?"

Jock slowly tilted his head to the side. "What you want?" Jock wheezed.

Justus casually took a banana from Jock's dinner tray and peeled it meticulously. "Damn cuz, look like you pissed somebody off," he mocked.

"Fuck you nigga!" Jock spat, with all the strength he could muster.

Justus shook his head. "Seems like you should be tired of trying to fuck shit, muthafucka. That's what got you laying in that bed now," he pointed out with the banana. Justus looked at his Rolex, crossed his legs, and leaned back in the chair. "I'm a little pressed for time so I'll make this quick. My old lady waiting on me to give me some of that good pussy. Oh wait, that's *your* old lady. That pussy under new management now, feel me?"

Jock gritted his teeth. "Fuck you."

Justus smacked Jock upside the head with the banana peel. "Listen up, it's a new day. Shit has changed. I'm not who you remember, and you not as tough as you think you are. Now I'ma say this as humble as I can, Jock." Justus moved his face so close to Jock that he could smell the banana on his breath. "I AM THE WRONG MAN TO FUCK WITH. Messing with Nikki is messing with me. That's mine now, playboy. You blew it. I'm giving you fair warning right now. If I ever hear that you around Nikki again ..." Justus blew into his face and shook his head. "I just better not hear it. You understand? Matter fact, if you see Nikki walking down the street you better cross over to the other side. Got it?"

Jock stared up at the ceiling, seething. He couldn't believe that the young boy who used to ride the bike in the neighborhood was coming at him like this.

"The only reason you still alive now is because of me. Remember that?" Justus stood to leave. He tossed the banana peel on Jock's chest. "And far as Diamond is concerned, don't let me catch you around her either. That's *my* daughter now. You wasn't doing shit for her anyway."

Chapter 20

The radiant Mexican sun shone heavily on Leader's bald head as he emerged from the airport. Leader was wearing a crisp grey linen suit, soaking his body in comfort. He would've been in a minor utopia if it were not for all the college students milling about, making him uncomfortable. They were everywhere. White. Black. Asian. Latino. Leader recognized more than a few entertainers as he maneuvered throughout the airport parking lot. He had been instructed to take a cab to bungalow #7. Leader quickly found a cab and was on his way.

This wasn't Leader's first time in Mexico. He had been a few times before on business, however he had never ventured out this far. What he was seeing now was a different part of Mexico, far removed from the norm. The Mexico he was familiar with was hostile to the faint of heart, filled with poverty, violence, and drugs (not particularly in that order). The thousands of teenagers he now saw would have been victims in Ciudad Juarez.

When Leader reached bungalow #7, he found

that it was isolated and quiet. He spotted other bungalows off in the distance, but each was far enough to provide just the right balance of safety and seclusion.

Leader exited the cab underneath a clump of shade trees. While the cabbie was assisting Leader with his one bag, Carmen emerged from the bungalow wearing a yellow two-piece bikini with a sheer sarong. The bright color contrasted beautifully with her brown skin, giving her an exotic look. "Damn." Leader muttered under his breath at the sight of such beauty. He tipped the cabbie, and bid him farewell in perfect Spanish.

When Carmen greeted Leader in perfect Spanish he really wasn't too surprised. In fact, he almost expected Carmen to speak Spanish since she was so proficient in so many other things.

Inside the bungalow was decoratively well-appointed yet still cozy. A small kitchen sat in the center of the front room, while a bathroom and two bedrooms were off to the side. The bathroom boasted a cylindrical shower and separate garden tub, while the bedroom contained a whirlpool. The fact that Carmen went all out was not lost on Leader, but he had no intention of utilizing the facility's fine appointments. He was here strictly for business, and business only.

"So what's up? You have some information for me?"

"Damn, aren't we curt," Carmen quipped.

"I came here for business. I didn't fly out of the country for bullshit." Leader was keeping things hard purposely. Firm.

"I understand." Carmen nodded. "I have some good news and some bad news."

"Look Carmen, don't bullshit me!"

"Hold up, hold up. I have the information, but you gotta wait a couple of days. I figured we can spend a . . ." Carmen's words faded into obscurity when she saw the look Leader was giving her, he didn't have to raise his voice at all, his raised eyebrows spoke volumes. "Leader just trust me on this. It will be worth it. Think of it as a paid vacation, then you can return to 'work'."

For Leader, it really wasn't a question. If Carmen could lead him closer to finding out who was onto him, he really was at her mercy. His obligation now surpassed just his own welfare. He now had Justus to worry about. He had introduced him to this life. He couldn't just leave him high and dry, without steady jobs as his outlet, for Justus would surely use his skills in a non-productive manner and thus would surely perish. He had already caught wind of Justus's escapades on the dudes that robbed Pug. He knew his son could perform only so many acts in town before authorities would realize they were dealing with a trained professional.

"Alright," Leader conceded. "But the same rules still apply."

"What? You mean no sex?" Carmen taunted. Leader nodded. "Of course not. After all, you are happily married, right?"

"That's right," Leader said.

"Good. So we're just two friends enjoying a few fun-filled days in paradise." Carmen flashed a

wicked smile then dropped her sarong, fully revealing her French-cut bikini. Seconds later, she
dropped her top, freeing bountiful 38C's. "Let's
go swimming!"

Damn, thought Leader. This was going to be
the longest two days of his life.

Pug and Justus cruised down Skibo Road, en
route to Cross Creek Mall in Justus's '71 Chevy 'vert.
The sound-system quaked the earth around them as
they proudly bumped hometown legend Qwess's
classic CD *Janus*.

Justus leaned back in the driver's seat like he
was napping while they waited for the light to turn
green.

"Yo, man, I still can't get over that shit you
did." Pug said.

"What you talking 'bout, dawg?" Justus asked,
lost in deep thought himself.

"I just wanna know . . . How the FUCK do you
hang a nigga by his intestines?!"

Justus stared at Pug. He didn't discuss business
once it was done. The past was the past, but since it
was Pug, he indulged him a bit.

"You said you wanted to send a message. Well,
I think the streets heard you."

Before Pug could respond, an H1 Hummer
pulled up beside them garnering all of the attention. The truck had to be sitting on 28-inch rims or
better because all they saw was chrome. Pug reached
for his .45 under his shirt, just in case something
popped off. He and his whole crew were in war

mode since they attacked Jock. Suddenly, the passenger window slid down slowly and a woman revealed her face.

"Which one of y'all is Pug?" The woman asked. Neither Pug nor Justus answered. They both knew drama was indiscriminate. A broad would bring heat just as fast as a dude these days, sometimes faster, and being in a drop-top made them tragically vulnerable.

"Who wanna know?!" Pug called out, making no attempt to hide the fact he was holding his heat at that very moment.

The woman giggled then answered, "Saigon."

"Saigon?" Both Justus and Pug repeated. Saigon was a rap superstar down with Fayetteville's premier record label, ABP. Pug recognized the name well. He used to tear her off before she made it big all over the world. He had not seen or heard from her in years. Saigon reached over the passenger showing her face, and Pug lost it!

"Ohhh shit! Pull over, nigga!" Pug ordered Justus, pointing to the Burger King parking lot. Minutes later, Pug and Saigon were catching up on old times and plotting on new ones.

While Pug conversed with Saigon, Justus struck up a convo with the passenger. She was a cutie, about five-five, borderline petite with a tacky weave. She was hardly Justus's style, but she was straight for the stroke.

Justus was gathering her particulars for a possible hit-and-run when he saw a ghost from his past exit Burger King and head toward a burgundy Honda Accord. He quickly dismissed himself and sprinted off toward the Accord. He caught up with her just as she was opening her car door.

"Panee?"

"Justus?"

She was a little thicker, hair a little longer, but it was still her.

"What's up?" They greeted each other in unison.

"Damn, gurl—"

"Damn boy." This was said in unison as well.

"You go ahead," Justus offered.

"No, you go."

"I insist."

Panee exhaled. "You look good," she complimented, admiring Justus's cocoa-brown slacks and cream silk shirt with the two-tone suede loafers.

"You look great!" Justus ogled Panee openly. She was wearing a tight pair of jeans and a tank top, accentuated with four-inch open-toe heels. Her toe ring glistened in the spring sun. Panee looked even better than Justus remembered.

"So what are you doing home?" Justus asked. "You home for spring break or something?"

"Believe it or not, I'm kinda back home for a while," Panee shared.

"Really?"

"Really."

"What happened?"

Panee's voice dropped a level. "Well, I kinda botched my scholarship at Spelman," she admitted. "I had to work two jobs to make ends meet so my studies ended up suffering."

"Whaaat?"

"Oh, it's true," Panee assured him. "So I had to come home for a semester and save some money. Now, I'll probably start at Fayetteville State next semester."

"Damn, I hate to hear you have to start all over," Justus said sincerely.

"It's okay."

"So, what are you doing for money now? You ain't stripping are you?" he joked.

Panee grinned. "Actually, yeah. I am." Justus's jaw dropped. "Pick your jaw up, Justus. I'm just joking, but I do work at Club Flesh four nights a week. I'm a waitress."

"Get the fuck outta here!" Club Flesh was the premiere strip club in town.

"Seriously. I've been working there for almost two weeks now. Worst case scenario, I only have to wear a thong, and it pays the bills so it works out for me." She shrugged her shoulders as if it were no big deal.

"Damn, what you want so bad that you gotta show a room full of niggas that pretty ass? Where ya' man at?" Justus openly let Panee see him admiring her pretty round bottom.

"Hold up, Jus. Before you even go there, I know all about you. You got a girl. Your name stay ringing bells. Hoes in the club wanna get wit' you and they don't even know how you look."

Justus chuckled, "Stop playing, girl. I'm low-key, so that can't be."

Panee put her hands on her hips defiantly. "Seriously, Justus, everybody knows how you ride for your girl. They say you got her driving Porsches and Benzes and shit. By the way, congrats on the twins," she smirked.

"Ohhh, you got jokes? I see."

"No jokes, just the truth. You *do* have twins, right?"

Justus nodded. "You got that."

For the next few minutes Panee joshed with Justus something fierce. He swore he scoped a tinge of jealously in Panee's eyes. He couldn't help but admire how beautiful she was, even though she was upset. She had gotten thicker in all the right places and despite loving Nikki, he couldn't deny what he felt. He wanted her. Real bad. She was the one that had gotten away. Until now.

"So Justus, did you really buy that girl that big house and all those cars?" Panee asked. "Because that's all I keep hearing about. Well, I heard something else too, but I ain't gon' say nothing about all that."

"Yeah, I bought the house and cars," he admitted. "But I don't know what you tripping about. All that shit supposed to be yours, but you bounced on a brother. Now look." He could tell his words touched Panee. Suddenly she seemed uncomfortable. "But look, I ain't tripping on the past," Justus quickly said before the mood turned sour. "I'm concerned with here and now. Let me take you out to lunch or something so we can catch up on this unfinished business."

Panee sighed loudly, "Even if I wanted to, I couldn't. I don't have time."

"Hold up. What you mean, '*If you wanted to*'?" Justus was offended.

"Don't get me wrong, I would if I wasn't in a relationship."

"Anyway . . ." Justus sucked his teeth.

"I'm serious, Jus. I don't have time."

"I bet you have time to get your ass dolled up and shit."

"What? That's different. A woman always makes time for the things that are important to her."

She noticed the strange look Justus gave her, and reminded herself of his monstrous temper. She didn't want to upset him. Surprisingly, it seemed Justus could keep a cool head.

"Damn. So now I've been reduced to being lower than a nail appointment?"

Panee laughed. "Boy, you crazy."

"Seriously though," Justus laughed. He had Panee smiling so hard he knew he was in. He spotted Pug coming over their way so he decided to wrap up with a strong finish.

"Give me your phone," Justus said. He took Panee's phone and dialed the number to his stash phone. He let the phone ring a few times, then ended the call. "Now we linked. All you gotta do is push this button right here when you wanna talk to me. Anytime, anyplace. I'm doing big things now. I wanna help you with your situation. A'ight? No woman I love should have to show her ass to a room full of vultures." Justus openly lusted over her nice shape. "That's for my viewing pleasure only." He smacked her on her plump ass and gave her the phone back.

Pug and Justus jumped back into the 'vert and pulled off into the warm sun with the music blasting. They both had secured some "strange" (pussy other than their wifey) so they were feeling good about themselves. So good that they never noticed the car tailing them.

When Leader returned to the bungalow from his morning run, everything was quiet. He detected the faint smell of scrambled eggs as he made his way through the bungalow. He paused at the bedroom door where a smooth sweet scent massaged his nostrils. He cracked the door and found the source of the smell.

Carmen was standing in front of the mirror, asshole naked, rubbing her beautiful body down with oil. Leader stopped and stared at her for a long while before letting his presence be known. Carmen didn't seem the least bit surprised. She gazed at Leader through the mirror, continuing to stroke her body with the oil. Leader met her gaze through the mirror, charging the environment to nuclear proportions.

Carmen craned her finger, inviting Leader over. "Can you help me please?"

Leader hesitated a moment but his masculinity overpowered him. He joined her at the mirror and took the bottle from her hand. He motioned to the bed. "Lie down."

Leader took his time rubbing the oil on Carmen, admiring every crevice of Carmen's toned body. Her skin was very soft despite her muscular frame. There was nothing he loved more than seeing the female form whipped to maximum capacity. Carmen's body was a work of art. She possessed the perfect balance between fitness and femininity.

Leader slid his hands between her sculpted shoulders and massaged her neck. Carmen moaned and squirmed. She sucked in a mouthful of air, and rubbed the insides of her thighs. She pushed her middle finger inside her wet vagina, pulled it out, and slid it across Leader's nose. She offered him a taste of her sweet nectar, but he refused. Carmen put the sticky finger to her mouth and sucked her own juices off.

"What are you doing?" Leader inquired, dismounting Carmen's back.

Carmen rolled over on her back and put her finger at the door of her opening. "Promise not to touch, and I'll let you watch," she cooed. Without waiting on Leader's answer, she began rubbing the lips of her slit until she was practically leaking juices onto the silk sheets. Leader watched, transfixed on the spot where Carmen's finger was going to work. *Even her pussy is pretty*, he thought.

Carmen worked herself into a frenzy, pinching her left nipple with one hand while continuing to plunge two fingers from her other hand into her pleasure center. Soon her moans claimed the room as she coaxed herself to climax.

Leader saw Carmen's juices ooze onto the bed like hot lava. He was beyond reproach or reason. His only reasoning was that he had already transgressed by watching the show. He shed his sweaty clothing and mounted Carmen. He slid inside of her eagerness with no protection and pounded away to climax, releasing his essence deep inside of her. He was so aroused by Carmen that even after he climaxed, his manhood was still rock hard. So, he pounded away again. This time Leader soaked in Carmen's pleasures. The first round was for him, a means to caress the impossible burning inside his loins.

This round was for her.

He gripped her small waist and drove himself deep inside her heaven as if he was drilling for oil. She cradled his head. Gazed into his eyes. Wrapped her thick powerful thighs around his legs. She collapsed her inner walls around his engorged member and milked him like a cow to climax. He moaned like he was being tarred and feathered as he released a river of semen inside her tight walls.

After three strong eruptions, Leader lay on top of Carmen, spent. Like black fog, guilt slowly crept in. He was disappointed for allowing himself to be manipulated. He had allowed another person's mind to trump his own. At that moment, he developed a strange blend of respect and hatred for Carmen. Respect for her cunning. Hatred for her craftiness. The two combined for a potent arousal.

As if sensing Leader sulking, Carmen took Leader's face into her delicate hands, "No regrets," she whispered. "We did what we wanted to do, and now it's over."

Leader knew not so deep down inside, Carmen was right. He had done what he wanted to do and it felt good. After being so constricted in his marriage for so long, the feeling of reckless abandonment felt refreshing.

However, his feelings were fleeting. He had come to Mexico for business, to discover who was

onto him. Thus far, he was not any closer to his
quest to find answers. Tomorrow would be his last
day in Mexico. He would get the answers he sought
before he left.

For tonight, he wanted more Carmen.

Panee was being held hostage in Fayetteville's
notorious hair salon, Beauty Palace, off of Skibo
road. The usual gossip was being spewed: who was
fucking who, who was driving what, who was getting money for real, for real, etc. Panee really didn't
care to participate in the gossip, but she had no
qualms with listening to it. She was really getting
fed up with the life she was living, and each time
she came through the doors of the salon, her feelings were exacerbated. Hanging amongst this caliber of women forced her to realize just how far
she had strayed from her life's ambition. Yet, it
wasn't over until it was over. As her mother always
told her: tough times don't last, tough people do.

Panee was dozing off in her chair when she
faintly heard the door open. Suddenly the women
in the salon started swooning. Panee opened her
eyes and saw Justus standing near the entrance with
at least two dozen roses in his arms. He was speaking with the receptionist when suddenly she pointed
in Panee's direction. Justus glided over and plopped
down in the unoccupied hair dryer next to her.

"Justus, what are you doing here?" Panee gasped.

"What does it look like I'm doing?"

"Following me?" Panee questioned.

"Nah, of course not, I just happened to be in

the neighborhood," Justus clarified calmly. "By the way, these are for you." He placed the roses on the floor in front of her.

"Justus, this is crazy! What's with all this?"

"Well, since you won't go to lunch with me, I decided to bring lunch to you."

"What are you talking about?" Panee thought Justus was really losing it since she didn't see any food inside the roses.

Justus casually glanced at his Cartier watch and replied, "You'll see."

While Panee waited, the resident aesthetician slid a foot tub in front of Justus. She slid his Gucci loafers off, and placed both feet into the steamy solution. Meanwhile, Kim wrapped his hands and prepped him for a manicure. After he was prepped properly, Kim left the two of them alone (as alone as two people can be in a room full of nosy, gawking gold diggers.)

"So, why haven't you called?" Justus asked.

"I've been busy, as you can see," sniped Panee, cutting her eyes at their spectators.

Justus took offense at her tone, "Damn, you shouldn't be so cold to old friends. I stay busy, but as you can see, I'm making time for what's important to me.

"So, now I'm important to you?"

"Always have been,"

"You have a funny way of showing it," Panee claimed.

"Look, don't persecute me for my past deeds. That was then, this is now. I realized my mistakes, and I've come to atone for them. Can you cut a brother some slack?" Panee could see some sincerity in his eyes, but he kept checking his watch every few seconds and that frustrated her.

"Got somewhere to be?"

"Nah," Justus responded, checking his watch again.

Panee sucked her teeth. "See, that's why I couldn't be with you, even if I didn't have a man. You have *commitments*." Panee said the word like it was a bad disease.

"I can handle my commitments, and I'm not concerned about your man," Justus assured her. He had heard about her man. Some old do-gooder, jelly-back, spineless negro. In Justus's eyes, dude was a pussy. "If he was any kind of man, your stomach wouldn't be growling like a gotdamn lion right now!"

"Funny, I don't see you coughing up no food."

"Au contraire." A Chinese deliveryman entered the salon while they were talking. Justus waved him over and paid him from a wad of cash in his pocket. The deliveryman left the salon and retuned a few minutes later with enough food to feed a housing project. Justus instructed the man to feed everyone inside the salon. He took the liberty of feeding Panee himself.

By the end of the afternoon he had achieved his goal. Panee agreed to let him take her out again the following day.

Chapter 21

Leader's final day in Mexico began innocently enough. He awoke, showered and meditated to cleanse his soul of the past night's transgressions. When he emerged from his room with clean energy, Carmen was nowhere to be found.

He fixed a light breakfast and ate. Still, no Carmen.

Around noon, he prepared lunch and ate. Still, no Carmen.

She returned just before sunset, fully dressed in a jogging suit and cross-trainers. Offering no explanation, she instructed Leader to get dressed in something comfortable and follow her.

They left the bungalow and hiked a trail up the mountain, deep into the woods. After hiking for about an hour, they stopped on a hilltop overlooking the many resorts. By this time, it was well past dark. Carmen took a seat on the damp ground while Leader continued to stand. Carmen produced a small set of binoculars from her pocket and peered down the hill onto the beach. The beach had to be at least eight hundred yards away. Leader saw nothing but a bunch of kids on the shore, drinking and having a good time. Carmen's binoculars consumed the distance between them and the revelers and allowed her to see everything the kids were doing.

Leader grew impatient. "What's up Carm? I didn't come to Mexico to spy on teenagers. You got that info for me or what?"

"Shhh . . . patience. I gave you my word. I'll deliver."

He watched her as she crawled toward a cluster of bushes and retrieved a black case made of steel. The case was nearly six feet long. Carmen flipped the case open to reveal the pieces to a Barret .50 cal. Leader watched in shock as she pulled the pieces out and assembled the weapon in record time. As she performed the systems check on the firearm, things began to make sense for Leader.

Carmen tossed him the binoculars. "Keep your eyes on the beach."

Leader kept one eye on the beach and the other eye on Carmen. She placed the long barrel inside the cradle of a tree branch shaped like a Y for stabilization. She spread her legs wide and took position behind the Barret. She attached her eye to the scope of the weapon and slowed her breathing.

Leader was impressed. The way she handled herself proved she was a professional. She handled the weapon with a sense of familiarity. She traversed the terrain as if she were used to navigating tough trails. The cool confidence. The perpetual patience. The calculated manner in which she hid the weapon. It was all becoming clear now. It wouldn't be long before Carmen manifested her true identity.

Leader shifted his attention to the beach. He pulled the kids on the beach up into his focus and waited to see Carmen perform.

Thoom!

The Barret roared to life announcing its path to destruction. Even with the suppressor attached, the cannon managed to rock the hillside. Through the binoculars, Leader saw a Mexican teenager lose his head as the .50 caliber round ripped through his neck.

Carmen fired another round.

Thoom!

Another teenager lost his head.

Carmen fired eight of the ten rounds in the clip of the Barret, decapitating each of her targets with laser precision. She nearly had the gun broken down by time the last body dropped. Leader marveled at the display. Eight shots downhill, into the wind, at night. She was good, *really* good. Now he knew who had taken the shot in D.C.

The only question was, why?

"It was me who intercepted your son's shot that day in D.C.," Carmen revealed. They were hiking back down to the bungalow after Carmen's performance. "It was the only way I knew to get your attention." Questions surfaced on Leader's face. "Allow me to explain," Carmen requested.

"I've been hearing about you for years now. In fact, you're the reason I chose this profession in the first place. I was hired to investigate the murder of a client's husband. The deeper I delved, the more I realized that you were so far removed from the actual killing itself that it was as if you weren't even there. I did find out about who paid you and how much you were paid. Simply put, I was intrigued. I mean, I was obviously in the wrong profession, right? Anyway, I never discovered who you were personally, but your name rang louder than the liberty bell in certain circles." Carmen spared Leader a look to see how he was taking everything in.

"The more I investigated the profession, the more your name surfaced, almost to mythic proportions. After a while my curiosity turned into admiration. I had never seen a man so powerful that other men shuddered at the mention of his name. I decided I wanted that type of power for myself. After all, isn't that why we all do what we do? Power?

"I completed my first contract just two years ago. Finding the mark was easy since that's what I already specialized in as a P.I. The elimination was a bit more difficult. In the end, I did what I had to do. After the first kill, the rest was easy, as I'm sure you know. I made *cleaning* women my specialty, reasoning that it would be easier for me to get closer to women than men. Plus, I was still cutting my teeth so I didn't want to take the risk of some male target overpowering me and turning the tables . . ." Carmen smiled in hindsight. She knew male or female didn't have a chance in hell with her now.

"The more proficient I became, the more known

I became. Soon, money chased me like a greyhound on a rabbit, and my stature grew. I became revered in certain circles. But no matter how well I performed, all the big money jobs went to the notorious Leader. So I made it my personal quest to find you. I was shocked to find out you were under my nose the whole time. When I approached you at the bar, I wanted you to acknowledge me more than anything. And you did, but for my sexuality not my talents."

Leader could hear the disappointment in her voice when she spoke. Her pace slowed as she recalled that day.

"I wasn't so sure I had the right person, but when you took the contract everyone was scared to touch, I knew I had the right person. I saw an opportunity to gain your attention and I took it. I knew you would have to acknowledge me because no one could take that shot like I did. No one besides you, of course. So, I seized the moment. You aren't mad at me, are you?"

Leader mulled the question for a moment. "Why not just tell me who you were?"

"Would you have believed me?"

She had a point. "Why bring me here?"

"I wanted to show you my skills firsthand."

Leader looked at her disbelievingly. "You already did that," he pointed out.

"True." She smiled. "I guess the real reason is that I wanted to seduce you."

Leader sped up his pace, and almost tripped over an object that lay in his path. Carmen grabbed him by the arm.

"Wait. Wait. Hear me out, please?" They both stopped on the trail. "My motives aren't just physical." She paused. "I want you to train me."

"You seem pretty well-trained to me." Leader jerked his thumb in the direction from which they came

"The judge's daughter?" Carmen scoffed, dismissively. "That was easy. I knew where she was going to be. I want to learn! I want to learn how to stalk a man like a lion, from start to finish. If I learned that then—"

"I'd be out of a job."

"No, no," Carmen swore, desperately. "We could be partners."

Leader had resumed walking so Carmen's words hit his back. Even in the darkness Leader could hear the desperation in Carmen's voice. He had already seen how far she would go to get what she wanted. Frankly, her desperation was unnerving.

"I don't know, Carm. I work alone. My son is my successor. He is who I train. Besides, we've gone too far on a personal level to ever be in business together."

Carmen waved her hand. "Please, that was just sex. Think about it, Leader. With us together, the best in the business, we could monopolize the market."

Leader agreed Carmen did have a point. With more help—experienced help—he would have his way with the market. He could demand more money, access more places. There could definitely be advantages to having Carmen on his team. But he was not greedy. He had no aspirations of monopolizing the trade, nor was he concerned with money. Shit, he was already rich! Money was always his reward, never his motivation. Ultimately, Leader was chained to practicality. He had seen too many men crash and burn by exiting their niche. His niche was slow and steady. He had no interest in being fodder for the generations to come.

"I don't know," Leader finally told her. "I have to get back in the loop on some things. Then I'll be able to give you a better answer. But I thank you for solving my mystery."

Carmen was not thrilled with Leader's answer, but it wasn't a "no," so she remained optimistic.

They returned to the bungalow. Carmen showered while Leader pondered on the events of the trip. When he was sure of his decision, he joined Carmen in the shower and gave her every ounce of passion he could muster. He ravaged Carmen like she was the last piece of ass he would ever get.

Because he never planned to see her again.

Chapter 22

"Ohh Justus, that was wonderful!" Panee exclaimed. She collapsed on top of Justus with his semi-flaccid penis still lodged inside of her vagina.

They were inside of a plush Miami hotel overlooking the sandy shores of SoBe. After a few dates back in N.C., Justus had flown them south on a whim. The whole trip had been a surprise—for Panee *and* Justus. He was campaigning hard for her affections and wanted to blow her mind. When most men spoke of taking their women to the beach, they drove down to Myrtle Beach. Justus was playing on a different level though. Miami was how he got down. He wanted Panee to see what she had let go. He was now a made man with more time and money than he could manage.

"I never knew I was missing out on all of this!" Panee admitted. She climbed from the bed and walked to the window naked.

Me neither, Justus thought, looking at Panee's magnificent body. She claimed her boyfriend was the only man she had ever been with. Justus was inclined to believe her because her pussy was super tight! She had heroin inside those walls and Justus was getting hooked with each stroke.

"Don't worry, you never have to miss out on it again," Justus promised. He hopped from the bed and followed her to the window. He wrapped his arms around her and his hard dick rested on the small of her back. "When we get back I'm going to get you a place. I'll put some money in your pocket so you can focus on school. But you got to quit that place. I'm the only one that get to see that pretty ass." He smacked her ass and his hand sank inside the soft flesh.

Panee gnawed on her bottom lip. "I don't know, Justus. Everything got a price and I'm not sure I am willing to pay yours."

Justus nibbled on Panee's ear and whispered, "It wasn't a request, baby."

This was a different Justus than Panee remembered. He had always been confident, but he was cocky now, demanding things and calling shots. He had bossed up his life and this new Justus was exciting to Panee.

"Justus, what about your family?" Panee challenged. "Like, where do they think you are right now?"

"I don't have them kind of problems," Justus lied. In truth, Nikki thought Justus was out of town with Pug. Pug was O.T. (out of town) with Saigon so everything worked out. "Let me worry about that?"

Panee exhaled and leaned her head back on Justus's shoulder. "Why me?"

Justus kissed the top of her forehead. "Why not you?"

"Seriously."

Justus shrugged his shoulders. "I don't know. I guess I've always had a thing for you. More importantly, I believe in you," he stated flatly.

"Do you?"

"Yeah. The only question is, do *you* believe in yourself?"

"I do."

"Well stop being stubborn and let me handle my business."

Justus rubbed on Panee's booty and palmed her soft cheeks. He pushed her against the window and hunkered down behind her. He spread her ass open and slid inside her from behind. Panee moaned and rocked back on him.

"Yeeeah," Justus hissed. "This good pussy mine now. Hear me? Tell me it's mine."

Panee reluctantly agreed. Justus had caught her at a vulnerable moment in her life and what he was offering was a way out. A way out of hardship, a way out of poverty, a way out of walking around with her ass hanging out for tips. So what, she would be the other woman. At least she would be taken care of. Plus, with Justus having a family of his own, she wouldn't have to worry about him being all crammed up under her. She could still live her life free.

Just as Justus and Panee were settling into a comfortable groove, Justus's phone began ringing incessantly. Justus let the phone go to his voicemail. He listened to the message a few minutes later. When he heard Pug's voice, he immediately was alarmed.

On the voicemail, Pug's voice was loud and clear. "Cuz-o, they say when daddy's away, baby girl will play. I heard ole' girl was with ole' boy again. You need to handle your business when you get back."

Pug said some other things as well, but all Justus heard was the first part of the message. Justus couldn't believe this shit! Nikki still thought this shit was a game. He vowed to show her otherwise. It never dawned on him that he was lying in a bed butterball naked with his mistress. All he saw was Nikki violating him by seeing Jock again.

"Get dressed," he ordered Panee. "We're leaving. Now!"

"What?"

"Bitch, you heard me. Let's roll!" Justus was already out of bed, on his way to the bathroom. Panee was confused.

She wondered, what in the hell had she gotten herself into?

Chapter 23

Leader was feeling pretty good about himself. He had successfully maneuvered out of a situation with Carmen, his dignity intact, and more importantly, his jobs back on track. In fact, he and Justus had a job lined up for the following day, which was why he was spending time with his wife and daughter, shopping as a family.

Cross Creek Mall was packed as usual on a Saturday, making it difficult for them to stay together. Keisha wasn't making their excursion any better, demanding that Leader buy her a pair of low-rise jeans.

"For the last time, Keisha, no!"

Keisha pursed her lips defiantly. Leader hated to see his precious daughter pout, so he stuck his hand in his pocket and fished out some bills. "I swear, you gon' get me a charge," he grumbled. "Bad enough them li'l hot-blooded boys already chasing you around."

Before Leader could pass Keisha the money,

Glenda stopped her. They argued for a while with Glenda winning in the end. As soon as Glenda turned her head, Leader slid Keisha a hundred dollars on the low for consolation. He was helping her pick out a more suitable outfit when his phone rang.

"Mr. Moore, please help me!" The voice on the other end cried. "Please come get Justus! He's hitting me!" Nikki screamed.

In the background Leader heard Justus ranting and raving at the top of his lungs. Justus's voice became clearer then suddenly the phone went dead.

Leader dialed her back. Justus answered the phone and assured his father that things were okay. Leader hung up and shrugged his shoulders. He was from the old school. What went on between a man and his woman was between that man and that woman.

World War III raged inside Justus's home. He had caught the first flight from Miami, rushed home, and put his foot in Nikki's ass.

"Justus, please don't hit me no more. I'M SORRY!"

Justus's nostrils were flared. The appropriate wife-beater he wore was tattered to shreds. His right hand held the leather belt he was using to whip Nikki into submission.

"Oh, you sorry now, huh? A mu'fucka treat you like somebody and this the thanks I get?!" Justus whacked Nikki with the belt across her back. "I bust my goddamn ASS to provide for you and you creep on me with the nigga who treated you like shit!"

"Justus, please don't hit me no more. I said I'm sorry!"

"Nah, you don't care. You want a nigga to beat yo' ass!"

"No, I don't," Nikki cried, shielding herself from yet another blow.

"Well, why you creeping wit' the nigga that beat yo' ass? Huh? Tell me Nikki!" Justus eased up from the assault to actually give Nikki time to answer this rhetorical question. Unfortunately, Nikki couldn't muster a response. "I gotta beat yo' ass for you to love me?"

"Justus, I do love you," Nikki pleaded, but her pleas fell on deaf ears.

Justus dropped his hands in a huff. "I'm done wit' it. You want that nigga, go be wit' him." Justus grabbed Nikki by her bruised arm, and started dragging her toward the front door, oblivious to the fact that Nikki was clad in her bra and panties. Nikki kicked and screamed the whole way, to no avail. Justus opened the front door and dragged Nikki toward it. She latched on to one of the brass pillars by the door and held on to it for dear life.

Suddenly, tears wailed from the opposite direction. Supreme and Power both crawled into the room, crying hysterically. Justus stopped dragging Nikki. He saw the fear on his sons' stunned faces. Was this the example he wanted to set for his seeds?

Justus dropped the belt and scooped his sons into his arms. He walked off, leaving Nikki on the floor sobbing.

"Justus, I do love you," Nikki cried out. "I would've never went to see him if you wasn't out with your WHORE!" Justus tensed up for just a brief second but Nikki caught it. "That's right nigga, I know about your whore! You going outta town on business? Yeah right. You were out with your whore!"

Justus never denied it. He prided himself on never lying to Nikki. He just didn't tell her the whole truth about things. He kept silent while Nikki, sensing that her blow stung, continued the onslaught:

"What, my pussy ain't tight enough? You had to go get some young tramp? What? Answer me, dammit!" Nikki went on and on until she finally said the unthinkable.

"Well since you don't want this pussy, I know who do."

Justus calmly placed the twins on the floor and turned to Nikki, were she lay on the ground. With no remorse, he kicked her over and over again in her side. Luckily, for Nikki, the buzzer to the front gate rang, and Justus saw Leader enter on the monitor attached to the wall.

"This ain't over, bitch. I'ma teach yo' ass a lesson," Justus promised, wiping spittle from the corners of his mouth, as he went to greet his father.

The second Justus opened the door, Leader knew all was not well. His son's eyes were clouded with the look of death. No words needed to be spoken. Justus led his father to his game room, his head laden with pressure and disappointment.

Leader racked the pool balls then passed Justus a cue. "Let's shoot a game," Leader suggested. "It's relaxing to the mind."

While Justus ran a few balls, Leader extracted a joint from his pocket. He took a deep drag, then passed it to Justus. Justus hesitated a second then took the joint. Leader allowed their buzz to set in before he spoke, offering Justus to sip from his cup of thoughts.

"Home is your sanctuary," he began. "When all the world is gone to hell, home should be your heaven, where you relax, release, relate. Home is everything. Home. Is. Everything. Understand?"

Justus nodded.

"Now home can't be your sanctuary if you ne-glecting it. You MUST take care of home, Justus," Leader emphasized. "You probably got some young trim somewhere, but don't get it confused: Nikki and those kids are where your home is. I know you young and full of cum, but you a man now. You got responsibilities. More importantly, you have to remember what you do for a living." Leader tapped his skull with his index finger. "Every big thing starts small first. What if you get ran in for a domestic violence charge? Now you a felon. Now you on their radar. No passports. Extra scrutiny. It doesn't make sense."

Justus dropped his head in shame. "I know Dad, but I just got these violent tendencies now. Maybe the job is getting to me."

Leader nodded. "It happens to all of us at some time or another, but you have to control the beast. That's the perpetual challenge of the job. It's all mental, son. Dreams? You see some of the jobs in your dreams?"

"Sometimes," Justus admitted.

"That too shall pass. It's the nature of the business. We can never go back to just being regular. You cannot *unsee* the things we have seen. So we have to find ways to cope. Me, I do yoga. You need to find you a coping mechanism, some type of hobby."

"Nine ball in the side pocket," Justus called.

"Son, beating a woman won't make her stay. If anything, it'll make her leave quicker. Understand?"

"Yes, sir."

"Now Nikki's upset. I'll talk to her, smooth things out. Let her know you made a mistake. You gonna go out and buy her something nice, some forgive-me trinkets, before we leave. When we return, you're going to treat her like she's the queen of Sheba. Not because I said so; because it's the right thing to do. Remember, on this level, it's family over everything."

Justus repeated. "Family over everything."

If only it were that simple.

When Justus and Leader returned home from dispatching yet another victim, Justus took Leader's advice, showering Nikki with ice, watches, chains, bangles—anything that could drip, he flooded it. In return, Nikki threw herself into their family. She also began filling out the financial aid paperwork necessary for her to attend medical school. Her ultimate goal was to become a pediatrician as she had expressed to Justus on numerous occasions. She had begun classes at Fayetteville Technical College to complete her nursing degree. Once

finished, she had plans to transfer to Fayetteville
State to complete more courses in preparation for
her ultimate goal. Justus supported Nikki 100% by
looking after the kids when needed. Things were
going well.

Justus also kept his promise to Panee, putting
her in a brand-new fully furnished condo. In turn,
Panee quit showing her pretty ass at the strip club
and began classes at Fayetteville Tech also. (She
was unable to attend Fayetteville State immediately, due to a course she dropped while at Spelman.) On a few occasions Panee ran right into
Nikki, and though she was certain Nikki knew who
she was, Panee never looked in her direction. Justus had given her marching orders, and they were
simple: Nikki was his wife, she was his "other wife."
Under no circumstances were she to look, speak,
touch, or even breathe in Nikki's direction. Of
course, Panee wasn't thrilled about the arrange-
ment, but the pros definitely outweighed the cons,
since Justus lavished gifts upon her like every day
was her birthday. She also accompanied him on
trips O.T. with Pug and Saigon.

Pug had started creeping with Saigon around
the same time Justus began creeping with Panee.
The two of them used each other as alibis. However, Jackie was not as naïve as Nikki. She just didn't
give a fuck. She knew Pug ran around on her, but
as long as he kept her laced, she had no reason to
trip.

Pug had easily become one of Fayetteville's
largest heroin suppliers. Riches, coupled with the
threat of extreme violence for transgressions, made
Pug an eight-hundred-pound Gorilla in the streets.

With his newfound wealth, he built a 7000-square-foot home near Justus, and upgraded his modest fleet of cars to a more prominent fleet befitting his new stature. His new collection included the requisite Cadillac sedan and truck, as well as the pink hummer Jackie had been nagging him about. To launder some of his money, he became a partner in a fledgling barbershop chain, and started a pit-bull kennel. Of course, the dogs specialized in fighting so they sold for top dollar. The dogfighting also became Pug and Justus's new pastime. The bloodshed appeased Justus's rapidly developing lust for carnage. He became Pug's best customer as they traveled all throughout the southeast, fighting dogs for tens of thousands of dollars. For all of Justus's worldwide taste and experience, he was still just a hood nigga at heart.

Leader continued to school Justus every chance he got, but between reconciling the guilt from his own affair, and getting contracts, he was emotionally swamped himself. He had not spoken with Carmen since leaving Mexico, but his buckets of wisdom warned him that Mexico was not the end. Therefore, he concentrated on fortifying his foundation, so it could weather the inevitable storm.

Trouble was just around the corner.

Chapter 24

It was an unseasonably cool summer night. Pug was riding shotgun in Saigon's brand-new Bentley coupe. Saigon pulled into the McDonald's on Skibo Road to grab a bite to eat before heading to Columbia, S.C for a concert. When they returned from inside, Pug decided to drive. He wanted to see how the European ride handled. He had almost purchased one himself, but didn't want the attention that was sure to come with such an exquisite automobile.

Pug exited Mickey D's, heading straight to Owen Drive to test the limits of the W-12 engine. He was already enraptured by the plush honey leather and rich wood that encapsulated them.

Turning onto Owen Drive, Pug gunned the engine to the tune of a lusty growl. When they turned onto U.S. 301 headed out of town, Saigon reached over, unbuckled Pug's thousand-dollar jeans, and whipped his manhood out. She stroked him a couple of times then dived headfirst onto his hard dick. The initial sensation of Saigon's warm lips caused Pug to swerve, but he quickly re-grouped, and allowed Saigon to find her rhythm.

Pug was feeling on top of the world. A broad that niggas the world over lusted after was giving him brain while he pushed *her* six-figure ride to unsafe levels! He pushed Saigon's head deep into his lap and prepared to shoot his load all down her throat. Just as he was reaching his climax, a car bumped them from behind, causing the Bentley to skid out of control. Saigon's teeth clenched down on Pug's hard dick.

"Goddamn!" Pug swore as he maneuvered the car to a stop.

"Sorry, Daddy," Saigon apologized, wiping her mouth and pulling her curly hair away from her face. She didn't seem the least bit fazed about her car, only that she had earned her thug's displeasure.

Pug, on the other hand, was heated. Whoever had interrupted his freak session was about to pay. And they crashed the Bentley? Pug palmed his Glock .45, and popped out the door with a vengeance.

The first bullet tore into his shoulder. Pug screamed, clutching his shoulder where he took the first shot. The next shot exploded into his chest. The sheer pain almost made him drop his weapon, but he maintained long enough to return a few shots of his own before being pinned to the open door by another volley of shots. He raised his weapon to fire again, and his shots flew erratically.

Saigon saw Pug absorbing round after round. She saw that he was in grave danger and sprang into action. She pulled Pug into the Bentley and climbed over him into the driver's seat. She pinned the pedal to the floor and the Bentley torpedoed forward. A couple of shots shattered the back window as they made their escape, but she held on, and escaped unharmed.

As Saigon piloted the Bentley, Pug lay slumped between the front and rear seats bleeding profusely. Blood leaked from his open wounds like a broken faucet. Unfortunately, Saigon couldn't tend to Pug. She had to ensure she lost any would-be pursuers. Once out of harm's way, Saigon headed straight to Cape Fear Valley.

As Pug drifted in and out of consciousness, two things kept him alive. One, was the prospect of revenge. The other was Jackie. She was under the impression he was out of town with Justus. If she found out the truth, she was going to kill him.

Justus lay across the plush bed he had purchased for Panee watching the flat-screen plasma T.V. Videos were on, and ironically enough, Saigon's new video was debuting. Justus chuckled at the thought of his cousin laying pipe to the beautiful mix of Vietnamese and Black at that very moment. Looking at Saigon's long pretty legs, and fat print in her leopard bikini, Justus permitted himself a quick thought about how good the sex must be. Crumbs from his potato chips frosted the sheets as he laughed at his own thoughts.

This was Justus's idea of relaxing. No stress. No nagging and a bird's eye view of one of the most beautiful asses to ever grace God's green earth. Panee made sure to keep her presence felt by walking around in a midriff baring wife-beater and purple lace boy-shorts. Her hair and nails were tweaked to perfection as always. Her three-inch heels made her tight butt stick out even more. Panee wasn't as thick as Nikki, but her ass was more round. Whereas Nikki's ass made a perfect S shape, Panee's ass exploded from her back like *PLOW*! Justus was in awe as Panee pranced around, teasing him in a sensuous manner. Apparently, she had learned a trick or two from her previous place of employment. Now it was paying off as Justus openly stroked himself through his boxer-briefs.

"C'mere, girl," Justus growled, lunging at Panee as she strutted by.

"Justus stop! You said you wanted peace and quiet."

"Unh-unh, I said give me a piece and I'll be quiet," he clarified.

"You crazy!" Panee chastised. She didn't resist Justus's advances this time. She welcomed his embrace lovingly, and stroked his chiseled torso. Justus loved when she did that. Panee always knew the right things to do to turn him on.

Justus teased Panee with his fingers until she became putty in his hands. His phone rang. Of course, they ignored it. When it rang the second and third time, Justus glanced at the caller I.D. and saw Pug's number all three times. He answered the phone, and his worst fears were confirmed as Saigon relayed to him the night's events.

Justus bailed from the house so fast he forgot all his personal effects. He even had to come back for his left shoe.

* * *

Things went from bad to worse when Justus arrived at the hospital. The first person he ran into was Nikki. She was obviously upset from the tears streaking her face. She gave Justus a look cold enough to chill water. He was supposed to be out of town with Pug yet here he was an hour after the incident occurred? Justus tried to get a situation report from Nikki, but she stormed away in the opposite direction. He started after her, but was bombarded on both sides by Aunt Gloria and Jackie. They each grabbed a shoulder and soaked it with tears.

While Jackie and Gloria wept, Justus looked around the hospital and spotted Saigon surrounded by a platoon of bodyguards. She was visibly shaken as she gave her statement to investigators. Justus freed himself of the wailers, and stepped to Saigon, who was now standing by the elevator with her hired muscle.

"'Sup, Sai," Justus greeted, softly.

"Hey, Jus," Saigon returned, suddenly.

"Listen, I know this isn't the time, but I need to know what happened. Who did this?"

Saigon sniffed, "I don't know."

She then proceeded to recount the night's events to Justus, omitting nothing. When she finished, Justus thanked her then returned to his people, which now included his mother, father, and a steadily growing mob of Pug's henchman. The mob grew louder and louder, until a wiry doctor emerged from the O.R. The angry mob quieted down to learn of Pug's status. Unfortunately, the results weren't favorable.

Pug died on the operating table.

The doctor went on to explain how loss of blood and trauma, and yada yada yada, contributed to Pug's death, but Pug's people only heard one thing.

Pug was dead.

Jackie went numb, as did Gloria. Glenda supported Gloria as best she could since she was grieving herself. Justus supported both of them as much as he could. The mood in the lobby turned somber as the impact suddenly hit home. Pug was dead.

Justus, who had killed over a dozen people mercilessly, finally felt the pains of grief that he had caused so many others. He couldn't grasp exactly what he felt. He had become desensitized to death . . . but this was Pug.

Leader observed the whole thing with the same detachedness he used when he was the reaper. He had long conquered the depth of death. He had long mastered his emotions. Sure, he hated to see Pug gone, but such was life. His primary concern was the effect this would have on his son and partner. He recalled vividly how losing the most important person in his life took him over the edge, made him the person he was. Leader had been unable to do anything about his grandfather's death at the time. In Justus's case, he could definitely do something about it! Leader was sure that Justus was reviewing scenarios of retribution at that exact moment. Leader wouldn't be surprised, nor could he blame him, but Justus had to be smart.

Before Justus left the hospital, he conferred with Saigon once more, coming up with nothing more than empty leads. It wasn't until he spoke with Pug's soldiers that he discovered who was behind the hit.

As it turned out, word on the street was that Jock found out who attacked him, and was talking big-shit about what he was going to do to Pug when he saw him. Unfortunately, Pug's crew had just found out earlier that day, and wasn't able to warn him in time. Now Pug had paid the ultimate price: his life.

Justus was so vexed he thought about doing something to Pug's crew for being so reckless and irresponsible. He decided against it, but he did decide he had had enough of Jock. He had spared Jock's life on account of Diamond. Now, there would be no more pardons. Jock wanted a war? He now had one.

Leader had intended to meet with Justus the following morning to possibly thwart any plans of get-back. However, he awoke to problems of his own.

"Hello?" Leader repeated through the phone receiver. It was a little after 6 a.m., and he was still befuddled so he wasn't sure the voice was who it sounded like it was. "Carmen?"

"That's right, John. It's me. How are you?" Carmen said, happily.

Leader looked at the phone. "What are you doing calling my home?"

"Don't act so surprised," Carmen retorted. "After what we've shared, it's not like we're exactly strangers."

"No, we're not," Leader admitted, then added. "We at least know each other well enough to know that this shouldn't be happening."

"What is 'this'?" Carmen challenged.

"This!" Leader spat through clenched teeth. Beside him, Glenda stirred. If not for the sleeping pills she had taken, she surely would have been up. "You calling my home," he clarified, lowering his voice a bit. "We're supposed to respect boundaries remember?"

"You got nerve talking about respect. After you just fucked me and left me like that!" Carmen was screaming so hard, Leader had to cover the earpiece. "What about 'I need to see you.' Can you respect that, John, huh?"

Leader rolled from bed, went into the guest bedroom before continuing. "First of all, you seduced me! You knew I was married. Now accept the consequences of your lust. Be a woman!"

"Be a woman? Be a woman? Oh, I will. In fact, I'm exercising my womanly rights right now!"

"Oh yeah?!" Leader taunted. "I can tell."

"Well, tell this: I'm pregnant with your child."

Leader laughed. "That's a good one. Old but good."

"Are you mocking me?" Carmen asked indignantly. "You think it's a game?"

"Look, it doesn't matter. I'm married." Leader was trying the smug approach.

"You're kidding me, right? John, you do NOT want to play games with me. I will ruin you!" Carmen ranted for the better part of five minutes before Leader silenced her.

"Like I said, what we had . . . we had. I'd appreciate it if you would leave me and my family alone."

"You have not seen me get started. I will crush you. I will bring you to your knees! I will—"

Leader disconnected the call. Too much drama. Too early in the morning. He had more problems, namely preventing his son from going renegade. He didn't teach him the things he did for him to squander it away on personal vendettas. Jobs were about money. Period.

While Leader pondered his issues, Justus was making plans of his own inside his basement armory. He had been holed up there since returning from the hospital. Thus far, he and Nikki had not spoken a word to each other, although she had been checking up on him through the night. Most of the time she found him doing the same thing, either crouched over his vast arsenal of weaponry, or talking animatedly into his cellphone while pacing a hole in the floor. The last time she checked on him, he sat on the floor, Indian-style, with his back to the door. His back shook violently as quiet sniffles escaped his body.

Justus couldn't recall the last time he had actually cried, but in the wee hours of that morning, he could no longer contain himself. His comrade, his ace, his brother, was gone.

After the rain came the planning. Justus had been calling in Pug's old favors all night long. By the time the sun appeared, not only did he have Jock's whereabouts, he also knew where his mother lived, his crew's hangouts (and their mothers' addresses too). Justus even had the location to Jock's new girl's house. He had every intention of getting the suckas back before Pug's body even grazed the earth.

Justus heard movement on the steps and turned to find Diamond.

"My mama said come eat," Diamond relayed sweetly. Looking at the precious child, Justus felt a little guilty about the murder plot concocted for her father. Yet, it was what it was. Dude had to go. Justus didn't make the rules. He just had to abide by them.

Justus followed Diamond up the stairs where he was ambushed by his twins, Power and Supreme. He scooped them into his arms and sat at the table to eat. During the meal, Nikki walked in and out of the dining room, refilling glasses, and bringing more food, but she never uttered a word to him.

Just as Justus finished his meal, Leader walked into the dining room, with Jackie closely behind him. Jackie was staying with Justus and Nikki until she recovered from Pug's death.

Leader took a seat across from Justus and stared at him until Jackie left them alone. Justus knew what this was. Leader was reading him.

"Are you sure this is what you want?" Leader asked, already knowing Justus's plans without having to ask.

Justus nodded.

"So you're willing to risk everything for a personal vendetta?"

"Yeah. After all, wasn't it a personal vendetta that got me started anyway." Justus shot Leader a snide look to accompany the comment.

"This is true." Leader admitted.

"Well . . ." Justus shrugged his shoulders. "This should fit in the same box."

Nikki walked into the room to refill their glasses and offered Leader a bite to eat. He declined, and Nikki left, but not before rolling her eyes at Justus.

"No." Leader answered without a second thought. "Personally, I'm against it, but it's your decision."

"I helped you when yours was personal," Justus hurled.

Leader was taken aback by Justus's forthrightness, but the irony of the situation was not lost on him. It allowed him to teach Justus another lesson.

"Listen and listen good: If you are not willing to die—or kill—for what's yours, what you love, then you're not deserving of it. What we did was for your mother, so it was just as much your beef as it was mine, maybe more so," Leader schooled.

"Well, Pug was my big brother. I loved him. Is that not worth your revenge?" the student reasoned.

For an answer, Leader suggested, "Let me tell you a story."

He proceeded to tell Justus the story of his great-grandfather, John Mo. Leader left nothing out, including the part about his father murdering his mother. When he was done, a single tear gathered in the corner of Justus's eye, but he refused to let it fall.

"So you see, this life chose me," Leader explained. For the first time, it seemed he was having second thoughts about the decision to teach his son.

"I guess it's like you told me a long time ago," Justus said, wiping his eye, "Leave the past in the past. I am what I am. It has to be done. This has to be done. No love lost for not helping, but this is going down."

Leader nodded his head. He grew to respect Justus that night. Justus was proving again and again that he had no qualms about putting in work. If anything, Leader was concerned with Justus's eagerness to do so, especially behind his emotions. Leader had warned his son about wearing his heart on his sleeve. He told him women dealt in emotions, men mastered theirs. He figured it would be one of those things he would have to learn on his own.

With Justus's decision final, Leader stood to leave. At the front door, he stopped to give his son a hug. "Be careful, my son. Don't forget we gotta be in Brazil two days after the funeral."

Before Leader left, he sized Justus up for a long time. Justus definitely wasn't the same person. The only question was, was he better or worse?

Chapter 25

It was a cool Carolina night. Justus hugged a tree inside a thicket just behind a house. He wore all black, including the mask that covered his face and was armed to the hilt. In his arm he carried an M-4 assault rifle, which was a civilian mode M-16 with a shortened stock and barrel. Strapped to his back was a riot-pump shotgun. Under his arms on each side were two .44 revolvers made of platinum with pearl handles. These two firearms were his pride and joy. He'd had them specially made. He knew they were ostentatious, but it didn't matter. No one who saw them ever lived to tell. He didn't plan on this being any different.

Justus eased his way to the back of the house, plastering himself to the rear wall, where he listened to ascertain how many people occupied the house. Apparently, a card game was going on, evidenced by the yelling of bets over the loud music. Justus could hear them clearly.

"Nigga, you ain't got no bread! I'll buy the pot every time," someone was saying.

"Ah, fuck you and that bitch you fucking wit!" someone else said.

"Leave her out of this, yo." The other voice warned.

"I'm just saying, dawg, the bitch been fucking since I was little. Hell, if the hoe had all that dick sticking out of her that been stuck in her, she'd look like a porcupine, nigga!"

The joke emitted a roomful of laughter before someone else said, "Play cards, damn!"

Justus figured at least five people were playing cards. He didn't know how many others, so he snuck around to peer through a window. He couldn't see anything more from there either. He figured he could cap all five with no problem, but if someone was in the back he would be wide open. Justus knew from his intel the house belonged to a crackhead. The fiend would rent his house out for the d-boys to sell, trick, or do anything else d-boys do. Justus knew Jock wasn't inside. Justus didn't intend for him to be there. He wanted to send him a message up close and personal.

Tired of waiting and guessing, Justus went to the power box and snipped the line. Momentary confusion claimed the house until the emergency lights popped on. Justus used those few seconds to make his move.

Justus shot the knob with the silenced M-4, then kicked it open with a three-round burst from the assault weapon. Panic ensued, as expected. Dudes fell face down to the floor like they were being raided. This made Justus laugh inwardly since he almost assumed the role of S.W.A.T. for this mission. Oh, how easy it would've been!

The unfortunate few who dropped to the floor scrambled to get back up when they saw Justus plucking their partners off one by one. Everywhere the red dot touched, a path of lightning followed behind it.

Justus was enjoying every minute of his reign of terror. The weapon jerking each time he pulled the trigger combined with the fresh smell of gunpowder was intoxicating. The screams coming from his victims made his dick hard.

Justus was in a zone until he felt a thud hit him in the back of his vest. He turned to retaliate but his weapon was shot from his hand, where it draped from its string under his left arm. The guy tried to squeeze off another round but his gun jammed. That's when Justus drew both .44's from his shoulder holster and pumped three holes the size of golf balls in the middle of his chest.

Justus complimented himself for using a revolver. No shells being spewed. Definitely no jamming.

Ensuring the rest of the house was clear, Justus slid through each room with both hammers drawn, looking for any sign of life. When he was certain the house was clear, Justus returned to each of his six victims and placed a single shot to the backs of their heads. When he was done, he extracted a bag of powder from his pocket, sprinkled it over his final victim then left the same way he came, disappearing into the night.

Jock was leaving his girl's house en route to his crack spot. Something was wrong. He had been paging and calling Winky all day to no avail. Same thing with Lex. They were supposed to re-up two hours ago. Last he heard from them they were going to "the spot" to play poker until they were ready to holla at their connect. Jock told them he was going to get his dick wet for a few hours. Told them to call when they were ready. Jock ended up falling asleep inside Jamika. When he woke up, it was ten after two.

His phone had not rung once. This was not right. Winky did not play when it came to money. So it was that Jock found himself speeding down Raeford Road at three in the morning. He was still drowsy and a little high from the blunt he had smoked earlier.

Jock turned the volume up on his system, letting the T.I. album quake throughout the Denali to wake him up. He dialed Winky's cell over and over the entire trip over. Still no answer. Jock leaned back, and let the music take him away.

In the back of the truck, Justus lay coiled into a ball. He was shed of his earlier armory but still wore his .44's over his bulletproof vest. He waited patiently for his time to act. In his hand, he held the instrument he planned on using to end Jock's existence.

Jock pulled onto the street his crack house was located on and turned down the music. Pulling up to the house, he immediately noticed all the lights were on full-blast. Jock thought this was odd, since the whole purpose of a crack house was to be discreet. He lit a blunt, contemplating his next move.

In the back of the truck, Justus slid directly behind the driver's seat and paused a second to inhale the euphoria of death. In a flash, he simultaneously lifted Jock's head with his right hand, while slicing his throat with the blade in his left hand. It happened so fast, Jock didn't have time to act. By the time he felt a hand on his forehead, he felt something sharp piercing his neck. He attempted to move but the powerful hands of his assailant kept his head riveted. Jock looked into his rearview mirror right into the eyes of Justus. Jock would remember those eyes anywhere!

Justus bore his eyes into Jock through the mirror as Jock's life left his body. He could feel Jock's warm blood ooze onto his arm, giving him an instant hard-on. Justus couldn't believe the power that coursed through his body. At this point, Justus felt omnipotent. Jock's gurgling, gaggling, and protests only heightened the feeling. Justus couldn't prevent deterring his tenants.

"Yeah nigga," Justus whispered in Jock's ear. "That's yo ass muthafucka! Look at me! I did this to you! I did it! ME!!"

Jock wheezed and wheezed, until his soul left his body quietly.

Satisfied that he was dead, but not satisfied with the results, Justus climbed into the front seat of the S.U.V. and unbuckled Jock's jeans. Pulling his pants down Justus placed his blade at Jock's penis and cut it clean off. Then he stuffed it in Jock's mouth.

"This will never get you in trouble again."

Nikki was up late watching television when she heard the buzzer sound. Seconds later, in walked

Justus still wearing his black, blending in with the shadows of the corridor. Nikki could feel his eyes boring into her from behind. Then she heard him leave, only to return minutes later, standing in the same spot. Nikki could sense the tension in Justus's aura. Frankly, it frightened her. She knew what Justus was capable of when pushed. She also knew he was scheduled to leave after Pug's funeral, regardless of what or how she felt. Business was first. Always.

Nikki went to meet Justus in the hallway. She noticed he was holding Power and Supreme in each arm. The closer she got to him, the more she smelled a foul odor like burnt copper. Nikki stopped short of the corridor, beckoning for Justus to meet her embrace, but he never moved.

Nikki finally grew tired and turned on the light in the corridor.

"Oh my god!" Nikki gasped. Justus's entire shirt was coated in dried blood. "Are you okay?!" Nikki snatched Power from Justus and began examining Justus more closely. "Justus talk to me! Are you okay? What happened?"

Nikki asked question after question while looking him over, but Justus remained silent. He was in shock. Although he was a professional killer, this murder disturbed him because it was personal—something he should have never done. No longer intoxicated from the thrill of the kill, the reality of his actions settled in. Diamond would now grow up without her father because of him. He had altered her reality forever in just one night, all because of jealousy. Maybe he wasn't cut out to be an assassin after all. He had broken a cardinal rule, he had used his tools of the trade for personal use, and now it was fucking with him.

When Nikki looked at his face again, a single tear ran down his cheek. "Oh my god, Daddy. What's wrong? Please say something," Nikki hugged Justus tightly, placing her head to his chest crying.

Nikki pulled Justus into their bedroom and ran bathwater while putting the boys to sleep in their cribs. When she was done, she stripped Justus naked and joined him in the tub.

Justus was in a trance, so Nikki washed him while he lay back in her arms. After a moment passed he began to talk.

"Please don't hate me. I did what I did because I love you. I love you more than anything. I know I fucked up but that's done. You are mine for life now. If a man isn't willing to protect what he loves, then he doesn't deserve what he loves," Justus reasoned, using his father's words. He turned to look Nikki right in the eye. "You belong to me and only me. A'ight?"

Nikki nodded.

"Do you love me more than anything?"

Again, Nikki nodded.

"Is it just us against the world? Are we family? Is this family the most important thing to you?"

"Yes. Jus. Yes. Why are you asking me this?"

"Because it's time you know who I am, or should I say, what I am. But I need to know that you have my back a thousand percent."

"Jus, you know I do! What is it?"

Justus turned back around in the water, doused the candles, and told her everything.

Chapter 26

Pug was laid to rest two days after Justus massacred Jock and his crew. Everybody who was anybody came to pay their respects. Pug's memorial service was being held at an affluent church on Bingham Drive. There wasn't too much space for the mourners to park so the procession quickly spilled into the streets, prompting police to monitor traffic. This fell right into their plans, as they already had installed undercover agents throughout the crowd to gather intelligence on Jock's crew's murders.

Justus, Nikki, Jackie, and the children arrived late, making a grand entrance as they exited the family car. Jackie wore a long black dress with high-heels and a black brim with a veil suspended from its front. Justus and Nikki both wore black with red accents. Nikki, a black skirt with a red rose pinned to the front. Justus, a black-on-black, double-breasted Armani suit with a blood-red tie. The children wore a variation of both.

As they made their way down the center aisle

to their positions in the front pew, all eyes were on
them. The unofficial verdict of the street was out,
and Justus was guilty. So, people throughout the
church watched him glide confidently down the
aisle. It wasn't that everyone knew. The few that
did gave so much deference to Justus that it created a strong magnetism to everyone within the
vicinity. Murmurs grew so loud that the preacher
was forced to pause during his sermon. He didn't
continue until Justus took his seat next to Leader,
who was comforting Gloria.

As Justus sat listening to the preacher's words,
he couldn't help but reflect on his actions. The
preacher was saying some real things, especially
the part about young lives being snuffed out pre-
maturely. Justus thought about all of the murders
he had committed. None of them affected him the
way Pug's death and his subsequent actions did.
His comrade was no longer here to ride with him.
Justus had a hard time accepting that fact, which
was ironic considering his familiarity with death.

The thing that was really troubling Justus was
his feeling about Jock. Justus didn't give a fuck
about Jock's crew, but Jock was a different matter
altogether. Hell, he knew Jock! Used to be cordial
even. Now he had killed Jock. Viciously. Now, Diamond would always wonder what happened to her
father. Justus was assuming it would eventually
weigh on her mind, when she grew old enough to
ask questions. Looking to his father at his side, Justus wondered if Leader ever experienced this
when a hit fell too close to home.

Leader noticed Justus staring at him and instantly knew what he was thinking. He could re-

member feeling the same thing years ago, which was why he made a personal policy to attend no funeral, but his own. However, with everything that was happening, he had to be present to observe the mood of the streets. And if these muthafuckas weren't street then there weren't any! The only way this crowd could be more street was if they were pavement! Leader stayed on top of things by keeping his ear to the pavement. No matter if he stayed on Jupiter for a week, if he wanted to know what was happening in Fayettenam (or any other city) all he had to do was go to the hood. And the mood in the chapel said it all: someone felt that he or Justus was behind the recent rise in the murder rate in Fayettenam. Or, as his old friend from Sherlock's fallen organization said to him earlier that day, "Chickens always come home to roost."

Nikki was listening to the preacher's words as well, but her mind was still reeling from the ton Justus had dropped on her. A hitman! She couldn't believe it. But the more she thought about it, the more it made sense. The heavy secrecy. The arsenal of weapons. The dreams at night. The fake passport that made him twenty-one. Nikki knew all these things were related, but she didn't know how. She always thought he was on consulting jobs with his . . . Oh my God! If Justus handled business with his father, that meant his father was a hitman too! Nikki couldn't believe her luck. She had jumped from the frying pan into the fire. She went from a man who sold drugs to a man who sold death. And now Jock was dead because of her, she thought. It never dawned on her that Jock had overplayed his own hand, thus being the cause of his own demise. Then the brutal way that he was found made Nikki cringe at the thought. His neck slit with his penis stuffed in his mouth! *Could her Justus be so cruel?* As much as Nikki wanted to say no, reality made her say yes, for it was she who comforted Justus when he came home soaked in Jock's blood. As for now, Nikki knew she and Justus were married until death did they part—literally. No, they had not had an elaborate ceremony. No, they had not had some stuffy preacher officiate a ceremony. The bond they formed was stronger than any words could cement. They were joined together by blood.

After the ceremony, everyone gathered at Gloria's house for the reception. Gloria still lived in Topeka Heights, because despite all the money Pug had amassed, Gloria still refused to let Pug move her from the hood. When the limos pulled into the neighborhood, followed by the long procession of cars, everyone who wasn't already part of the convoy joined in, to either be nosy or pay their respects to the mourning family.

When dudes affiliated with Jock's old crew saw Justus emerge from one of the limos, they ice grilled him. A couple of the more ambitious dudes stepped in his direction, but backed down when Leader slung his arm around Justus's shoulder and walked him inside. Justus wasn't worried anyway because underneath his fancy suit he wore both of his platinum .44 revolvers in his shoulder holsters, and he was begging to set them ablaze again—especially on these dudes. As far as Justus was concerned, they were all guilty, and were subject to the same punishment as their comrades.

"It wasn't as easy as you thought it would be, huh?' Leader said to Justus once they were inside.

"Nah," admitted Justus.

"I told you a long time ago: every big thing starts small first. Now because you brought your job home with you, you can't even be comfortable in your own town now."

Was this advice or a rebuke? Justus couldn't tell. "So, whatchu saying?

"I'm saying you fucked up!" Leader exclaimed.

"How did I mess up?"

"You brought unnecessary heat down on us."

"Unnecessary?"

"Yes. Unnecessary. I told you when you make moves it should always be about business! Anytime!"

"But this wasn't business," Justus attempted to explain but was cut short.

"Bullshit! Anytime you use what I taught you its business. You tried to mixed business with personal, which was why you fucked up!" Leader made sure to drive his point home. He hoped he wasn't coming down too hard on Justus, but he had to learn. He couldn't have Justus playing vigilante with the valuable skills he possessed.

"Wasn't it you who said protect what you love?" Justus wondered, more than a little confused.

"I said *protect*. Pug is dead! Now I got love for the brother but we could kill a hundred fools and it wouldn't bring him back. What you want to be: a vigilante or a rich businessman?"

Justus didn't answer so Leader continued.

"I know what this is about though. Let me find out you got a tender dick!"

Justus gasped. Someone knocked on the bed-room door.

"Yeah! Be out inna minute!" Leader yelled. "Let me tell you something: Don't you ever let some funky piece of pussy be your downfall, son."

Now Justus was pissed. "It's not even about that!"

"It might as well be! I told you: perception is reality. In case you haven't heard, the word on the street is you killed that dude over Nikki. They say she got you whipped.

"Now I brought you too far along for some bullshit to bring us down. And it *is* us! If you go down, I go down. Is that what you want to happen over a piece of pussy?" Leader snarled.

"No," Justus reluctantly answered. He didn't approve of Leader degrading Nikki, but now was not the time to fight that battle.

"A'ight then. Fix it. Fast." Leader pointed at Justus forcefully. "After we come back tomorrow night I want you to lay low for a while. Let this blow over, maybe take a vacation or something."

"A'ight," Justus conceded. He didn't like the way Leader was playing him and if not for him being his father he'd have to handle his business. Justus did realize that he'd have to solidify his relationship with Nikki though. She held a key part of his life in her hands. Justus had to admit Leader was right on that point.

Later that night while Nikki showered Justus went into his safe, extracted fifty grand and began placing it in neat stacks on the bed. When Nikki emerged from the shower, he intercepted her in the bathroom and dried her off while showering her with kisses.

"What's wrong?" Nikki was shocked with the sudden display of affection.

"Nothing. Can't I show love to my lady? Come on," Justus led her to the bed.

Sprawled out on the bed, arranged to spell the word "LOVE" was the fifty grand Justus had removed from the safe.

Nikki gasped. "What's this?"

"It's yours. If anything ever happens to me I want you to be able to maintain. So, this is the money for school. Take it and use it," Justus explained. "And if anything ever happens to me, like I'm killed or something—"

"Don't say that, Jus!"

"I'm just being real. If something happens, here's a key to my safe-deposit box." Justus passed the key to Nikki. "Only if something happens could you get in. I want to make sure you're straight. A'ight?"

"A'ight."

Nikki felt warm and fuzzy inside. Justus always told her he would take care of her, and he remained true to his word. So, what if it was blood money? In one way or another all money was blood money, Nikki rationalized. Justus was just playing the cards he was dealt. Nikki felt that Justus murdered Jock's crew on the strength of her alone. For that, Justus earned her undying support. Nikki vowed she would do anything in her power to protect her family. Anything! No woman, man, or child would come between their union.

Chapter 27

Glenda rolled her Jaguar into her spacious driveway, stepped out in her silk suit and checked her mailbox. Inside she found a large, thick manila envelope addressed to her without a return address. Glenda immediately checked the post office stamp and realized it was sent from Florida. Curious, because she didn't know anyone in Florida, she opened the envelope right there. What she saw shocked her.

A letter read:

Today begins the rest of your life. It's time you wake up and see what your husband really is!

Accompanying the letter, Glenda found pictures of grotesque crime scenes. One picture showed a close-up of a head with the back blown out. The accompanying picture showed a close-up of Leader firing a high-powered rifle. Putting two and two together, Glenda surmised the insinuation that Leader was responsible.

The next picture clearly showed a disguised Leader firing shots into a man's back from a silenced pistol in broad daylight. Glenda continued to flip through the photos. Each flick showed more scenes of Leader causing death. In some of the pictures Leader was obviously younger, maybe by ten years or so. When Glenda got to the last few photos, her knees went weak. They were photos of Leader receiving fellatio from Carmen. Another showed Leader pounding Carmen from the back. Yet another showed Leader licking Carmen's vagina like ice cream.

Glenda dropped the packet to the ground and braced herself on the mailbox. All types of thoughts ran through her head. Foremost was, *where was he now? Was he on a real business consulting trip, or was he consulting death? Was Justus in cahoots with him? Were they in danger?* So many unanswered questions.

Glenda gathered herself, went inside and perused the contents of the envelope over and over again. Each time she passed through a photo, more questions were raised in her head.

By the time Leader walked in the door at two a.m. that morning, Glenda was all cried out and ready for action. She met Leader at the door with a look cold enough to freeze the sun.

"What's up babe? What are you doing up?" Leader asked, knowing something was up.

"Don't babe me, motherfucker! What's this!?" Glenda smacked Leader in the face with the manila packet. "Huh?! Tell me!?" She poured the contents on the floor. Leader bent to pick them up, but she kicked him in the stomach.

Leader backhanded Glenda to the floor. "Fuck is wrong with you?"

"What, you gonna kill me too?" Glenda stammered, wiping the blood from her mouth.

When Leader rifled through the photos his heart sank. He recalled every single hit displayed in each picture. Some of them were five years old or older. When he got to the picture with him and Carmen, a groan escaped his mouth.

"That's right, nigga! That's yo' ass caught red-handed! What you gotta say for yourself. Huh? What?"

Leader looked at Glenda with disgust. Lucky for him, the phone rang keeping him from having to respond.

Who is this calling my house at this time of night, Leader thought to himself. He picked up the receiver from the wall.

"Trouble in paradise?" The voice asked. Leader immediately recognized Carmen's sultry tone. "I told you I will bring you to your knees you mother-fucker! You don't know me, but you will in due time. Yes, you'll know exactly who I am!"

Leader lost it, "You stupid bitch! I'ma break your neck!"

"Ooh. Promises. Promises."

"Now you listen—

"Hello? Hello?" Glenda had snatched the phone from Leader, but Carmen hung up.

"Oh, so now your bitch calling my house? You got some nerve."

Glenda went on and on, but Leader never responded. Finally, he grew tired of her ranting. He turned on his heels and headed toward the door.

"Oh, so where you going? To Florida to be with your whore? Huh? To kill somebody else now, Mr. Murder?!"

Leader froze on a dime. "You acting real childish, Glenda," he said, turning to her face her. "Now I fucked up. Yes. I know. We got problems, but we WILL work them out 'cause leaving is not an option.

"I'm gonna leave for a few days so you can clear your head. I'll call with the number to where I'll be so when you're ready to talk we can. In the meantime, what you saw in these pictures stays between us. All of it. Understand?" From the way Leader looked at Glenda, she knew this was not a question. It was a statement. Glenda didn't respond but she was no fool. She knew what the deal was. Violating him was cause to become like the victims in the pictures. Leader held his stare a few more seconds then left with the packet in his hand.

The following morning Justus went over to his parents' house to speak to his father about something that happened on the previous night's job, and found his mother swollen in disarray. It was obvious she had been crying and her right eye was bruised.

"What happened?!" Justus cried, taking his mother's face into his hands, examining her wound.

"Oh, you don't know?" Glenda replied sullenly.

"No!"

"Your father happened, that's what. The affair! The murders! The lies!"

Justus froze in his tracks. Glenda noticed his

apprehension. "So, you do know?" she dropped her head.

Justus obliged her. "Look I don't know nothing about no affair." He said softly.

"Oh, so you're a murderer too?"

Justus was silent.

"My god. My god. What is going on? This can't be happening." Glenda murmured to herself.

"Look, none of that is gonna change anything." Justus stated defiantly. "It is what it is, Mom. I can't turn back the hands of time nor do I want to."

"Son, what are you saying?"

"I'm saying. Dad showed me the way."

"Your dad, huh. What'd he show you, how to be a whore!" Glenda slammed the pictures onto the coffee table, illustrating her point. Justus glimpsed his father in the compromising positions and his heart went cold. "There's more." Glenda prodded, plopping more flicks on the glass. "What you think about your dad now?

Justus was stunned. "Where did you get these?"

"From your father's whore. He threatened me. Said if I tell anyone, he'd kill me, but I'm not scared of him."

Justus grew aware of his mother's implications and attempted to placate her. "Mom maybe you're speeding. Maybe it's not like that."

"Like what? Maybe he can keep his dick in his pants!"

Justus had never heard his mother use such language. His aunt, yeah, but not his mother.

"Calm down. Look I'm gonna talk to him. Maybe it's a big mix-up. Ya know they can do all kinds of stuff on the computer nowadays. Don't do anything rash until I talk to him."

"Where is he?"

Glenda looked at Justus, pain evident in her eyes.

"Don't worry, I'll find him. Just be cool. We'll fix this. We gotta, ma. We all we got: This family. Separation is not an option."

That's the same thing Leader said, thought Glenda. When Justus said it, she knew she had lost an ally. Leader had corrupted her son. She thought hard about revealing another family secret, but decided she'd save that nugget for another time.

Unfortunately for her, she wouldn't have a chance to do so.

Justus left his mother in a fit of rage. He needed some space. Some time to think. So, he headed over to his sanctuary, his home away from home. Panee.

When he arrived at Panee's place, the lights were off and the blinds were shut. Justus thought this odd since Panee was always home during the day. Justus grabbed his sport coat from the passenger seat, put it on to cover up his weapons, then quickly exited his C7 Corvette.

Putting his key into the lock, he thought he heard a male's voice. Then just as quickly it faded. Justus attempted to push open the door, but the chain lock was engaged so he was only able to see through a portion of the foyer. Unfortunately for Panee, it was enough for him to see her in lingerie running toward the back with Timberland boots in her hand.

Uh-oh. Justus didn't wear Timbs anymore.

BLOOOM!

Justus blew the chain lock off with one of his .44's then kicked the door off its hinges. Storming into the house with both weapons drawn, he first spotted Panee cowering on the floor, her eyes plastered on the bedroom door. Justus cautiously approached the bedroom door, listened briefly, then kicked it open with weapons pointing in each direction.

He spotted him tucked in the closet with his knees drawn under him. He was naked except for socks and a pair of black boxer-briefs. He wore braids in his hair and pure fear on his face. His eyes were transfixed on the platinum barrels of Justus's guns.

Justus reached in the closet and snatched dude out by his braids.

"Pl-please don't kill me, man," the scrawny guy begged. Panee bust into the room and screamed when she saw Justus with the guy's hair in the same hand he held his gun.

"Justus wait . . . Don't do this."

"Do what?"

"This . . . Not like this. He's innocent. He doesn't know about you."

"Oh, so it's your skanky ass I should shoot," he pointed his other gun at her. She drew her hands to her face in defense. Justus didn't shoot her, he chastised her, "You stank hoe. After all the shit I did for you. When the world gave you it's ass to kiss, I picked you up. And you do me like this wit' a broke, punk-ass pussy muthafucka?!" Justus was heated. "Look at him! He can't even protect you! He more a bitch than you!"

The dude was speechless. Inwardly, he prayed for his life.

"Do you have any IDEA the things I do for you to live like this? You trifling whore!"

"Hey man that's en—" The guy tried to speak, but that was all he got out before Justus smashed the butt of the gun into his head and fired a round simultaneously.

"Aaah!" Panee screamed when her paramour crumpled to the floor and began pissing on himself.

"You silly muthafucka!" Justus yelled at the fallen lame. He aimed his pistol at his head. The red beam danced around his eyes. Justus was in a daze, begging for a reason, beginning to feel the power that accompanied a kill.

"FREEZE!! DROP YOUR WEAPON!!"

Justus turned and saw a dozen Cumberland County and City of Fayetteville police officers with guns pointed at him. He shot Panee a death glare before surrendering.

"Shit."

Chapter 28

Justus was processed at the downtown Fayette-ville jailhouse, better known as Cumberland County Detention Center. Through the whole fingerprinting ordeal, complete with mug shots, Justus hoped his story held up. He had told the police he was a security consultant for major executive firms. He was twenty-two years old and his guns were legal. Justus pronounced his words professionally, provided phony registration for his weapons, and a phony driver's license with his real birthday, but an exaggerated year. As a result of this, he was just being charged with assault, reckless endangerment, and discharging a firearm into a private dwelling. For now.

After Justus was processed, they allowed him to make a phone call. He didn't want to call Nikki because she would want to know what happened. His mother was going through a crisis also, so he didn't want to upset her. And of course he didn't know Leader's whereabouts. So he phoned his Aunt Gloria. He told her the short version of what hap-

pened, told her NOT to tell Nikki or his mom, and
call back at the jailhouse at six. It was still early in
the day so Justus anticipated he would make the
night court session, get a bond, and be out.

As it turned out, he didn't make the night
court session due to an already full docket (apparently everyone was acting up in the 'Nam.) Justus
was transferred upstairs to GP or General Popula-
tion. He just knew things were too good to be true.

The C.O. escorted Justus to a cell-block after issuing him a blanket, mattress, one sheet, and a hygiene kit which consisted of a comb, toothbrush,
one bar of soap, a washcloth, and towel. The cell-
block consisted of four two-man cells in a straight
line with a large six-man cell at the end. All were facing a glass window that ran the entire length of the
wall, enabling the prisoners to look outside at
downtown Fayetteville. Unfortunately, there were
bars that ran parallel to the window. The bars were
closest to the cell block, and a walkway between
the windows and bars allowed C.O.'s to walk
through to observe the cell block without actually
going inside. On one end of the "rock" was a T.V.,
radio, and two tables for activities. On the opposite end, was another television, but it was always
out of order.

Justus carried his things into cell #4. Much to
his surprise—and pleasure—he was the only one
assigned to the cell. He placed his mattress on the
bottom bunk, threw his hygiene kit in the sink,
and plopped on the bed. He never made the bed
up. He didn't plan on being there long. Justus laid
down on his back, looking up at the iron-cast bunk
above him and thought about how he got into his

predicament. He knew he shouldn't have fucked
up with Nikki again. He should have kept his
promise to leave Panee alone. Now look at him.
As soon as he was released in the morning, he was
going to scoop her and the kids up, and take them
out of town somewhere until the word on the
street subsided.

Justus's keen senses felt someone watching
him. He raised his head a little to see, and noticed
a skinny, bald-head dude at his cell door. His jump-
suit was pulled down to his waist, exposing at tatted-
up torso, and his feet occupied bright orange shower
shoes. He leaned against the bar, casually watching
Justus.

Justus had never been to jail, but Pug had told
him enough stories for him to know he had to let
it be known off the rip: he was not the one to fuck
with.

"Sup, dawg," the guy responded, flashing a
starter kit of gold teeth.

"You know me or sump'in?"

"Naw."

"Then why da fuck you staring at me, dawg?"
Justus could still get gutter. Living well hadn't
spoiled him too much.

"You look familiar that's all."

"Yo, you don't know me, dawg."

"I'm saying tho . . . You look like the dude on
the news, dawg. Yo' name Justus?" The guy asked
pointing his finger at Justus.

"Fuck you talking 'bout?!" Justus exploded
from the bed.

"Dawg, you on T.V. right now." The guy gestured toward the corner. Justus stood to investi-

gate. Before he made it to the corner where the
T.V. sat, he saw his mug shot plastered across the
television screen.

"Damn!!!" So much for Nikki not knowing.

> *Again: shots were fired inside an upscale apart-
> ment complex. No one was seriously injured. De-
> tails are sketchy.*
> *But it appears the incident stemmed from a do-
> mestic dispute. One man was taken to the hospital.*
> *The man who was taken into custody is named
> Justus . . .*

Nikki flipped the plasma television off before
slamming the remote to the floor.

"Can you believe this shit!" Nikki screamed to
Jackie who was sitting right beside her watching
the whole ordeal unfold. "Nikki, I love you. Nikki
it's me and you babe. Family first,' " she mocked.
"The whole while he was sponsoring that trick!
Oooh!"

"Calm down, Nik. You know how it is. Shit.
Here, hit this," Jackie passed Nikki the blunt full of
the purple haze they had swiped from Justus's
stash. Since Pug was gone, Jackie spent her days in
a haze-induced stupor. "You know dude's gon'
have chicks on the side. Your man is paid, so expect it. Hell, he keep you laced and he's a great
provider so just accept it. Don't he bring the dick
home to you every night? A'ight then."

Nikki heard what Jackie was saying, but she'd
rather be hot. Justus had betrayed her trust. Again.
She took the blunt Jackie offered her and toked
away her problems.

Nikki's phone rang. She looked at the caller I.D. and decided to let it continue ringing. It stopped then shrieked again five minutes later. It was Jackie who answered the phone.

"Hello," she barked. "Hold on . . . here." She passed the receiver to Nikki.

"I don't want it."

"Here," Jackie insisted. Nikki finally accepted the phone.

"Hello?'

"Nikki? Baby Girl?"

"What Justus?"

"Look, don't be upset. It's not like it appears."

"Oh, you ain't in jail for fighting over another bitch?"

"Nah yo."

"Hmph. That's what it appears like to me. That's what it appears like on T.V. too."

"Baby Girl, it ain't like that."

"How I'm supposed to feel Justus? You got me looking stupid as shit!" Nikki exploded into the phone.

"Hold up. Hold up. My aunt Glo on the three-way."

"Don't worry 'bout me, Nikki." Gloria chimed in from the third line. "Curse his dumb-ass out."

"Aunt Glo?"

"Aunt Glo my ass! Go 'head Nikki." Nikki continued to wear Justus out until she was tired. Justus, being in the wrong, had to accept it. When she was done, he continued his spiel.

"Baby Girl, listen I need you down here with Aunt Glo first thing in the morning. All that other sh-stuff we'll deal with later, but I must get out of here. A'ight?"

"Okay."

"Good. Now look inside my closet and—hold-up—Aunt Glo, put the phone down a second." A clunk was heard through the line. "A'ight. Look inside my blue gators and," Justus paused. "Aunt Glo!?"

"Alright. Alright," Gloria really put the phone down this time.

"Look inside my burgundy gators, get the key, and go inside the wall safe. Get ten stacks. You never know what these people will try. Got it?"

"Yeah, Jus."

"A'ight. See you in the morning. I love you."

"Whateva." Click. Nikki hung up the phone. She was giving Justus hell, but deep inside she knew she wasn't going anywhere. Jackie was right. Justus did take care of her. He kept her laced in the finest fashions. He kept a well-maintained roof over her head, and their garage looked like a car lot. Her personal fleet made her look like a mathematician with all the numbers she pushed: 430's, 600's 750's. All the luxury cars represented in her stable. So, while she wasn't going to let Justus forget his transgression, she was going to hold him down. No matter what.

The following morning Justus was snatched from his cell bright and early, and taken to a room where he waited with a gang of other guys. When it was finally his turn, he entered a room where there was a T.V. monitor with a bench in front of it.

From the television, a voice said, "Take a seat on the bench son." Justus did as instructed. The voice belonged to a judge. On the screen he sat behind a bench in a courtroom somewhere far off.

This was to be Justus's arraignment.

Justus couldn't believe how impersonal the so-called legal system was. The judge read the charges off like he was reciting ingredients off a box. In the end, his bond was set at $50,000. North Carolina law required 15%, so he was looking at $7,500, cash. Justus chuckled on his way out the door. Shit, he almost had that much in his personal property already!

As expected he'd be home in no time. When he returned to his cellblock he tried to call home, but couldn't get an answer. He assumed it was because they were already en route to bond him out. Leaving the phone corner, Justus noticed a new guy had been brought in. He looked vaguely familiar, but Justus couldn't place where he knew him from and he didn't lose a second trying to figure it out. He just retired to his bunk to wait on his name to be called.

He dozed off and the next thing he heard was, "Moore! Bag and Baggage!!"

Justus recognized his name, but not the command that followed. It wasn't until the new guy from earlier called him by name and told him, did he know he had made bond.

"You need help, man?" New Guy asked. For some reason he was treating Justus with deference.

"Nah, I'm straight."

"A'ight. Take care," New Guy responded then added, "And tell Nikki, Chuck said what's up."

Justus froze in his tracks. "Whatchu say?"

"Nikki your wife, right?" New Guy asked.

"How you know my wife?" Justus's tone let him know the wrong answer could be detrimental to his health.

"Naw, man. It ain't like that," New Guy replied, suddenly getting scared, "I'm from Grove View. I used to stay beside her back in the day. She's like my big sister. I remember you too," Chuck stated matter-of-factly. The way he said it let Justus know he was implying something.

"Oh yeah?"

"Yeah. You good peoples." Chuck extended a pound. After a brief hesitation, Justus dapped him up.

"Moore, let's go if you going!" The C.O. called out. Justus stepped through the door, without pause.

Downstairs, after receiving his personal property, he met up with Nikki, Jackie, and Gloria in the lobby. They had a balding black guy with them. Justus assumed this was the bondsman. He was right. As the bondsman informed Justus of the conditions of his release, Justus looked at Nikki carefully.

Damn she fine, he thought.

Nikki was wearing a blood-red two-piece skirt suit with black four-inch pumps. Her hair was pulled up into a bun and her juicy lips modeled lipstick the color of her suit. She looked like a lawyer.

After Justus signed the papers they left the precinct.

Outside on the sidewalk, Justus was hugging Nikki while they headed toward the truck, whispering apologies in her ear. Out of nowhere they were accosted by two tall white men in dark suits.

"Justus Moore?" One of them asked digging into his pocket.

"Yeah—why?"

"We have a warrant for your arrest. Deputies take him into custody."

"Man what the—get off me!" Justus pleaded as the deputies snapped cuffs on him.

"You're under arrest for the murder for Jacques McNeil. You have the right to remain silent. Anything you say . . ." Justus looked to Nikki. "Call a lawyer."

Nikki burst into tears.

Chapter 29

This time when Justus went before the judge things were drastically different. Judge Blake scowled at Justus from his bench as he denied him bond. After that, Justus was shackled, then manhandled over to the County side where inmates were housed to await trial.

The following morning, Justus was snatched from his cell bright and early and taken to a holding cell, where he waited a full two hours on hard concrete. From there he was taken to an interrogation room, where he waited another hour in silence, shackled to a chair. When his patience was too thin to measure, he dozed off, only to be awakened by two visitors.

Justus immediately pegged the two men as D.T.'s. As always, one was black and one was white. The white detective looked like a marine reject all the way down to his spit-shined loafers. The black detective was dressed like a hip-hop star, draped in platinum jewelry, walking on Timberland boots.

"What's up, my brother?" The black detective

greeted then added. "I'm Jason." Justus remained silent. "we're here investigating a murder. Ah, maybe you can help us out here." Justus still didn't speak as he looked off into space. Jason motioned for his white colleague to step out. When he was gone, Jason pulled a chair close to Justus.

"Look here brother, these are some pretty serious allegations against you," Jason stated. "Now these crackers wanna see you fry. Me . . . I wanna help you get the best deal possible, but you gotta help yourself or these muthafuckas gonna hang you."

"These muthafuckas?" Justus finally said.

"Yeah."

"Well you wit' 'em, so I guess that makes you a muthafucka too."

Detective Jason chuckled. "Nah, I'm just a black man trying to do my job, which is to help brothas get outta tough situations."

"You wanna help me?"

"Yeah."

"You wanna help me?"

"Yeah!"

"Well take these cuffs off and open the fuckin' gates!"

"Now you know I can't do that," Detective Jason sighed. "For god's sake, you cut a man's dick off and stuffed it in his mouth!"

"I ain't do shit."

"Allegedly."

"Won't you allegedly get the fuck outta my face!" Justus turned his chair to the side.

"A'ight little brother. Can't say I ain't try to help." Detective Jason stood and let his partner in.

The detective rushed in and got in Justus's face like a drill sergeant spitting, "Oh you wanna play tough you little shit! Huh! You gonna tell us what we wanna know! You're gonna confess to this goddamn murder right now so we can all get the fuck outta here! I got a hot meal waiting and an even hotter wife. If I have to miss either one I'ma fuck you up but good!"

Justus sucked his teeth.

Whap! The chair smacked the floor full-force with Justus in it. The suddenness of the attack surprised Justus and he started to react, but didn't wish to reveal his hands. His plan was to play the sheep for now. He knew murder interrogations were recorded so he wanted to appear as docile as possible so as not to show any sign of a propensity for violence. Nevertheless, the wolf would appear when he exacted retribution on the bastard who had his knee in his chest at the present moment.

"You think I'm playing, cocksucker! I will beat you all night long. Now CONFESS!"

"I don't know what you're talking about," Justus pleaded through jagged breaths, "I'm a businessman."

The detective cackled loudly before sitting Justus back up in the chair. "I like you kid. You're clever and you've got balls . . . But it's my job to castrate niggers." With that he smacked fire out of Justus causing him to fall again.

The beating went on for forty-five minutes, but Justus's steely resolve never faltered and he never showed weakness. Justus never even let out a whimper as smack after smack rained across his face.

Justus wasn't allowed to call his lawyer or anyone else for three days. Each day Nikki came to visit only to be refused entry. When she finally did get to see Justus, it was through a glass. He wasted no time issuing orders.

"Use that money I gave you to get this lawyer," Justus ordered Nikki through the telephone. "His name is Hamin Shabazz and he's supposed to be the best lawyer in the south. Have you seen my dad? What did he say?"

Nikki's jovial mood suddenly turned sour. "Jus, I don't know how to tell you this, but we haven't heard from your father since the day this happened."

"What?"

"Yeah."

"What about my mom?"

"She hasn't heard from him either."

"Why she ain't been up here?" Justus wondered. Nikki hesitated then answered.

"She said she didn't want to see you like this . . . or you see her like that."

"Like what?" Justus stood up.

"Jus, her and your father have been having problems."

"And?"

"And let's just say I know where you get your woman beating tendencies from." Nikki chuckled. Justus did not. "Anyway, he hasn't been home since their incident."

Justus took the news in. *What was going on?* he thought. Surely, Leader knew about his situation. Did Leader think he was going to turn foul? Justus had to see what was up.

"A'ight, check this" Justus began. "Write this

number down: 1-888-486-2200. That's Pop's emergency cell. Tell him what happened. Tell him I need him to get me out A.S.A.P., alright?'

"What about the lawyer?"

"Just holla at Pop. He'll take care of all that. Kiss the boys and tell my mom not to worry. I'll be home soon."

Nikki stood to leave.

"Nikki," Jus called through the receiver. "I love you. Stop looking like that. Everything will be okay. Promise . . . Now let me see that smile." Nikki flashed the pearly whites. "That's my girl." They ended the visit touching palms through the glass.

Later that night, as Justus received his dinner tray, one of the trustees who brought the food kept eyeballing him. Justus recalled that since he had been there, the same guy kept eyeballing him each time he brought the trays. Justus decided to find out who the guy was. He sought out Rico's table then sat down to eat.

Rico was a guy who had been in the county for two years, awaiting trial on two bodies. Rico knew everything about the place, so if anyone knew the trustee it was him.

"Sup Killa," Rico greeted Justus as Justus sat to join Rico for supper.

"Chillin." They both ate in silence for a while until Justus broke the ice. "Want this apple, yo?"

Rico looked up from his food, momentarily eyeing Justus suspiciously. When Justus passed his test, Rico took the apple.

From there a rapport was established. For the next few days, Justus did the same routine, always giving Rico some food from his tray. The food was shit, but Rico seemed to love it. Finally, on the fourth day, Justus gently slid the question to Rico.

"Who is old-school that be bringing the trays, dawg?"

"Which one?" Rico asked, licking his fingers clean of the pork chop Justus had given him.

"The smooth old-head with the wavy grey."

"Oh, you mean Top!"

"I guess," Justus shrugged.

"Yeah, that's Top. He been bidding a minute, dawg." Rico confirmed, letting his eyes drift off into space.

"What's up wit' him?" Justus quire.

"Old-school been here 'bout three, four years. He came back to be a trustee from state. Nigga done did like eighteen years."

"Word?"

"Word."

Justus took a moment to let the thought of doing eighteen years sink in. Damn, nigga been bidding since he was two! Justus pictured what he was facing and shuddered.

"Why?" Rico was asking.

"Nah, dude just be eyeballing me, that's all."

"Oh, you straight," Rico stated dismissively. "If dude had beef witchu, you'd know. He don't fuck wit' nobody now, but word is he got a string of bodies."

Justus listened intently and thought about what Leader had told him: "Keep secrets in the breast because those who gossip to you about others will gossip to others about you."

In the span of a week, Rico had told Justus

enough to do Top harm. Damn, Leader was a genius.

The following day, while out for recreation, Justus finally got a chance to holla at old-school, Top. Justus was standing on the fence when, surprisingly, Top approached him. Top didn't say anything at first. He just stood beside Justus, observing him. Out of his peripheral, Justus was doing the same.

"Where you from, Youngblood?" Top asked, soothing the tense air. Justus looked at Top head-up, sizing him up, and responded, "Grove View."

Top nodded, then after a brief pause asked. "Who your peoples?" Top spoke real polished, but to Justus it seemed there was a high amount of rage just beneath the surface.

"The Daniels," Justus answered. Top nodded like he already knew the answer to his question. When Justus was about to ask Top some questions, he abruptly walked away.

Later that night, when supper came, Justus opened his tray and realized he had extra food. Justus knew exactly where the extra food came from. Rico spoke up, confirming Justus's guess when he said,

"Old-head been asking 'bout chu." Justus just listened. "He said he know your peoples."

This got Justus's attention. "Word? Who?"

"Say he know your old man." The mere mention of Leader caused Justus's blood to boil. Thus far, Leader still had not gotten back in touch with Nikki.

Justus didn't respond to Rico, allowing the sub-

ject to change for the remainder of the meal. The
following day on the rec yard Justus approached
Top as he sat watching a basketball game from behind his dark shades.

"Sup' Top."

"Alright Youngblood. What's happening?'

"Nothing much," Justus lied. A ton of shit was
on his mind. "You never told me where you was
from," Justus said, trying to float in the question
he really wanted to ask.

"Little bit of everywhere," Top offered vaguely.
"You wanna know how I know your old man, huh,"
he said suddenly.

Justus was surprised, but Top had pulled his
card, so he came straight with the old-timer.

"Yeah. Actually, I do."

Top chuckled, "It's alright. I'll tell you. But
first, how is your mother doing? Glenda, right?"
Justus nodded. Top zoned out for a second remembering old times. "Yeah, your mother was a
looker back in the day. Bet she still fine."

Justus blanched.

"I remember when you was this big—"

Top measured a foot with his hands. "Then I
saw you on the T.V, I didn't recognize you, but I remembered the name. When I saw you come in, I
automatically looked at you. You look just like your
daddy looked when he was your age. I knew it was
you. If only Ralo could see you now . . ." Top's
voice trailed off as he reminisced yet again.

Who is Ralo, thought Justus.

"Me and your daddy was inseparable. Top and
Ralo. Ralo and Top. Fucked me up when he got
killed."

"Killed? What the fuck?"

"That dude ain't have to do him like that. I wish I could catch him now. After all this time, the damn police still say they don't know who did it, but I do."

Top was talking irrational, or so Justus thought, so he finally said, "Man, I don't mean no disrespect, but I believe you got the wrong dude, cause my daddy ain't dead."

"What you mean, Youngblood. I was on the streets then. Matter fact, that was right before I came to the joint," Top corrected.

"You probably was too young to remember, but I remember like it was yesterday. Ralo was my ace."

Justus didn't like how he was coming so he stood to his full six-plus feet, looked at Top and said, "I don't know no fuckin' Ralo. My daddy named Leader."

"Leader?" Top hissed, then repeated the name like a bad omen. "You say Leader your daddy?"

"Yeah. You say you knew my mom, I'm surprised you didn't know that. They been together for the last twenty years."

"Your mom married Leader?" Top grabbed his head like he was getting lightheaded. Justus took a step back. He didn't like the way this was going down.

Top continued, "I can't believe this. She married that nigga?!"

"Come on, Old-school. Don't say too much about my dad," Sure, Leader was shitting on him, but Justus wasn't about to let anyone else talk reckless about him.

"Youngblood, that ain't your daddy. Your daddy

was named Ralo," Top's voice dropped an octave. "Your step daddy killed Ralo over your mother, when you was a baby . . ."

"Man, I'm gone." Justus attempted to walk off, but Top cuffed his arm, preventing him from leaving. Justus shot him a warning with his eyes. Top returned it. Justus relented.

"Listen Youngblood, I don't play no games and I usually don't meddle in people's business, but I got to pull your coat on this. Leader killed Ralo over your mother. Don't believe me? Ask any oldhead from around your way. The streets know. Nobody don't wanna say anything because of who Leader is. They scared, but I ain't. Fuck Leader."

Justus observed Top closely. His eyes burned with passion when he took his shades off. His breathing was rapidly increasing. Justus didn't want to believe him; Top's story was more than a little farfetched. Yet it was too farfetched to be made up.

"I don't understand why you telling me this. I mean, you say you know who my father is, but you telling me something that could be detrimental to your health," Justus reasoned.

"Like I said, fuck Leader. I'm telling you because you deserve to know who your real daddy was. Ralo was my best friend. Quiet as I kept, I took this life sentence for Ralo. So, that's what he meant to me." With that said, Top walked off, leaving Justus lost in his cacophony of thoughts.

Leader slowly crept through the spacious loft located on Chicago's affluent West Side. A couple weeks' worth of tracking and investigating finally came to fruition. He had finally found where Carmen rested her head when she was not out terrorizing the world.

Leader had left Fayetteville the hour he and Glenda had their spat and subsequent fight. He left on a mission to find Carmen to get into her life as she had done his. It was senseless to argue with Glenda until he had proof that what he and Carmen had briefly shared was over. Then he and Glenda could start over. Then he and Glenda could start their reconciliation phase. Drastic measures came from drastic situations, which was why he intended to take Carmen's head, absent her body, back to Glenda to show that she was no longer a problem. That in itself would make a huge statement. Glenda already knew what he did for a living now, so much so because of Carmen. So, since Carmen was the cause of Glenda's epiphany, her life would serve as the sacrifice.

It took Leader almost two weeks to locate Carmen's home, but after much back tracking and work he had found her lair.

Leader slowly tripped up the carpeted stairs with his silenced revolver drawn at the ready. The television was on upstairs, and Leader could see movement through the shadows created by the T.V.'s light. As Leader reached the top of the stairs, he made out Carmen's silhouette sitting up in the bed. Wasting no time, Leader crouched, aimed the red beam at her head, and pulled the trigger.

"Pop!" An explosion greeted Leader's gunshot, and the lights sprang on revealing the source of the explosion.

A dummy with a balloon head sat in the bed,

taunting Leader. The wig from the balloon now sat on its lap, a string with one end running from the light-switch, another attached to a lock of hair. Leader wasn't convinced Carmen wasn't there, so he assumed combat mode, searching the room carefully. When he was done, he brought his attention to the dummy. Attached to its chest was a note that read:

"You can come into my house uninvited, I can come inside yours. See you in N.C.," *Damn!* Leader thought as he rushed out the door.

Justus strolled to his post in the visitation room and greeted his wifey and Aunt Glo. Sitting on the stool, he lifted the receiver to speak. Nikki was up first.

"Hey Love, how you holding up?" Nikki touched her thumb to the glass.

Justus blushed. "It'll be over soon. Did you talk to that lawyer yet?"

"Yeah, but Mr. Shabazz said he can't touch your case for less than thirty grand. Fifteen up front."

"No problem. What's up with the bond?" Nikki sighed deeply. "He said you may have to sit for a couple more weeks to get a bond reduction, but for the fifteen, he'll make it happen." Justus didn't want to sit in jail, but he understood the way the system worked. "A'ight. You heard from my dad?"

"No. Not yet."

"How's my mom? Why she didn't come?"

"Her and Keisha been spending a lot of time together. She said she'll be over in the morning.

Keisha spending time with her friend Alayna tonight, so first thing in the morning she'll be here."

"Hey baby. How's everything?" Gloria said in
her drawl.

He looked at his aunt for a long time before
asking, "Do you know a dude named Top?" Gloria's face underwent a mélange of emotions until
recognition appeared on her face.

"I knew a guy years ago named Top. Why?"

Justus could tell she was hiding something so
he prodded on. "About my height, light skin, curly
hair?"

"Oh, honey, I wouldn't know. That was years
ago." Gloria's light skin betrayed her as it flushed
lightly around the cheeks. Justus saw the guile, and
kept digging.

"Well he says he know you," he bluffed. "And
Mom . . . and Dad. But the dad he knows is named
Ralo." Gloria's jaw dropped, letting Justus know he
had dropped a bomb. Justus relayed Top's story to
Gloria. As he told the story, veil after veil fell from
his eyes. As each syllable released itself from his
mouth, Justus's existence became more and more
frail.

"It's true isn't it?" Justus asked when he was
done recounting the story.

"Jus, baby. Why are you digging up the past?
Leader raised you, he's your father. All—"

"It's TRUE isn't it!!"

The C.O.'s glanced in Justus's direction, so he
lowered his voice, then repeated the question.

It was apparent that this was a long-lost family
secret. Gloria's face was in pain as she nodded her
head. She hated for Justus to find out this way. She

had told her sister years ago to tell Justus when he was old enough to understand. Gloria knew the old adage was true: What happens in the dark comes to light. Always.

"Ralo was your father," Gloria finally admitted. "But I don't know if Leader killed him or not. That's a street rumor. Truth is, your father was a powerful man. He had a lot of enemies. No one knows for sure if Leader killed him."

Inside, Justus was a bundle of emotions, outwardly his face was poker. Just as he was about to pose a barrage of questions his visit was terminated.

Later that day on the rec field, Justus humbled himself to Top, and Top proceeded to tell Justus all about his father. According to Top, Ralo was a "street general." Standing about six-foot-two, weighing about two-hundred and forty pounds, Ralo was like a bear; if you didn't kill him, he would kill you. It was safe to say no one wanted to cross him. He and Glenda were lovers from an early age. Ralo saw Glenda and knew he had to have her. Ralo used to talk Top's ears off, espousing the joys of Glenda. When she grew pregnant with Justus, Ralo was ecstatic, and chose Top to be the unborn child's godfather. Unfortunately, Top never got a chance to be a godfather to the child, as he went to prison soon after he was born. Justus demanded to know what happened between Leader and Ralo. Top was reluctant to tell him, but being that he was never able to pass on anything else to his godson, he figured he could pass on the legacy of what really happened to his father. So, Top and Justus sat down on the basketball court while Top spilled his secrets:

"I don't know when Leader and Ralo first really had beef, but all I know is one night we were out and someone—I forget who it was—told Ralo some brash New York cat was pursuing his old lady. Me and Leader didn't know each other, but apparently, him and Ralo already had words before. Anyway, we go to ths li'l juke joint and see the nigga pawing on your ma. Leader got heated, went over to Glenda and tried to kiss her or something. Meanwhile Ralo sees all this from the sideline. When he's had enough, he goes over, pulls Leader off of Glenda—SMACK! SMACK! Hit 'em a few times. Leader tries to fight back, but Ralo pulls his piece. Puts it right in Leader's face. Everybody in the spot goes quiet, and I realize where we at, so I pull Ralo back. We leave the joint in my Hog.

"Couple weeks later, I got locked up for this square me and Ralo had to put down. They wanted me to snitch on Ralo, but I ain't a rat, ya dig?"

Justus nodded, continuing to meet Top's dead-gaze head-on.

"Anyway, I wear the hit for the body, Ralo goes free while I get life. Before I even left the R&E center in Central Raleigh, I get the news Ralo was killed. Someone had broken into his home, stabbed him in the neck from behind, then blew his brains out. Shot him three times in the head."

Top shook his head and shuddered at the thought.

"I found out later by some jitterbug that came

down in the system that the dude who did it worked for Sherlock."

"Sherlock?"

"Yeah. Ya heard of him?"

"Little bit. Say he's legend," Justus said.

"Yeah. That's why Leader never got charged. Sherlock had police on his payroll and Leader was Sherlock's #1 enforcer. Plus, everyone was scared. Shit, Ralo was thorough, so naturally the person who took him out would rise in stature. Nobody never came forward, and Leader got away."

Top raised his hands signifying the end of his story.

Justus was blown away by what he'd just heard. Now that his Aunt Glo had confirmed what Top told him about Leader being his stepfather, he had no choice but to believe Top about this also.

So, Leader had killed his father. Even though Justus had never met his father—or couldn't recall anyway—it still felt funny, knowing someone had extinguished the source of his lineage. Justus couldn't help but think of the irony of his killing Jock over Nikki, and Leader killing Ralo, because of his mother. Guess the fruit didn't fall far from the tree. Only difference was, Leader had actually killed his father.

Justus was depressed that night as he laid in bed. He hadn't even eaten dinner. He had no appetite. He just couldn't get the situation off his mind. It seemed everywhere he turned, death met him head-on. Leader killed his father then replaced him with himself. Just as he did Jock with

Diamond, except Nikki helped him indirectly. So, what was Glenda's role in all of this? She allowed him to believe Leader was his father all these years. What did she know about this? Justus was confused, but he knew Glenda held more pieces to the puzzle. To what puzzle, he didn't know. All he knew was he'd know when he found it.

First he had to talk to Glenda.

Chapter 30

Glenda was done sulking. It had been weeks since she heard from her husband and frankly, she missed him. Moreover, she needed him. So many explosions were going off in her life, what with Justus being locked up, charged with murder. Gloria had told her Justus found about the "secret," and Keisha was having sex. Just last night Glenda had found a condom in Keisha's trash can inside her room. Glenda was so furious she sent Keisha away with Gloria.

Now Glenda was all by herself, lost in thought. As she waited for her bath water to finish running, she scurried around in her silk robe getting elements together for her sensual bath. Candles? Check. Roses? Check. Floetry CD? Check.

Just as she was going upstairs, the doorbell rang. Glenda didn't have the slightest idea who it could be at this time of day. No one ever called or came by after six p.m. Weekends were her time. Glenda glanced at the clock on the wall on her way to the door. *This better be good*, she thought. It was 7:50 p.m.

Looking through the peephole, she saw a black uniform. Her knees got weak instantly. She prayed Leader was okay as she snatched the door open. A very attractive female greeted Glenda. Even with the uniform on this woman was stunning . . . and vaguely familiar.

"Glenda Moore?" The officer asked.

"Yes," she answered. Then it struck her where she recognized the woman from. Leader's pictures! Unfortunately, it was too late. Carmen sprayed something in Glenda's face, causing her to collapse on the threshold.

Leader looked around the spacious cabin of the truck he drove, imagining a million different ways to stuff Carmen's body inside safely without notice. He was currently on I-95, consuming highway at a rapid pace en route back to N.C. The words on Carmen's note rang prolifically in his head. "See you in N.C."

He didn't know how Carmen knew he would find her home. Then again, he did. Carmen was just as skilled an assassin as he was. Maybe she wanted him to find her lair, so she'd have time to do what she wanted to do. Only question was, what did she want to do? His first thought went to Glenda, but he immediately dismissed the thought, since Justus was there. Justus would never allow anyone to harm his mother. That, Leader was willing to bet his life on. Leader never contacted

Justus while he was gone, partly because his communication devices were left back home, and mostly because he wanted his indiscretions to be forgiven. As he had told Justus time and again: A real man doesn't make excuses, he makes results. Surely, Justus had seen the damage he had done to Glenda's face by now. And surely Justus would be pissed by the affair he'd had, but by Leader killing his paramour, he intended to show them that she meant nothing to him. More importantly, he could guarantee it wouldn't happen again. Thus saving his family and regaining face . . . By doing so, he knew Glenda would forgive him . . . Eventually Justus would understand also. After all, Justus did kill his woman's baby's father for the same reason: to prevent future affairs from happening. Leader felt Carmen was stupid for coming into his domain. She was making things easy. Or so he thought. He didn't know she brought nothing but difficulty.

The room was dark and quiet. Those were the first things Glenda noticed as she slowly glided back into the world of the living. The next thing she noticed were her bound limbs. She couldn't remember much. Oh yea! The woman from the pictures. She had come into her home. Something about a police uniform also reverberated in her brain. Oh yes! That was why she opened the door. She thought something had happened to Leader.

"Wake up, Sunshine," a voice sang from the darkness. "Are you awake?" After a blinding light had been turned on, Glenda realized she was in her basement. Bound. Gagged. And suddenly terrified.

The woman, whose name she recalled was Carmen had changed from her policewoman get-up and now wore a black Lycra pantsuit. The material clung to her every curve accentuating her wide hips, curvy bottom, and ample bosom. Glenda could even see a six-pack pumping through the suit. As beautiful as Glenda had to admit Carmen was, any sex appeal the outfit would have exuded was eclipsed by the calf-high combat boots she wore. The boots along with the black leather gloves and balaclava she wore over her head made Carmen anything but sexy. She looked downright terrifying.

"Do you know who I am?" Carmen sang, bending down to look Glenda, who sat in a high-backed chair, eye-to-eye. "Oops, I forgot! You can't talk" Carmen removed the gag from Glenda's mouth. "Now speak." She smiled.

Glenda coughed," I know who you are b-bitch." She sputtered, remaining defiant under pressure.

"You're Carmen."

"Ahh, that's where you're wrong." Carmen raised her index finger in protest. "Carmen was your husband's mother."

"I know that, bitch." Where was this going?

"Do you?" Carmen chuckled then allowed silence to permeate the air. "What else don't you know?"

"Quit the games. If you're not Carmen, who are you?

"I am the product of a broken heart! The re-

sult of grief. Of murder. A widow. But most of all, I
am everything your husband forced me to be ten
years ago."

Glenda was beginning to lose hope. The woman
in front of her had obviously flipped. Glenda didn't
know how long she had been tied up, but she
knew someone had to realize she was missing.
Someone had to come over soon. Maybe even
Leader. Until then, she had to stall this lunatic.

"Woman, what are you talking about? You
couldn't have known my husband ten years ago."

"Oh? Allow me to explain." Carmen turned
her back to Glenda, looking far-off into space, and
began talking.

"My real name is Chantell Sims. I was a young
bride married to my college sweetheart ten years
ago. My husband, Antwann, owned his own business. A pharmaceutical firm. He was only twenty-
one years old when he started the firm. You see, he
was somewhat of a prodigy, wanted by all the top
pharmaceutical firms, heavily courted. But he
chose to go into business for himself. For us. *Black
Enterprise* magazine even called him one of America's Top Minority Businessmen," she offered a
sentimental smile. "I didn't know his seed money
was a loan from the Nigerian mafia. But your husband made that fact all too real.

"One night, as we lay in bed, an intruder entered our home. We had top-notch security systems
but none of them were alerted. We didn't know
someone was in our home until a man stood over
our bed, pointing an assault rifle at my husband's
head . . ." Glenda could tell "Carmen," or Chantell

Sims, was reliving the moment. Her voice trailed off more and more with each syllable. "Your husband pulled that trigger as easy as blinking an eye. Snuffed out my husband's life. Snuffed out my life. I was pregnant with our first child. Six months. Needless to say, after seeing my husband's brain on our pillow, I went into shock. The doctor's heroics weren't enough to save our child. I wasn't able to attend my own husband's funeral, because I wasn't strong enough to be released from the hospital.

"All I could think about in the hospital was revenge. I didn't know the first thing about violence." She chuckled at the thought of how far she had come. "But it's amazing what you can train your body to do."

Carmen turned around to face Glenda while she told the rest of her story.

"The police couldn't gather any leads and ruled it as another of the many Chicago homicides, but I knew better. Someone had sent death to my husband. So, using my skills as a P.I., I stumbled upon a far-reaching network of professional assassins. It didn't take long to figure out that the only way to find my husband's killer was to become a part of this close-knit network. I originally was just going to "fake-the-funk," but the guy who plugged me in said I had to complete a job to gain trust. So, I had to complete a job to gain trust. So, I did . . . And to be honest, it felt good. It felt empowering. I mean, you hear people, like strippers and what not, saying that doing what they do feels empowering. Like, we all know it's immoral, so what's so empowering, right? Well, now I understand what

they mean. Whether illegal or not, nothing—
NOTHING—feels more powerful than taking a
human life. I mean, that instant. POW!" Chantell-
Carmen Sims snapped her fingers. "You're like
God."

In the pregnant pause that ensued, Glenda
wondered why this woman was revealing so much.
Glenda didn't want to empathize with her. She'd
fucked her husband then invaded their home with
ill intent. Still, Glenda couldn't help but feel Carmen's plight.

Carmen continued, "Anyway, as luck would
have it, your husband turned out to be a legend in
the trade. Untouchable. A ghost. His works were
well-known, but he was a myth. It took me ten
years to track him down. Ten years . . . but I did it.
Unfortunately, no one informed me how hand-
some he was. When I finally did meet him, I didn't
want to shoot him anymore. I wanted to fuck him
to death. So, I did, and believe me, it was everything I imagined, as I'm sure you know already."

Glenda fought to escape her restraints.

"You bitch!!" She spat.

Carmen waved her hand., "Oh please. Cut the
dramatics. You'll never feel him again. I told you
everything I did so you'll know why you're dying.
See, the world isn't big enough for the both of us,
so since I'm with child, you have to go."

The messages repeated the same news again
and again. Leader couldn't believe his eyes. Justus
arrested for murder, denied bond. The messages

were almost two weeks old. That meant Glenda
was all alone.

Leader hadn't been in town a good thirty minutes before finding things out. He had stopped by
his secret apartment to retrieve some items to defend his home base if Carmen showed up. Now,
with the knowledge he possessed, there was a
sense of urgency getting home.

When he arrived home, he found Glenda's
Jaguar parked in the driveway. This was good. She
usually was home in bed at this time of night anyway. At 11:30 p.m., Glenda was sure to be in bed.
Leader parked his car and went inside. Immediately his instincts went off. Something was not
right. He couldn't put his finger on it but he knew
something wasn't right. Drawing his .45, Leader
closed his eyes, allowing his other senses to mag-
nify, and crept through the house. Checking all
bedrooms, he saw no sign of Glenda. Then, ever so
faintly, he heard a voice murmuring in the basement. He could hear the agony present in the dis-
tant pleas, so he ran cautiously to the stairs. It was
there he discovered a semi-automatic pistol lying
precariously on the top step. He scooped it up
without a second thought, checked the pipe. It was
empty so he stuffed it in his waistband, and continued on.

Leader paused at the basement door momentarily until he heard Glenda's agonizing moans.
He kicked the door off the hinges, cleared the
dark room with his weapon, before cutting on the
light. What awaited him wrenched his heart from
his chest.

Glenda was lying face-down in a pool of blood. Even from twenty feet away, Leader could see the gaping hole in the back of her head. It wasn't a bullet wound, it looked more sinister, as if someone had literally torn a chunk out of her skull. Miraculously, she was still alive.

Leader rushed to his wife's side. Turning her over, he saw that it was probably a matter of time before she checked out. Her eyes possessed a far-off stare, her face was already beginning to ashen. Then suddenly recognition: Glenda's eyes returned to the land of the living.

"C-Carmen wa-was h-here," Glenda wheezed. Leader cradled her head in his lap.

"Baby hold on," He pleaded.

"NO!" She managed forcefully. "You must g-go," she continued. Glenda said something else, but Leader couldn't decipher the words.

Glenda dug deep, gathering all her remaining life, and barked, "Go! She set you up!"

It was then that Leader heard the sirens. He was upstairs, yanking the front door open, when it dawned on him what Glenda meant. So much for help.

"Freeze!!! Drop your weapon and surrender!" Leader didn't realize he still held his pistol in his hand, until the police's spotlight illuminated it.

"Backup is on the way! You'll never make it out alive! Surrender now!!"

Leader summed up his situation quickly knowing time was of the essence. He then made his decision.

Pop! Pop! Leader licked two shots at the cops before slamming the front door shut. Seconds later, a volley of shots rained in through the front door. Leader continued to low-crawl through the house towards the back door. He ensured the cops weren't in back waiting for him. When he saw that the coast was clear, he peeled through the back door and tore off through the backyard.

Chapter 31

Justus did his last rep of push-ups, then pushed up from the floor with power. Yes, even in jail he had to stay in shape. Today, however, he did his routine with extra sauce, for today was a good day indeed.

He was going home.

After almost three long weeks of confinement, Justus was being released on bond. It took a lot of finagling (and of course money) but Shabazz, the lawyer he had retained, had finally pulled his coup. Even though defendants charged with capital crimes weren't guaranteed bail due to the severity of the offense, with the right amount of money put into the right hands, things weren't too hard to obtain. In this case, freedom. Justus was finally convinced Leader was yet right again! America was about two things: The haves and have-nots. And most of the time the haves luxuriated on the blood, sweat and tears of the have nots.

Getting dressed, Justus went outside his cell to wait for the breakfast trays. He wanted to say his good-byes to Top, and see if there was something he could do to assist him with his situation. After all, Top had given him something no one—including Leader—ever had given him: the truth. For that, Justus felt indebted to him.

While Justus waited, his thoughts drifted to Leader. He couldn't understand why Leader had abandoned him. Surely, Leader knew of his plight, what with the media coverage and all. Justus was finding it hard to deter the bitterness beginning to form in his heart.

Justus decided to watch some television to pass the time. On his way to the corner, he saw that the dude called Knowledge was holding the tube hostage with the news. It was futile to ever argue. Knowledge always watched the news. Everyone in the pod knew.

Justus sat idly, catching up on current events in the world, when to his surprise, his house appeared on the screen. Well, his parent's house.

"Yo, turn that up!"

Knowledge complied while looking at Justus skeptically. The news reporter was motioning toward the house while repeating her earlier statements:

> *Police are still searching for the man believed to have killed his wife by bashing her head with an automatic pistol. The pistol was found on the scene.*
> *According to police the suspect dropped it while fleeing from them . . .*

A middle-aged balding white man came on-screen to say a few words. He was introduced as Captain Taggert. The reporter asked him for a brief account.

> *Uh, after we received a tip from an anonymous caller about an intense domestic dispute, officers responded to the scene just as the suspect was leaving. The officers attempted to apprehend the suspect, but he fired on them.*
>
> *The officers returned fire. The suspect fled through the house and got away.*
>
> *Upon entering the house officers discovered the body of a woman in the basement. There was too much blood to positively I.D., initially.*
>
> *We now have her name. She was the woman who lived in the house. Glenda Moore, the suspect's wife . . .*

A beautiful picture of Glenda flashed across the screen.

"Nooooo!!!!!" Justus's primal scream echoed throughout the cell block when he saw his mother's picture. He began pounding the table emphatically, screaming louder and louder. The guards rushed in to detain him.

Ironically, it was at that exact point that he made bail.

"Moore! Bag and Baggage."

Chapter 32

Glenda was laid to rest in a beautiful ceremony three days after Justus's release. Family from all over the nation came to say their good-byes. Glenda was well-loved, and even more respected. Her sister Gloria took it hardest. First, her son Pug. Then her sister. Justus offered her his shoulder, but not much else. His mind was 99% focused on Leader.

As yet, Leader still hadn't shown his face, all but convicting himself. In Justus's eyes, he was already guilty, and just as he played judge, jury, and executioner to that kidnapper that fateful night years ago, he planned on doing the same to Leader when he found him.

The police were scattered about the funeral, hoping to catch sight of Leader. They didn't really believe the murderer would show up at the funeral, but stranger things have happened.

As Reverend Butkus Bucks delivered a gut-wrenching eulogy, an oversized black woman wearing black, with a charcoal-colored wide-brimmed hat, complete with a veil, listened intently while constantly observing her surroundings through the veil.

At least that's what the world saw. Leader had snuck in with the first wave of mourners and taken his seat. Since then he hadn't moved. He observed the numerous undercover officers file in and take their places. No doubt they were looking for him. He observed Justus and his family enter the church, grieving. Justus was remaining strong in appearance, but Leader could read his body language and see he was hurting. He wanted so bad to console his son, but by the way Justus scrutinized every mourner, he knew Justus believed the hype being splattered across T.V.'s statewide. Justus thought Leader was guilty also. As much as he wanted to vindicate himself, now was not the time. Too many emotions. However, Leader did leave a memento in Justus's home to send him a message just in case he wanted to get stupid and play vigilante. He was innocent, of this crime anyway. Yet he knew all too well: perception is reality. Therefore, he planned on distancing himself until he could create a better perception. Leader noticed the procession to view the body had commenced. This was his cue to move. He had no inclination to see his wife in a box with bad makeup on. He wanted to remember her the way she was. Beautiful.

Keeping his eyes on his son Justus, Leader stood to join the crowd, then make his exit. Just as he was about to turn the corner to leave the church, Justus looked up from his funeral program . . . right at Leader.

Oh shit. Show down.

They both froze. Justus's eyes narrowed, sizing

up the womanly figure with the masculine gait. Justus reached for where his pistol would usually be, finding the spot vacant. Nikki sensed the tension and followed Justus's gaze. She saw the woman, but nothing else. She was not trained to recognize disguises. After a tense few moments, Justus decided to stand down. He didn't wish to desecrate the memory of his mother with more violence.

Seeing Justus concede, Leader spirited out the church into the midday sun.

When Justus and Nikki arrived home later that evening they were exhausted. All the mourning had made them weary, particularly Nikki, who seemed to be taking things harder than Justus. Justus had yet to break down fully. His mind was all too much on Leader. He knew it was only a matter of time before Leader showed his face. If not soon, Justus planned to go search for him. Fortunately, the former presented himself in the form of a DVD.

Justus was putting his weapons away in his armory, after putting the twins to bed, when he discovered a DVD on top of his ammo box. Confused about the source of the DVD, Justus confronted Nikki, who was banned from his armory. She emphatically denied ever entering his armory, prompting Justus to view the disc in private.

Justus turned on the disc, and nostalgia crept up on him as he saw himself emerge on the screen. It was somewhat blurry, but he recognized the scene quite well. It was etched in his memory forever.

It was the night he killed his first man. On the screen, Justus could see himself hovering around the man as he sat in the chair tied up. He could be seen looking away, as if talking to someone, but Leader never materialized on the screen. Justus saw himself raise the gun to the back of the man's head then look away. He looked at the screen while reliving the moment in his head. That night seemed so long ago. So much had changed since that night. Yet Justus still flinched when the man's head exploded in a cloud of red dust on the screen.

While Justus recalled the night in vivid reflection, it wasn't remiss on him the reason he was even looking at the recording. Leader was sending him a message. He had been there, and he held the trump cards.

After getting a close-up of Justus in his moment of murderous pondering, the screen went blank. Seconds later, a picture of Leader materialized on the screen. He was sitting in a chair, the same chair Justus sat in at that very moment. Leader's face was calm, and he still wore the woman costume. Looking the camera directly in the eye, he spoke, "Justus, my son, I hate that it has to come to this. Before I go any further, I want you to know I didn't kill your mother. I love her and would never do anything to harm her. We're family . . ." Justus observed Leader intently, looking for all of the signs of a lie that he had been taught. Then it dawned on him: if Leader knew the signs well enough to teach them, then surely he could manipulate the signs to appear he was being truthful.

On the screen, Leader continued, "I heard about your situation and I'm sorry to hear about it, but you're smart, you'll persevere.

"When I saw you today, it hurt my heart that you could think I'd do something like that to your mother. As I said before, I didn't do it . . . but I know who did. As do you. Since I brought this on the family, it's my responsibility to see that things are reconciled. So I'm going to find who's responsible and make them suffer. I want you to help me, so I made a little motivation . . ." Justus couldn't believe his ears. The nerve!! "The tape you just previewed is one of many. I realized that you may take a while to graduate from the prison of your emotions, so I made some insurance a while back, just in case you flipped on me. I see I wasn't too far off in my assumption. Call me dirty, p'noid or whatever, but it is what it is, and this is what it has come to. So, here's what's going to happen: At four a.m., you are going to meet me at the farm. There, we're going to discuss plans of action to track down our now-mutual adversary and use her to clear our name. Resistance is futile. See you soon. Love you." Justus was about to replay the DVD when he heard three beeps. Seconds later, smoke enveloped the DVD. Justus attempted to save the disc, but by the time he retrieved the disc from the player it was unsalvageable. Looking at his watch, Justus saw that it was already well past midnight. That meant he had three hours to get ready for his show down with his stepfather.

There was never a question of whether he was going to meet Leader or not. The implications were clear. If he didn't meet with Leader, the police would get a copy of that video and lord knows what else. If he tried to kill Leader—or succeeded—

then, the police would get a disc. Therefore, he had no choice. With the charges levied against him already, a video of him killing someone would surely revoke his bond and possibly box him in forever. So. It was that Justus had to play Leader's game until an opportunity presented itself.

Chapter 33

Leader crouched in the bushes beside the dusty trail leading to the farm. Looking at his tactical watch, he saw Justus only had ten minutes to show up. It was never a matter of "if." It was always when.

Not to disappoint, Justus rounded the bend at exactly 3:55 a.m., and doused the lights. He was loaded for bear, with his body armor encapsulating him, while his trusty 357s occupied an armpit on both sides. In his arm, he held an M-4 assault rifle equipped with a night-vision scope and an infra-red beam attached to its muzzle.

Justus exited the vehicle quietly. He estimated a 200-yard trek to the farm itself. He decided to walk, so as to surprise Leader. Knowing Leader, he was sure to have a few tricks up his sleeve, especially with the farm being his turf. So, Justus wanted to minimize his exposure, and increase his chance of a victorious confrontation by using the element of guerilla warfare. In guerrilla warfare, you made your weaknesses into strengths by exploiting your opponents' weaknesses. In this case, Justus's weakness was him being alone and lacking intel on what awaited him. Therefore, he had to do recon.

Justus planted his eye to the scope attached to the rifle, and scanned the woods, looking for any irregular heat signatures within them. Satisfied, he began his long walk.

From his perch inside of a tree, Leader observed Justus through his night vision goggles. The red beam emanating from the barrel shone like a Christmas tree through the power of the NVSs. When Leader saw the beam swoop in and out of the bushes, he smiled. He knew Justus was checking his surroundings.

Damn, I taught him well, Leader thought. As Justus crept down the trail. Leader walked parallel to him, just a few feet away, the entire time. When Justus neared the farmyard, Leader decided to test him. He tossed a rock behind Justus on the opposite side he was situated on.

Justus stayed in his crouch, death-still, for a full two minutes.

Leader needed a diversion to get in place for the next step of his plan, so he pushed the button on a transmitter inside this cargo pocket, and waited.

Justus was beginning to see the courtyard of the farm when he heard steps in front of him. Out of nowhere, an apparition appeared glowing brightly through his NVGs, or night-vision goggles. It was running toward him on four legs rapidly. Justus wasted no time pumping a three-round burst into it, dropping it with a loud yelp. As he moved closer to inspect his fallen victim, Justus picked up more movement out of his left peripheral vision. He quickly swung his weapon in an arc, attempting to line up his sights with the figure running through the woods. Unable to acquire a good sight picture, he squeezed off a few rounds in frustration. He then continued cautiously into the courtyard of the farm.

Justus wasn't more than a good two feet onto the grounds, when he heard Leader speaking through a megaphone. Justus ran to the big barn to take cover until he could locate Leader's whereabouts, and to his disliking, Leader's voice followed him inside there as well.

"Come out with your hands up so we can talk about this like men!" Leader bellowed.

"Fuck you!!!"

"Come on, son! You're trapped here now. You can't leave here unless I let you!!!"

"You can't either!" Justus yelled, then licked off a burst of shots to illustrate his point. His goal was to keep Leader talking until he could ascertain where he was speaking from. Until then, he was content to hole up inside the barn.

Unfortunately, Leader had other plans. He had been watching Justus from his control room ever since he had made his hasty retreat. To the casual observer, the farm looked like a throwback from the nineteenth century. In reality, it was a state-of-the-art compound, equipped with the latest in electronic surveillance and technological advancements. The farm even boasted its own security system, complete with six-inch naval guns, March IV automatic grenade launchers, .50-cal machine gun posts, and an underground bunker.

This was Leader's place of refuge, if ever he had to hold court in the street. Right now, he observed Justus's every move by way of thermal imaging. Justus's heat signature was red-hot, signaling he was nervous.

Leader was tired of playing games, so he slipped through a few doors and ended up directly above where Justus crouched inside the barn.

"Let's quit the games, son." Justus heard Leader's voice above him, no longer amplified by the megaphone, and he almost shit his pants! Here was his adversary right above him in the flesh. It never occurred to Justus that if Leader wished him harm, he would've been dead by now. All he saw was red vengeance, so he rolled onto one side and fired through the balcony.

Leader heard the report of the rifle, but never flinched, as he was not in harm's way. However, he did rethink his plans since it was obvious Justus didn't want to talk.

Below Leader, Justus peeked from under his cover, saw the coast was clear, and darted out into the open, headed out of the barn.

That's when Leader seized the moment, and fired a shot into Justus's back. The sheer impact knocked him to the ground but he stumbled to his feet and kept running.

Leader tore off behind Justus, jumping from the balcony effortlessly, and taking off.

Justus dropped to one knee swung his rifle around and fired on Leader. Leader ducked behind the barn entranceway and Justus ran across the courtyard to the horse stable.

Just as Justus was opening the saloon door, he felt his shoulder get nicked.

"Ahh!" he screamed. Justus touched his shoulder, but no blood appeared on his hand. Justus made it just inside the stable, when suddenly the room started spinning. His weapon grew heavy so he dropped it, reaching for his pistols instead. But to his dismay, the room spun faster and faster, until he could no longer stand. Justus saw Leader at the door, about to enter, then he fell flat on his face.

Leader entered the stable cautiously. He knew that his tranquilizer had hit its mark, but sometimes it takes longer for some to go out than others, especially when they were in optimum shape, as Justus was. Leader kicked Justus a couple of times to see if he was conscious. Satisfied that he was out, Leader hoisted Justus's limp body over his shoulder and trekked across the courtyard.

Leader was halfway to the barn when he felt a sharp prick in his neck. Immediately, his legs collapsed, causing Justus's body to fall on top of him. Leader valiantly fought the darkness threatening to consume him, but the looming blackness was too much. His last thought before surrendering to the abyss was how could he be so careless. The last thing he saw confirmed the assumed perpetrator:

Carmen's high-heeled stiletto pierced his chest.

Justus awoke first in a fit of rage, thrashing and bucking to get free, to no avail. It didn't take long for him to realize that the more he moved, the tighter his restraints grew. Assessing his situation, Justus surmised he was back in the barn. His back lay flat against the wooden wall, his feet crossed and bound at the ankles, while his hands were tied behind him, between himself and the wall. The material used to secure his hands was made from some type of thin metal, so narrow that when Justus moved, it began to puncture his skin. A metal collar about three inches thick was looped around his muscular neck, drilled into the barn wall, making it almost impossible to look anywhere but straight ahead.

Justus's last memory was running from Leader then being shot. He thought it rather cruel that his own father would attach him to a wall in such medieval fashion. Justus craned his neck to the side, and thought he saw another person next to him, attached to the wall in the same manner, but due to the limited sunlight cascading through the balcony, and the excruciating penalty paid for turning his neck, he couldn't be sure. Therefore, he recalled some of Leader's instructions on using other senses when one was impaired, and attempted to smell. Unfortunately, all he smelled was animal shit. Then he heard what sounded like Leader call his name.

"Leader?"

"Yeah," Leader responded groggily from beside Justus.

"What's going on? Why are you tied up?" Justus inquired. Attempting to remain calm and defiant Leader groaned, "Cause this bitch is crazy."

"What bitch?"

"Carmen."

"You mean the woman you cheated on Mom with. What's she gotta do with this?"

"Everything. See, you don't understand. I didn't kill your other mother. She did."

"Oh, there you go," Justus groomed. "Trying to shift blame. Just be a man. Admit it you killed my mother the same way you killed my father back when I was a baby!"

Leader's jaw dropped. *Did he say what I thought he said?*

"What you say?"

"You heard me, nigga! You killed my father. My REAL father. That's right muthafucka I know!"

Leader's card being pulled, he dropped his head. "Who told you?"

"Justus, damnit, who told you?" Leader demanded.

"You know a dude named Top?"

The name brought back memories. "Top? I knew a Top before."

"Yeah, well he still remembers you vividly," Justus informed him. "He remembers you killed his best friend."

Leader drew a blank. He didn't have time to revisit past enemies. He was more concerned with escaping the iron clutches of the present one.

"See, son, you're too emotional. Here we are, lives on the line, and you wanna talk about past bullshit," Leader explained. "We need to focus on getting out of here."

"You're a trip. Your life was on the line the minute I found out about my mom. I don't know who else you pissed off or whatever, but you better hope they kill you because I damn sure am. And it ain't gonna be nice." Justus swore. The severity of their situation never dawned on him so he continued his threat campaign. Above all else, he wanted to hear Leader admit he killed his father.

"Listen to yourself, going against everything I trained you to be. If you really wanna know, yeah, I killed Ralo! The sorry mu'fucka. He was no good for your mother. He wasn't going to do anything but cause her more heartbreak."

"And you were better!?" Justus spat.

"You tell me!" Leader returned, attempting to look at Justus, the restraints preventing him from doing so. "I raised you as my own son. You never wanted for anything, and frankly, I deserve some respect."

"Respect? You killed my biological father, taught me to be a killer, all for your own selfish motives. You took away my innocence!" Justus was beginning to break down. All the pressure was becoming unbearable for him. "And you want respect?" Leader remained silent, so Justus continued, "You wrecked my life—"

"I made you a man!"

"You made me a killer like you!"

"I made you rich like me!" Leader boomed. "Who else you know your age that live like you?"

"But at what cost?" Justus questioned. Tears began streaming down his face. "Can't you see I'm not happy."

Leader scoffed, "You were happy until a few days ago." Leader thought he heard someone, so he shut up. When things were okay he spoke again with intended finality, "Bottom line: I made you through. Simple as that."

Justus didn't offer a response. It was obvious his guilt trip was beginning to penetrate Leader's conscience—as was his plan. With Leader lost in the realm of emotions, he would be a few steps off his well-honored square.

Thus allowing Justus a recourse in his defense, while he had his opportunity to up his offense. Despite Leader being forthright about Ralo, Justus still believed he killed his mother.

A pregnant pause in conversation gave way to an explosive outburst from Justus, "Why don't you stop playing games and let me loose . . . so we can handle our MUTHAFUCKIN' BUSINESS!!!" Justus thrashed and kicked desperately trying to escape his reins. He was convinced this was yet another ploy of Leader's, done to regain control by manipulating his mind. And Justus wanted no part of it.

"You say you didn't kill my mother. Then how come you were the only one around? The last one to see her alive?" Justus queried.

Leader had had enough. "Justus, for the last time I DID NOT KILL MY WIFE! Now we need to try to get out of here before this crazy bitch comes back."

"What crazy bitch?"

"I believe he is talking about me." Carmen sauntered inside the barn wearing a full-body Lycra catsuit with black boots. Her long hair swung freely about her shoulders. Her makeup was flawless. If not for the long Chinese sword she held in her left hand, it would've appeared that she was going on a date.

"And he's right, I am crazy. Let me tell you

why." Carmen proceeded to reiterate the same story she'd told Glenda before she sent her to her bloody death. The entire time Carmen retold her story, Justus listened intently, while Leader searched for a way to escape.

"I see death has finally found its way to your doorstep," Carmen commented after completing her story. "Your father is right. He didn't kill your mother, but her death is just as much his fault as it is mine. You see, he made me what I am." She raised her arms grandly. "I used to hate it, but now I love it! I have ultimate power and I owe it all to him. A strong love fueled by tremendous respect . . . which is why it's so special for me to bring to an end a legend, and a possible legend-to-be. Little ole' me. Can you believe it?" Carmen was obviously ecstatic with herself as she pranced around the barn just out of reach from her prisoners. Then she grew serious.

"Now it's time to end this. A lifetime of sadness, a lifetime of seeking revenge. It's finally coming to an end. But first . . . you must die," she pointed her blade at Justus. "I set you on a path to claim your destiny. The ultimate plan foiled because you can't remove your heart from your sleeve. When you thought Leader killed your mother you was supposed to retaliate! But I watched you at the funeral cower like a mouse. You will never be the man your father—or stepfather— was. E-yah!" Carmen slashed Justus's torso with her blade, peeling his chest open like a zipper. "You must pay for your weakness."

"Carmen! Leave him alone!" Leader thrashed violently in his restraints. "It's me you want."

Leader motioned his head at her large belly, accentuated by the tight clothing she wore. "We can raise that child to be the best assassin this world has ever seen. Me and you. We can do it doll."

Carmen offered a smile. She knew when her leg was being pulled. "Sounds sweet, my love, but unfortunately, it doesn't sound true."

"No, no, it is true. Me and you, babe. Just let the boy go. Look at him, he's bleeding to death." For the first time since his grandfather had passed, Leader was beginning to feel something he never felt before: remorse. So, with every tactic he could muster, he begged for young Justus's life, as it slowly slipped away in a fountain of blood. "Look at him Carmen. He had nothing to do with this. I did that to you. He's innocent."

"So was O!" Carmen screamed but she regained her composure. "But you know what I learned? In war there is always collateral damage. My child was collateral damage."

"Do you want what happened to you to happen to his family? He has twins. Do you want them to grow up seeking revenge?" Carmen chuckled, "Funny you should seek pity for a life. Have you ever spared a life?"

"I spared yours."

"Did you? Did you?" Carmen was right upon Leader, jabbing the point of her sword into his stomach hard—but not hard enough—to puncture. "Nah. You didn't save my life. You gave me a new one. Back then and now," she rubbed her stomach. To her left, Justus moaned in agony as his life slowly slipped away by the second. "Now, it's my turn to give you a new life, my love. First pain then love."

That said, Carmen glided over to Justus in one stride, cupped his face in one hand while plunging her sword through his stomach with the other.

That was how she left Justus. Staked to the wall. To his credit, Justus didn't scream or whine or holler. He took his blow like a soldier, looking into Carmen's eyes for as long as she would allow, just as he did to his countless victims.

Beside him, Leader broke down. His insides were crushed, and he began to see the error of his ways. He thought he was imparting a gift to his son. Something to make up for what he took. Something to make him as close to being a god as this world would allow. Ironically, Leader didn't feel very god-like now. He felt helpless. That, to him, was almost more cause for remorse than his own son's life. Leader had always called the shots. Even his name suggested so. Now, to feel so inferior was alien to him. He couldn't save Glenda's life. Or Justus's life either . . . just like he couldn't save his grandfather many years ago also. It seemed like he had come full-circle, all because of the beautiful woman who stood before him.

"I wore my make-up for you," Carmen was saying as she removed a revolver from her bosom. "This was the date of dates. A date with destiny. I hope you like it." She coiffed her hair. Walking up to Leader, she placed the revolver to his temple. This made him jump, but then he positioned his temple to the barrel of the revolver, prepared to go out like only a trooper could.

"I have now completed my mission," Carmen rhapsodized. "Good-bye." She blew his brains all over the wall.

Pinned to the wall, Justus heard everything. When Carmen blew Leader's brains out, Justus cried on the inside. He waited for his last moments to arrive, but they never came. Instead, he heard Carmen sobbing profusely. She stood sobbing for what he judged to be minutes, but it felt like a lifetime. Then there was silence.

After a few moments, Justus heard Carmen's steps as she left the barn. He attempted to move, but the stakes drilled into his body prevented any movement. So, pinned to the wall, hatred rooted in his heart, he vowed to pay Carmen back. If he survived. His body was numb, and the excruciating pain shooting through his brain short-circuited his sight. But he still had his hearing.

And his breath.

And a will to live.

DON'T MISS THE FIRST BOOK IN THE
CRESCENT CREW SERIES

Street Rap

For Reece and Qwess, being rap superstars
was the dream, but in real life, nothing moved
without the money. So they formed the Crescent
Crew, an outfit of young, ruthless hustlers that
locked the Southern drug trade in a stranglehold.
They're at the height of their power when
Qwess is offered a record deal from a major
label. He accepts and makes plans for his whole
crew to go legit, but Reece enjoys his position as
king of the streets and has no desire to relinquish
his crown . . .

Available wherever books are sold

Enjoy the following excerpt from *Street Rap* . . .

Chapter 1

The black Tahoe crept onto the rooftop of the parking garage overlooking downtown Fayetteville and stopped. The driver lumbered his hefty frame out of the truck and stood to his full six-foot-seven-inch height. He flipped the collar up on his heavy mink coat, readjusted the sawed-off shotgun tucked beneath his arm, and scanned his surroundings for danger. Satisfied that the area was clear, he tapped on the passenger window of the truck. The tinted window eased down halfway, and a cloud of smoke was released into the air.

"It's clear," the giant reported.

"Good. Now go post up over there so you can see the street, make sure no funny biz popping off," the man in the truck instructed.

The giant hesitated a moment. "You sure about this? I mean, I don't trust these dudes like that," he said.

The man smiled. "You worry too much, Samson. Nobody would dare violate this thing of ours again. Look around you, it's just us and them. This is crew business, and this shit has gone on long enough. Tonight, it ends, one way or another."

The window glided up, and the giant assumed his position near the edge of the parking garage.

Behind the dark glass of the Tahoe, two men sat in the back seat sharing a blunt while a brooding hip-hop track thumped through the speakers. The men casually passed the blunt and enjoyed the music as if they were at a party, and not on the precipice of a drug war for control of the city's lucrative narcotics trade. Although partners, each of the men was a boss in his own right. Their leadership styles were different—one was fire, the other was ice—but it was the balance that made their team so strong.

In the back seat of the Tahoe sat Qwess and Reece, leaders of the notorious Crescent Crew.

"Yo, that beat is bananas, son!" Reece remarked to Qwess. "You did that?"

Qwess nodded. "You knowww it," he sang.

"Word. You already wrote to it?"

"I'm writing to it right now," he replied. He pointed to his temple. "Right here."

"I hear ya, Jay-Z," Reece joked. "So, anyway, how you want to handle this when these niggas get here?"

Qwess nodded. "Let me talk some sense into them, let them know they violated."

"Son, they know they violated."

"Still, let me handle it, because you know how you can be."

Reece scowled. "How I can be? Fuck is that supposed to mean?"

"You know how you can be," Qwess insisted.

"What? Efficient?"

"If you want to call it that."

Headlights bent around the corner and a dark gray H2 Hummer came into view. The Hummer drove to the edge of the garage and stopped inches in front of Samson. He spun around to face the truck. The giant, clad in a full-length mink, resembled King Kong in the glow of the xenon headlamps.

Inside the truck, Qwess craned his head over the seat to confirm their guests. "That's them," he noted as he passed Reece the blunt. He climbed from the back of the truck and tossed his partner a smirk. "Stay here, I got it."

Qwess joined Samson while men poured out of the Hummer. When the men stood before Qwess, someone very important was absent.

Qwess raised his palm. "Whoa, whoa, someone's missing from this little shindig," he observed, scanning the faces. "Where is Black Vic?"

One of the minions stepped forward. He wore a bald head and a scowl. "Black Vic couldn't be here tonight. He sends his regards." The man thumbed his chest with authority. "He sent me in his place."

Qwess frowned. "He sent you in his place? Are you kidding me? We asked for a meeting with the boss of your crew, and he sends you?"

The man nodded. "Yep."

Qwess shook his head. "Yo, get Black Vic on the phone and tell him to get his ass down here now."

The minion chuckled. "I see you got things confused, dawg. You run shit over there, not over here. Now are we talking or what?"

Samson took a step forward. The other three men took two steps back. Qwess gently placed a hand on Samson's arm. The giant stood down.

"I need to talk to the man in charge," Qwess insisted. "Because we only going to have this conversation one time."

"Word?"

"Word!"

Suddenly, the back door to the Tahoe was flung open, and all eyes shifted in that direction. Reece stepped out into the night and flung his dreads wildly. Time seemed to slow down as he diddy-bopped over to them, his Cuban link and heavy medallion swinging around his neck. He pulled back the lapels on his jacket and placed his hands on his waist, revealing his Gucci belt and his two .45s.

"Yo, where Victor at?" Reece asked.

Qwess scoffed. "He ain't here. He sent *these* niggas."

Reece looked at each man, slowly nodding his head. "So Victor doesn't respect us enough to show his face and address his violation? He took two kis from my little man, beat him down. My li'l homie from Skibo hit him with consignment, and he decided to keep shit. Now, we trying to resolve this shit 'cause war is bad for business—for everybody, and he wanna say, 'fuck us'?"

"Black Vic said that you said 'fuck us' when you wouldn't show us no flex on the prices," the minion countered.

"Oh, yeah? That what he said?" Reece asked. He shook his head and mocked, "*He said, she said, we said . . .* See, that's that bitch shit. That's why Victor should've came himself. But he sent you to speak for him, right?"

The bald-headed minion puffed out his bird chest. "That's right."

"Okay." Reece nodded his head and looked around the rooftop of the garage. "Well, tell Victor this!"

SMACK!

Without warning, Reece lit the minion's jaws up with an open palm slap. Samson lunged forward and wrapped his huge mittens around the neck of one of the other minions, who wore a skully pulled low over his eyes. Qwess drew his pistol and aimed it at the other minion in a hoodie, while the soldier in the passenger seat of the Tahoe popped out of the roof holding an AK-47.

"Y'all thought it was sweet?" Reece taunted. He smacked the bald-headed minion again, and he crumpled to the floor semiconscious. "I got a message for Victor's ass, though."

Reece dragged the man over to the Hummer and pitched his body to the ground in front of the pulley attached to the front of the truck. He reached inside the Hummer to release the lever for the pulley, then returned to the front of the Hummer. While the spectators watched in horror, Reece pulled bundles of metal rope from the pulley and wrapped it around the man's neck. Qwess came over to help, and when they were done, the two of them hoisted the man up onto the railing.

"Wait, man! Please don't do this!" the minion

pleaded. He was fully conscious now, and scrapping for his life. Qwess cracked him in the jaw and knocked the fight right out of him.

Reece fixed him with a cold gaze. "*We* not doing this to you, homie. Your man, Victor, is," he explained. "His ass should've showed up. Now, of course, this means war."

Reece and Qwess flipped the man over the railing. His body sailed through the air, and the pulley whirred to life, guiding his descent. His banshee-like wail echoed through the quiet night as he desperately tugged at the rope around his neck. Then suddenly, the pulley ran out of rope and caught, snapping his neck like a chicken. Both Qwess and Reece spared a look over the edge and saw his lifeless body dangling against the side of the building.

Reece turned to face the others. Slowly, he slid his thumb across his naked throat, and the AK-47 sparked three times. All head shots.

This was crew business.